# silver threads

THE MEMORY HOUSE SERIES, BOOK FIVE

BETTE LEE CROSBY

SILVER THREADS
*Memory House Series, Book Five*



Cover design: damonza.com
Formatting by Author E.M.S.
Editor: Ekta Garg





ISBN-978-0-9969214-6-6

BENT PINE PUBLISHING
Port Saint Lucie, FL

Published in the United States of America

For Coral Russell

*My genius, friend and partner.*

# silver threads

# Somewhere Far Away

On the day Jennifer Green was born, a pile of stones was placed alongside her scale of life. A few were the dark gray of sorrow, but most were a pale blush color. The largest stone was the rose hue of a sunrise. That one would be placed on the scale the day she married Drew Bishop.

Even more brilliant but a wee bit smaller was the pink stone glistening with specks of silver. That one would bring Jennifer a baby girl named Brooke. The Keeper of the Scales smiled. Seeing such happiness laid out before him was pleasing to his eye.

Since the beginning of time the Keeper alone has been challenged with the task of keeping each person's scale in balance. A bit of happiness and then a small stone of sorrow, until the lives he has in his charge are measured evenly.

You might think such power is universal, but it is not. There is a silver thread that crisscrosses the landscape of scales and connects strangers to one another. Not even the Keeper of the Scales can control the events traveling through the thread. The only thing he can do is try to equalize the balance once it has been thrown off.

**Like Jennifer Green, each of** the Coggan twins was also given a pile of stones at birth. Tom Coggan used up the blush-colored ones in his early years—wasted them on frivolities like Patsy, the blond stripper who worked at the Boom Boom Club. During those years the Keeper tried to balance Tom's life by dropping one gray stone after another onto the scale, but the weight of whiskey and good times far outweighed the gray stones.

Before Tom's thirty-fourth birthday, only a single piece remained in his pile. It was neither a blush-colored stone nor a gray pebble but a large black rock. The Keeper of the Scales gave a saddened sigh, lifted the rock and dropped it onto the sorrow side of Tom's scale.

With a resounding thud Tom Coggan's scale came crashing down and landed on the silver thread that connected him to the woman who had ten years earlier become Jennifer Bishop.

# Clarksburg, Alabama
# February 13, 2013

That Wednesday morning Jennifer Bishop awoke with yet another migraine. When the alarm on her cell phone rang, the sound seemed sharp as a razor blade in her ear. This was going to be one of those days when she wanted nothing more than to remain in bed with the blinds drawn and an icy cold cloth folded across her forehead.

Had Drew been at home she would have asked him to drop Brooke off at school, but he was traveling again. This time it was Atlanta or maybe Chicago. He'd left a schedule, but she'd paid little attention to it. This was a week like all the others; five or six days of being on the road then home for a day or two and gone again. What difference did it make if he was in Dallas or Topeka?

Jennifer tapped the Calendar icon. Just as she thought: there was a Brownie meeting after school. With her head pounding like this, there was no way she could spend the afternoon shuttling Brooke and her friends from school to the meeting and then from the meeting back home.

Tracy Edwards, Lara Stone and Jennifer took turns carpooling the girls from place to place. Today it was Jennifer's turn, but with this migraine it would be impossible. She texted Lara.

"Killer headache. Can U take carpool? I'll do the next 2."

She tapped Send then reluctantly swung her legs to the floor and started toward the bathroom. After splashing a handful of cool water on her face and pulling on a pair of jeans, she went back and checked the messages.

"No prob," Lara's text said. "Feel better."

Jennifer tapped out a quick thank you then stuck the phone in her back pocket and headed toward Brooke's room. Her eight-year-old daughter had inherited Drew's ability to sleep through almost anything. She gave the girl's shoulder a gentle shake.

"Brooke, honey, it's time to get up."

In the same way her daddy would have done, Brooke opened one eye, mumbled, "Okay," then closed the eye and dug deeper into the pillow.

"Really," Jennifer said. "You've got to get up. Mama has a headache this morning, and we're already running late."

Brooke gave a sleepy stretch and sat up. "Do I have to take the bus, or are you gonna drive me?"

"It's raining, so I'll drive you. On the way home I can stop at the drugstore and pick up my prescription."

Jennifer bent and kissed her daughter's forehead. "Hurry up now. No crawling back into bed."

Brooke gave a guilty giggle and pushed back the covers. Although she had her mama's easy smile, her personality was that of her daddy: serious minded and studious. She never had to be reminded of homework or tucking a sweater into her backpack. It was done before anyone asked. The night before she'd laid out the clothes she planned to wear to school that day, so she was dressed and downstairs in fifteen minutes flat.

After a quick bowl of cereal, they were in the car and headed for school.

**JENNIFER KNEW THE DROP-OFF LINE** would be long on a rainy morning, and it was. One by one the cars inched forward and kids scrambled out. Three cars ahead of her a Buick tapped the bumper of the SUV in front of it, and all hell broke loose. The agony of waiting for the SUV owner to come around and inspect the bumper, that quite obviously had no damage, escalated when the woman behind the Buick began blowing her horn.

Jennifer groaned. "My head is killing me. Can't you just jump out here?"

Brooke's eyes grew big and round. "No. It's against the rules."

"The walkway is right there," Jennifer pleaded. "Five, maybe six feet away."

"Rules are rules, Mama. If I get out before—"

"I know." Jennifer gave a weary sigh. "Missus Lombardi will come over here and read me the riot act."

Brooke nodded.

There was no escaping or bypassing the drop-off line. The cars were bumper to bumper. Jennifer couldn't pull out even if she wanted to, so she sat there with a sharp pain hammering against the inside of her head. Her only thoughts were of getting to Dunninger's Drugstore, grabbing her refill of Relpax and returning home where she could lie down in a darkened room and wait for the migraine to subside.

After what seemed an eternity, the cars began to move and they pulled up to the walkway. Brooke leaned forward, kissed the side of her mama's cheek then reached for the door handle.

As it swung open Jennifer said, "Don't forget, you're riding with Ava's mom to Brownies."

"I thought it was your turn."

"It was. Lara's doing me a favor, so don't forget to thank her, okay, sweetie?"

"Okay." Brooke nodded then she slammed the door shut and hurried along to join a group of classmates.

The sound of the door ricocheted through Jennifer's brain like a bomb blast. The migraines were getting worse. This one was close to being unbearable. Pulling out of the drop-off line and circling around behind Clarksburg Middle School, she fixed her eyes on the car in front of her and used every last bit of energy she had to push on the gas pedal and keep moving.

**Tom Coggan was out of** money and out of options. He had until five o'clock to get three thousand dollars to Antonio or have both legs broken. He hadn't had a fix since yesterday afternoon, the ringing in his ears wouldn't stop and his gut was killing him. He had the shakes so badly he could barely get the mug of coffee to his mouth. After two tries, he tossed the cup into the sink and watched it splinter.

He'd already pawned his watch, and the only other thing of value he had was the gun. He could pawn that too or use it to get the money he needed. The gun would maybe get him fifty bucks—not enough to pay off Antonio or get a fix—so he decided to go for the alternative. He had nothing to lose; he was as good as dead anyway.

Tom's first thought was the liquor store. Liquor stores always had a fair bit of cash on hand, and he could snatch a bottle of booze while he was there. He pulled on his jacket, dropped the gun into the right pocket then stuffed a length of cord and a wool cap into the left. As he moved toward the door he grabbed his sunglasses and put them on.

It was seventeen blocks to the liquor store. Since he had no car, he had to walk. The rain was barely a mist when he started, but after three blocks it began to pour. Twice he stopped and thought about going back, but then he reasoned that the rain was a good thing. It would keep people at home. The liquor store would be empty and all that much easier.

By the time he turned onto Atlantic Street, the plan was clear in his mind. He didn't have to shoot the clerk. He could leave him tied up, and that would allow time enough to get clear of the area. Wearing the sunglasses and hat, he was unrecognizable.

Tom smiled as fat raindrops dripped off his collar and rolled down his back. He was convinced it was a good plan. All he had to do was get in and out with no violence, and then he'd be home free.

No violence. That was the thing. That's where Tom's brother, Eddie, had made his mistake. As soon as that clerk ended up in the hospital, the cops came looking for him. Tom had warned Eddie a dozen times or more, but Eddie had chosen to listen to Cassidy and ended up in jail.

*Stupid; just plain stupid.*

Good thing the cops didn't bust their chops looking for a snatch-and-run. Over and over again Tom reminded himself, no violence.

It was 8:20 when he got to the liquor store. The door was locked. "Closed" the sign said. "Open 10AM to 10PM, Monday through Saturday."

Tom reached for his wrist to check the time then remembered his watch was gone. It was at the pawnshop along with his cell phone, bowling ball and a number of other things.

"Damn," he mumbled.

He stood there for several minutes and rattled the door handle as he cussed it for being locked. Finally he turned and started down Commerce Street.

The bakery was open, but there were three women inside. Not good. Besides a bakery wouldn't have much cash, and he had no desire for gooey muffins. Two blocks down he saw the green neon sign for Dunninger's Drugstore and headed in that direction.

Tom felt for the gun in his pocket and smiled again. A drugstore was as good as a liquor store. Better maybe. Once he had the clerk tied up he could help himself to a bit of morphine or oxycodone to take the edge off.

**DUNNINGER'S DRUGSTORE HAD BEEN ROBBED** the summer before, and Albert Dunninger lived with the reminder of it. He'd been knocked out cold and shoved into a storeroom while the thieves pilfered through his drawers of drugs. After God only knows how long, they'd emptied every container of painkiller, antidepressant, tranquilizer and sleeping tablet then scattered bottles of vitamins across the floor. By the time the police arrived, Albert had a huge lump on his forehead and was so traumatized that he had to be hospitalized for a week.

The drugstore had remained closed for the full month of August, and before it reopened in September Albert had gotten himself a Beretta 92. He kept it in the drawer beneath the cash register. At first he'd worried the gun was too heavy and perhaps too powerful for an amateur to operate, but he'd solved that problem with shooting lessons and one solid week of target practice.

**THE MINUTE ALBERT SAW THE** stranger walk in he became suspicious. Why would somebody be wearing sunglasses on a day with pouring rain? And a wool cap pulled low over his brow when it was barely fifty degrees?

He stood behind the cash register, eased the drawer open an inch and then two. He didn't reach for the Beretta but stood there watching and waiting.

**TOM CIRCLED THE STORE, LEAVING** a watery trail behind him. He stopped and browsed a display of candies then moved on to cold remedies. As he walked he glanced down one aisle and along the other.

He was soaked through to his shirt but feeling good. Already he could imagine himself with a pocket full of money and enough oxycodone for a real high. Once he was certain there was no one else in the store, he turned toward the cash register at the back counter. He slid his hand into his pocket, wrapped it around the handle of the gun and fingered the trigger.

*No violence.*

Tom's nose was red, swollen almost, and runny looking. In an effort to get the pharmacist to turn away so he could grab him from behind, Tom said, "The doctor called in a prescription, and I'm here to pick it up. Jones; Bill Jones."

In that moment Albert could have pulled out the gun but he hesitated, thinking maybe he'd made a mistake judging the fellow. He stepped back from the drawer and asked, "What's your date of birth?"

Tom wasn't prepared for the question, and it unnerved him.

"February fifth," he answered nervously.

The moment the words were out of his mouth he realized he'd made a mistake in giving his actual birthday. He yanked the gun from his pocket and said, "Don't move, and you won't get hurt."

He moved closer to the counter, the hammer cocked and his right arm locked into position. The revolver was pointed at Albert's face.

Albert heard the front door open and waited for a moment of distraction. His Beretta was less than a foot away. All he needed was the split second when the man turned to glance back.

The only thing Tom heard was the ringing in his ears.

Jennifer Bishop came down the cold remedies aisle staggering beneath the pain of the migraine. At the end of the aisle, she rounded the corner and stepped in the trail of water Tom had dripped across the floor. Her foot slid out from under her. She grabbed for the shelf and knocked over an end cap display of Hockmeyer's Cough Syrup.

The sound of bottles clattering to the floor was louder than the ringing in Tom's ears. He whirled around, saw her standing less than two feet away and fired. Before her body hit the floor, Albert grabbed his gun and fired a second shot. That one tore through Tom's brain and splattered parts of it halfway down the aisle. The last thing Tom Coggan saw was a big black rock hurtling through space and aimed right at him.

By the time the EMTs arrived, both Tom Coggan and Jennifer Bishop were dead.

# The Phone Call

Late that morning two uniformed policemen stepped onto the front porch of the Bishop house and rang the doorbell. They waited for several minutes, and when there was no answer they began knocking at the doors of the nearby houses.

Jennifer's next-door neighbor, Marta Feldman, was watching *The Price is Right* when she heard the knock. Just as Drew Carey was about to reveal the correct price of the Whirlpool dishwasher the knock sounded again.

"I'm coming," she called out then snapped the television off and headed for the door. When she saw two policemen standing on her porch, she clutched her hand to her heart and gasped.

"Don't tell me something's happened to Walter!"

Looking a bit puzzled, Officer Scott repeated, "Walter?"

Marta gave a fearful nod. "Walter Feldman, my husband. Has something—"

"We're not here about your husband," Scott cut in. "But we do need to ask a few questions about your neighbor..." He glanced down at his notes. "...Jennifer Bishop."

"Jennifer?"

He nodded. "Do you know if Missus Bishop lives with anyone?"

"How could I not know? I'm right next door." Marta stepped out onto the porch and glanced up and down the street. "If you want to know something about Jennifer, why don't you ask her?"

"There's no one at home. All we need to know is—"

"Drew, her husband, lives with her. They have a daughter."

Marta liked Jennifer and her little girl too. She was none too anxious to give out information they might want to keep hidden. Her brows pinched into a suspicious frown.

"What's this all about anyway?"

Without answering the question, Scott asked, "Do you know how we can get in touch with Drew?"

"No, I do not," Marta replied in a bristly tone. "And I'll not say another thing unless you tell me what this is about. If Jennifer is in some kind of trouble—"

"No trouble," he said, "but there's been an accident. Missus Bishop's cell phone had her home number on it but wasn't programed with an emergency contact, and we're trying to figure out who to get in touch with."

Marta's hand flew to her mouth. "Dear God. What kind of—"

Without giving her the chance to finish her question, Scott again asked about the husband.

"Drew works for a printing company and travels a lot," she said. "He comes home every week or two then goes again."

"Do you know how to get in touch with him?"

"Me? Of course not. But if you have Jennifer's cell phone his number is in there. Brooke might have it, but she's just a child and I doubt—"

"Brooke, is she their daughter?"

Marta gave a reluctant nod. "She comes home at about three o'clock, except on days when she has after-school activities, then it's later. Four maybe. Or five."

"She'll need someone to stay with her," Scott said. "Do they have family nearby?"

Marta shook her head. "Not close by. Jennifer's parents live in California, and Drew's daddy...well, I forget where he lives, but it's nowhere around here."

"Any close friends you know of? Or should we just get Child Welfare Services?"

"Child Welfare?" Marta exclaimed. "How can you suggest such a thing when I'm standing right here? Jennifer and I are neighbors! What makes you think I would allow Child Welfare to take my neighbor's daughter?"

"Are you saying you'd be okay with watching the girl until we can get in touch with her father?"

Marta defiantly thumped her hands on her hips. "That is precisely what I am saying."

"Thank you, ma'am," Scott said. "You've been very helpful."

Both policemen turned away before Marta could ask anything further.

"Call in and have them check the listing for Drew Bishop on her cell phone," Scott told his partner as they climbed back into the squad car.

**AS SHE STOOD AND WATCHED** the patrol car pull away, Marta could feel her heart thundering. She had a sixth sense about trouble and knew this was bad. Very bad. Although the officer gave no details, it was obvious something terrible happened to Jennifer. The probability was she'd been injured or, God forbid, was now dead, and there was no telling how long it would be before Drew returned home. Marta's thoughts went to Brooke. She pictured the child's big blue eyes and trusting smile.

The girl was only seven years old, eight at the most. Too young to have a next-door neighbor tell her something bad had happened to her mama.

Marta stepped back inside and closed the door. Wondering

what to do, she stood at the window watching the walkway to the Bishop house. After a long while she decided that at least for now she would keep the news from Brooke. She would stand at the window and watch for the school bus, and if Brooke didn't get off of the bus she would continue to stand at the window and watch for one of Jennifer's friends to bring Brooke home. As soon as a car pulled into the driveway she could hurry out and tell Brooke her mama said she should stay with her until someone got home.

Several times Marta ran through the scenario, anticipating the questions Brooke might ask and coming up with answers that had the sound of legitimacy. Once the pieces were eased into place, she stood at the window with her eye fixed on the bus stop at the corner.

**DREW BISHOP WAS ON HIS** way from Macon to Atlanta when he got the call. There was construction on Route 75, and the traffic noise was worse than usual. The screen flashed "unidentified caller." He pushed the Talk button and said, "Drew Bishop."

"This is Officer Scott of the Clarksburg Police Department—"

"Speak louder," Drew said. "They're working on the road, and I can hardly hear you."

"I said there's been an accident. Your wife, Jennifer, was at the drugstore and there was a robbery—"

Drew pulled to the side of the highway and stopped. "Is she okay? Was Brooke with her?"

"Your daughter wasn't with her," Scott said, delivering the most positive news first. "But Jennifer was shot."

"Shot?" Drew's voice trembled. "Is she—"

"I'm sorry, Mister Bishop, there was nothing anyone could

do," Scott said sympathetically. "She was gone before the EMTs got there."

Scott explained that Marta Feldman had volunteered to take care of their daughter until Drew got home.

"Does Brooke know?" he asked.

"No," Scott answered. "Your wife's name has not been released to the press yet, and we've not given Missus Feldman any of the details so I doubt she'll say anything. I think it would be better if you were the one to tell your daughter."

Drew pictured Brooke side by side with her mama, and he could already feel the heartache of delivering such news.

"I'll get there as quickly as I can," he said. "I'm east of Atlanta right now, and the drive will take about five hours."

After giving a few more details, Officer Scott's voice was gone as suddenly as it had come. The screen flashed, "Disconnect call?" Beneath the question there were two options, "Yes" and "No." Drew ignored them and dropped his forehead onto the steering wheel, his heart thundering in his chest and his breath coming in thin ragged puffs. In what felt like a single heartbeat, his world had fallen apart and his life forever changed. It seemed almost unreal, like a nightmare he should somehow be able to break free of.

Three short days ago he'd held Jennifer in his arms and felt the warmth of her love. She'd kissed him goodbye and playfully nibbled at his ear.

"Hurry home," she'd said, "because you never know what trouble I could get into while you're gone."

She'd laughed, and even now he could hear the echo of that laugh.

*How could it be that someone so alive is suddenly gone?*

A flood of thoughts passed through his mind as he looked back on that morning: Brooke, still wearing her pajamas, wiping sleep from her eyes hugging his neck and kissing his cheek.

"Goodbye, Daddy," she'd said. Sometimes she complained about him leaving but not that morning. Everything had been good that morning and now, just three days later...

*Brooke. Oh, God, poor little Brooke.*

He reached forward and pressed the Start button. He had to get home. Quickly.

As he made his way through the construction traffic, Drew placed three calls. The first two were canceling the appointments he had scheduled.

"Family emergency," he said.

The third call was to Marta Feldman. As he listened to the phone ringing he thought back on the day Jennifer had programed that number into his cell phone. They'd gone to Virginia Beach for a long weekend, and halfway there she'd remembered the geraniums on the front porch.

"They'll die without water," she said and then called information to get Marta's phone number.

That's how Jennifer was. She knew how to ask someone for a favor and make them feel good about doing it.

"You're a sweetheart," she'd told Marta and promised to bring her a box of taffy.

That day he'd teased her about fussing over a few potted plants, and she'd laughed. It was a laugh that filled the car with the sound of happiness. It was a laugh he'd never again hear. Drew's eyes blurred, and he blinked back the tears that began to roll down his cheeks.

The phone rang several times before Marta picked up. She answered in a hushed voice.

"Marta, is that you?" Drew asked.

"It's me," she said. "There's been an accident, have you heard?"

After a long pause he finally answered, and the sound of a sob could be heard in his voice.

"Yes, the police called me."

"Don't worry about Brooke," Marta said. "She'll stay here with me after she gets home."

"She doesn't know yet, does she?"

"No, I thought it would be easier if you told her."

"Thank you, Marta. Thank you for everything."

Drew wanted to say thank you for watering the geraniums, but he didn't. Instead he leaned on the horn then pulled out and flew past a slow-moving U-Haul. "I'll be there in a few hours."

Marta heard the sound of the horn again.

"Drive carefully," she warned. "Brooke needs you."

"I know," he answered wearily.

As he continued down Route 75, he couldn't dismiss the thought of those damn geraniums. He kept remembering how Jennifer had thought to bring home the box of taffy, and he'd not even taken time to walk across the lawn and say thank you.

A sorrow greater than any he'd ever known settled into his soul, and he began to realize what a vast emptiness Jennifer had left behind. Yes, he would miss her, more than he'd miss an arm or a leg, but he wasn't the only one. There were so many others who'd feel an emptiness in their lives: all the friends and neighbors she'd taken time to care about. People like Marta and Walter. And then there was Brooke, a child as connected to her mama as the sun is to the sky.

Brooke most of all would feel the pain of Jennifer's absence.

**IT WAS AFTER TEN WHEN** he arrived at the Feldman house, scooped the sleepy little girl into his arms and carried her home.

That night, long after he'd tucked Brooke into bed, he sat in the living room trying to sort through his thoughts. Trying to think of what had to be done. As he looked at the future the way Jennifer would have done, he came to the realization that he could no longer be an absentee father. He now had to be both father and mother to Brooke.

When he carried his suitcase upstairs to the bedroom, he saw the bed with the covers still folded back. He sat on the side of the bed, touched his hand to the pillow that still held the imprint of where she'd laid her head and cried.

# Drew Bishop

*How in God's name can something like this happen? That's what I keep asking myself. How can it be that one minute your life is fine, perfect maybe, then the bottom falls out and you're left wondering how you're going to make it through a single day?*

*Everywhere I look I see Jennifer—standing in the kitchen, calling out to me from the upstairs hallway, sitting on the side of Brooke's bed, telling stories and kissing her good night.*

*Seeing Brooke's face is like looking at Jennifer in a mirror of the past. She's the spitting image of her mama. They're alike in a thousand different ways: the blond hair, the expressions, the giggly laugh and maybe most of all the eyes. When I met Jennifer the first thing I noticed was the blue-green color of her eyes. I don't know of another person with eyes that color…except Brooke.*

*There were so many things I never told Jennifer, and now I wish I had. We always had something more important to talk about. A new dishwasher, a bill that was due, plans for the weekend. Now none of those everyday things matter. Instead of talking about those things, I should have told her when I'm far away in a strange hotel room I picture her and Brooke and wonder what they're doing at that exact moment.*

*Jennifer knew I loved her, but I so seldom told her how much. I never thought to call just to say she was the heart and soul of me, the heart and soul of our family. I never thought to say without her I would be an empty shell. I never thought to say it, because I never thought it would happen. You don't expect a woman as alive and vibrant as Jennifer to die. You just never expect it.*

*All these years we've been together the days have flown by. Weekends came and went in the blink of an eye. Now time all but stands still, and I'm stuck in this God-awful minute. This minute of knowing that Jennifer is gone, and in the morning I'll have to tell Brooke. If it's this difficult for me to accept, I can't begin to imagine how hard it will be for her.*

*Even though I know what is in store, I pray God will give me the words I need. I pray He'll help me tell Brooke in the gentlest way possible so I don't break her tiny little heart. I know such a thing is impossible, but still I pray.*

# When Morning Comes

Brooke put her hand on her daddy's shoulder and gave a gentle shake.

"Where's Mama?" she asked.

Drew felt a tightness clutch his heart when he saw his daughter standing alongside of the bed, her face just inches from his.

"Good morning, sweetheart," he said and pulled himself up on one elbow. "You're up very early."

"Where's Mama?" she repeated.

There was no easy answer. Drew thought he'd have more time to pull the right words together, to say what he had to say in a way that was less painful. He sat up, swung his legs to the floor and took her small hands into his.

"I love you, Brooke," he said soulfully, "and your mama loves you too. She once told me if she had to choose the most perfect little girl in the world it would be you. Not in a hundred million years would she ever want to leave us, but sometimes things happen, things we can't—"

A frightened look settled on Brooke's brow. "Did something happen to Mama?"

Drew gave a solemn nod. "Yes, baby, it did."

He felt the churn of his stomach as he began to explain. "Yesterday a bad man did an evil thing, and your mama got hurt—"

"Is she in the hospital?"

"No, I'm afraid not, honey."

"Then why didn't she come home?"

"She wanted to. God knows your mama would be here if she could. She loved you more than anything on earth, but she didn't have a say in what happened."

Brooke bit down on her lip as it began to quiver. "Is Mama coming home today?"

"No, baby, she's not," Drew replied softly. "Your mama's not ever coming home again. She can't. God took her up to heaven."

"Only dead people go to heaven."

"Yes, Brooke, that's true." He wrapped his arms around her, pulled her to his chest and held her.

"You're squashing me," she said and wriggled free. "You're just saying that to scare me. Mama's not really in heaven...is she?"

Brooke's eyes became watery as her voice turned to a trembling mix of fear and childish demand for truth.

A long sigh rattled up from Drew's chest. It was heavy with the sorrow he himself felt.

"I would never try to scare you, and I would never say such a thing if it weren't true."

"Don't say that!" Brooke angrily pushed back and looked up at Drew with tear-filled eyes. "Where is Mama really?"

"In heaven," he repeated.

The tears overflowed Brooke's eyes as she stood there looking up at him.

He gently pulled her into his arms and whispered, "I'm sorry, sweetheart."

He kissed the top of her head and breathed in the scent of the vanilla bean shampoo Jennifer used. He held her close, and she buried her face in the cradle of his neck. With his hand on her back he could feel the heave and pull of her tiny body as she sobbed. Her tears continued for a long while, soaking into his tee shirt and cracking his heart into a hundred million pieces.

When the tears finally slowed she asked about what happened.

How could Drew possibly explain this tragedy to a child when he barely understood it himself? He reached for the simplest version he could find. The truth was too harsh, too cruel to tell, so he tried to soften it.

"There was a robbery at the drugstore," he said. "The policeman told me your mama must have walked in and startled the robber. The gun accidently went off, and the bullet hit your mama."

The tears filling Brooke's eyes spilled over and again ran down her cheeks. Drew gently pulled her into his arms and tried as best he could to comfort her.

"The doctors tried to save your mama," he said, "but they couldn't."

Brooke continued to sob, holding tight to him just as he held tight to her. With her small body so close, he could feel the tiny heart shattering. He wanted desperately to say something that would be of comfort, but there simply was no comfort to be had. Not for him, nor for her.

They remained locked together for a long while, but in time her sobbing slowed to a broken-hearted sniffle. When that happened, Drew led her to the bathroom and wiped a cool washcloth across her face. He kissed her forehead and promised he would always be there for her.

"I know I'm not your mama," he said, "but I'll do the best I can."

"What about when you're working?" she asked. "Who's going to take care of me while you're working?"

It was a question that caught Drew off guard.

"We'll work something out," he answered.

"Please don't make me go live with Miss Marta."

"You won't have to live with anybody but me. How's that?"

With her blue-green eyes still watery, she gave a somber nod.

Drew knew then his life was never going to be the same. He could no longer go town to town calling on clients, attending industry conferences or flying to Chicago to check on a press run. He now had a responsibility greater than all of those things. His daughter, a tiny lookalike of her mama, was now his sole responsibility.

There was no one else.

Jennifer's parents lived in California, and both were still working. They'd come for a week, maybe two, but in time they'd return home. They were lawyers with a life of their own.

His dad was a bachelor and not someone who could be counted on. Drew's mom died the year he turned fourteen, and he could still remember the cloud of gloom that settled over the house. His dad wrapped himself in a cocoon of sorrow and ventured out only to go to work. In the evening he'd sit on the sofa and drink beer as he cursed the fate that had brought him to this point. It was as if Drew had ceased to exist along with his mom.

Meals, when there was one, consisted of Chinese food scraped from a container or canned spaghetti. Although Drew felt the loss as much as his dad, there was no one to turn to for comfort. Those were bad years for everyone. Drew, then a freshman in high school, got mixed up with a wild crowd. The night he got arrested it was Margaret Thompson, his history teacher, who he called for help.

Brooke deserved better. He had to make it better. Somehow, someway he had to learn to be the kind of parent she needed.

**THAT MORNING AS THEY SAT** across from one another at the breakfast table, Drew told his daughter that she was the most important thing in his life.

"I won't be traveling anymore," he said. "I'm going to find a way to work out of the house, so I'll be here every afternoon when you come home from school."

She pushed a few Cheerios to the side of the bowl and looked at him with an expression he knew as Jennifer's.

"You swear?" she asked suspiciously.

"Cross my heart," he replied.

**THE WEEK THAT FOLLOWED WAS** a frenzy of activity. The house was filled with people, and Drew's cell phone never stopped beeping and buzzing. Those who didn't call texted message after message. "How can I help?" they asked. "What can I do?" He tried to keep up with answering the messages, but before long it became impossible.

Jennifer's parents flew in and Drew's dad came with his latest girlfriend, a woman twenty years his junior. Marta whirled in and out a dozen times a day, and each time she arrived carrying something: a casserole for supper, clean sheets for the guestroom, a stack of freshly laundered towels.

"You really don't need to do this," Drew told her but she poo-pooed the thought and left, promising some sweet rolls for the next morning's breakfast.

The neighbors came in droves, and they too brought food: cakes, pies, trays of cheese and sandwich meat. Lara Stone, Ava's mama, brought a chicken dinner complete with mashed potatoes and gravy.

"I knew Jennifer had a migraine that morning," Lara said

through tears. "I should have offered to pick Brooke up and drive her to school. If I'd done that Jennifer might still be alive."

"It's not your fault," Drew replied grimly. "I'm the one who should have been home instead of off in Atlanta."

It seemed everyone owned a piece of the guilt for what happened, even Brooke. Sitting side by side with her friend Ava, she whispered that it was her fault for not taking the school bus. When Drew heard that, he took Brooke aside and told her it was absolutely not her fault.

"Your mama drove you to one place and another because it gave her joy," he said. "She wouldn't have wanted it any other way."

Alyce Abrams, Brooke's teacher, was one of those who came. She knew Jennifer, apparently quite well. She took Drew's hand in hers and spoke about how Jennifer frequently helped out on class projects.

"She was someone I could always count on," Miss Abrams said. "And the children, why, they absolutely adored her."

This was yet another part of Jennifer's life that he knew nothing about. She had so many parts. Helping hands, a loving heart, a giving soul. He had known only one small part of this woman he'd loved: the part that was his wife. He'd missed knowing the woman that these other people had known, and now he was left to fill the emptiness of a spot he knew so little about.

Before Miss Abrams left she knelt and hugged Brooke.

"Don't worry about your schoolwork," she said. "I'll send this week's lessons to the house, and your daddy can help you to get caught up."

Drew heard this, and it added to the enormity of the tasks he seemed to be inheriting.

For him the loss of Jennifer became more pronounced with every day that passed. Long after everyone else had retired for the night, he circled through the rooms, picking up a forgotten dish, emptying one last ashtray, doing the small everyday chores he'd seen her do a thousand times. As he wiped the kitchen counter or straightened the bathroom towels, he remembered her doing these same things, only for her it seemed so easy. She did it with such nonchalance. A single stroke and the counter glistened, whereas he'd sponged it three times and still there were odd spots of jelly or ketchup.

**ON THE DAY OF THE** funeral, Brooke clung to him with a ferocity he'd never before seen. Throughout the service and even at the graveside, she'd not said a word. At the very end she'd held to his hand as they moved forward and placed the two roses atop Jennifer's coffin. That's when she began to sob hysterically. Drew lifted her into his arms and carried her back to the car.

That night she climbed into his bed and slept beside him, in the exact spot where her mama had once laid her head.

# THE WEEKS THAT FOLLOWED

Sorrow is a thing that, when shared, becomes less bitter. In the early weeks following the funeral, a constant flow of Jennifer's friends and neighbors stopped by the house. They came and dropped off a casserole or a few grocery items they thought Drew might need. They stayed for a cup of coffee and chatted. They messaged Drew, asking if Brooke need a ride to the Brownie meeting or a pickup for dance class. They listened with a sympathetic ear as he spoke of how he found it hard to accept she was gone, and oddly enough having those strangers fill part of the day somehow made his sorrow more tolerable.

But as days turned into weeks and weeks into months, they stopped coming and returned to the busyness of their own lives. Little by little the text messages, phone calls and visitations became the exception rather than the rule.

The only ones who still came were Brooke's friends, little girls who needed milk poured and snacks prepared. Once they arrived he'd have to set aside whatever he was doing to microwave some popcorn or cut the crust from a peanut butter and jelly sandwich, or fix the broken door on a dollhouse, or find the string kite they'd played with last summer.

When Brooke was at school, Drew had the emptiness of the day to face alone.

He'd gone back to work a week after the funeral but no longer traveled from town to town seeing customers. Instead of face-to-face meetings, he called or video chatted. He dropped Brooke off at school, then returned to the house and sat at the kitchen table wearing jeans and a tee shirt. The table became a desk of sorts with folders stacked on top of each other and sticky notes stuck to the wall. His business day began when he opened his laptop to discover what new crisis or complaint was waiting, and he cringed when the doorbell chimed in the middle of a call.

"Aren't you at the office?" customers would ask, and then he'd have to explain the situation all over again.

The button down shirts and sport jackets he once wore hung in the closet and gathered dust. There was no more wining and dining the buyers; no more entertaining them with clever stories and jokes. There was only a brisk phone conversation or, worse yet, a video conference where someone mentioned the kitchen sink in the background and laughed. He once might have chuckled himself, but now he'd lost the ability to laugh at such things or make idle chatter over football games, world events and groundbreaking new technology.

"Are you happy with the spring catalog?" he'd ask, but inevitably there would be some small sticky point that presented a problem. The blue was too blue, the black not sharp enough, the overrun too large or the delivery a day late.

"We missed having you at the print run," they'd say. Then Drew would again apologize and explain that he was still trying to work things out.

"I'll be there next time," he'd promise, but he generally wasn't. The closest printing facilities for Southfield Press were a day's drive away, and when it was a rotogravure run it meant a flight to the west coast. Even if he was willing to hop on a plane and fly back on the red eye, there was always the problem of Brooke. She had gone from a giggly little girl to a solemn child who rarely smiled.

"I miss Mama," she'd say a dozen or more times a day.

"I miss her too," he'd reply, and even though he was in the middle of trying to estimate the price for a full color sixteen-page newspaper insert, he'd find himself rethinking that day and feeling the pain of it all over again.

Every morning he drove Brooke to school and was always there to pick her up at the end of the day.

"How was school today?" he'd ask, and she'd answer with little more than a shrug.

As they drove home in silence, he often thought back on the little girl who used to greet him when he returned from a trip. Back then—back when they still had Jennifer—Brooke was always full of chatter about the things they'd done and places they'd gone. Before the dirty clothes he'd carried home were dumped in the laundry basket she'd be telling him about a visit to the library, a spelling test or some weekend event Jennifer had planned for the three of them.

Now Brooke had almost nothing to say. In the evening she sat at the dining table with her school books open and her mind elsewhere. She'd sit in the same spot for hours doodling circles or squares in the notebook where she was supposed to be working through math problems.

Several times Drew offered to help, but after their initial experience she grimaced and shook her head.

The first time he'd offered she'd nodded. He sat alongside of her explaining how to find the sum of 486 and 637 by adding the six and seven together then carrying the one over to the next column.

"We're not supposed to do it that way," she said and burst into tears.

In between her huffs and puffs of frustration, she finally explained that they had to break the numbers into hundreds, tens and ones, then add up all the components. Not only did she have to come up with the right answer, but she also had to show the thinking she'd gone through to get to it.

This breaking numbers into digital units thing was foreign to anything Drew had ever known, and the process seemed extremely unwieldy.

"But why?" he asked. "Why would anyone go through all that when it's so simple to add two numbers together?"

Her answer was another bout of tears and the complaint that he was only trying to confuse her.

"Mama knew to do it like Miss Abrams told us," Brooke said through angry tears. "How come you don't?"

Drew could do nothing but give a baffled shrug.

All those years Jennifer had led him to believe he was the backbone of their family, when in truth she was. She alone held the secret to making everyone happy.

Before three months had passed, the hours of doing homework had grown into a gigantic bone of contention. With her mouth pulled into a pout, Brooke sat on one side of the table pretending to study while he sat on the opposite side scrolling through emails on his phone or leafing through a newspaper he'd already read.

"When you finish your homework, we can have a bowl of ice cream," he'd suggest, but even that was to no avail.

Finally when the clock struck ten, he'd tell Brooke it was time for bed and say she could finish in the morning. Of course she never did, and in early May Miss Abrams sent a note home saying she'd like to meet with Drew.

"It seems we have a problem in that Brooke's grades have fallen dramatically," she wrote.

**THE FOLLOWING THURSDAY HE PICKED** Brooke up at school, drove her home and then asked Marta to come over and stay with her while he went back for the meeting with Miss Abrams.

"I'm eight," Brooke complained. "I don't need a babysitter."

Trying to humor her, he said, "I know you don't. Marta is only going to be here in case of an emergency."

Brooke's chin dropped as her mouth opened in a huge O, and her eyes grew big and round. "What kind of emergency?"

"I didn't mean a real emergency," Drew replied quickly. "I just meant in case you wanted her to fix you a bite to eat or help with homework. Something like that."

"She doesn't know how to do math, and I don't like what she gives me to eat."

Drew raised an eyebrow and gave her a look of questionable belief. "You used to love Marta's cookies."

"No, I didn't. I just pretended so I could be polite."

"Well, keep pretending and be polite for a while longer, because I have to go to this meeting with Miss Abrams."

"Why can't I go with you?"

"Because she wants to speak to me privately."

"I'll wait in the car. I can bring my book and study while I'm waiting."

"I'm not going to leave you in the car all by yourself."

He kissed her cheek and said he'd be back in no time at all, but as he started to go he saw the fear in her face. He turned back, hugged her another time and then wrote a number on the inside cover of her notebook.

"This is my cell phone number," he said. "If anytime, not just today but anytime, you get frightened you can call me. When you do, your name will flash on the screen and I'll answer no matter where I am or what I'm doing."

She gave an apprehensive smile. "Honest?"

"Cross my heart," he said and kissed her again.

**THAT AFTERNOON MISS ABRAMS HAD** little to say other than what she'd already said in her note. Brooke's grades had taken a dive.

"She used to love reading and writing, but now she has no interest in it at all. In fact, last week she didn't even turn in her essay on zoo animals."

Miss Abrams ultimately suggested Brooke might benefit from seeing a psychologist.

"We as lay people have no real concept of the psychological trauma a child goes through with the loss of a parent," she said.

"Actually I think I have a pretty good idea," Drew replied. "We've gone through a lot together, and somehow we're managing."

"Managing for a child isn't the same as thriving. Until recently Brooke was always an excellent student, so I have to believe this drop off is because she's still suffering the trauma of losing her mother. Maybe if she spoke to someone who could rationalize this—"

"Rationalize?" Drew echoed with a note of sarcasm.

"You know, explain that such feelings are normal."

As she continued Drew drifted into his own thoughts. The painful truth was that normal no longer existed for them. Their little world had slid off its axis and spun out of control. The best he or Brooke could hope for was to simply hang on, and perhaps sooner or later life would right itself.

Until then he was all she had, and he would be there for her. If he had to learn the new way of doing math he would. He would try to be both mother and father for Brooke. He would learn to cook the foods she liked, start sorting laundry by colors and do all the thousands of other things Jennifer had done.

Somewhere deep within his heart he knew Brooke didn't need a psychologist; what she needed was a mother. But the problem was he had no idea of how to be one.

# Drew

*Last night after Brooke went to bed, I sat up for a long while wondering what I was doing wrong and how I could best fix it. I know Brooke misses her mama, and I don't have Jennifer's way of comforting her. I try, but it's not the same.*

*Sometimes I do something the way I think Jennifer would have done it, and Brooke gets upset.* That's NOT how Mama does it, *she says and stands there with her arms folded across her chest and a mad look on her face. It would be easy enough to think she's angry with me, but that's not really it. What she's angry at is the unfairness of life, and I can't really blame her. I'm angry at it myself.*

*It was after midnight when I remembered that incident when Brooke was just a baby. Jennifer had the flu and was so sick she couldn't even get out of bed. I was tending the baby. That evening Brooke started crying, and I just couldn't get her to stop. I walked the floor with her for hours, patted her back, changed her diaper, jiggled a rattle in front of her and did everything I could remember seeing Jennifer do, but she wouldn't stop crying.*

*Finally I went in and asked Jennifer why it was that she could calm Brooke whereas I couldn't.* I'm doing everything you do, *I told her.*

That's the problem, *she said.* Stop trying to be me and just be the real you.

*For a few minutes I stood there wondering what that was supposed to mean. Then I thought about other times I'd taken care of Brooke and remembered what it was that made her happy. I zipped her into a snowsuit, buckled her into her car seat and we went for a nice long ride. And just like always, she was sound asleep in less than fifteen minutes.*

*Remembering that made me realize I've been trying to do everything the way Jennifer did but all I've done is made a mess of it, which ultimately only makes Brooke miss her mama more. What I need to do is come up with some new thoughts, different ways to do things so Brooke and I can become closer. I'm not a good mother and I probably never will be, but I can be a really good father and perhaps for now that's enough.*

# Thirty-Six Years Ago In West Virginia

Sally Hawkins was not only a hopeless romantic; she was also as gullible as they come. When Billy Crowder stuck his hand up her skirt saying how he was crazy in love with her and had to have her, she believed him. There in the back seat of a Pontiac that smelled of whiskey and stale smoke, she could almost see a little house with a railed fence and him coming home to her every night.

Of course such a dream didn't last; before the week was out he was walking arm in arm with Jean Marie Mosley and saying he was going to marry her.

Sally was devastated but not nearly as devastated as she was a few months later when her belly began to swell. Her mama and daddy were church-going people who had zero tolerance for harlots, so she knew she had to do something and do it quick.

In her fourth month she went into downtown Charleston and got a job waiting tables at a south side gin mill. That's where she met Otto Coggan. He was sitting at a table alone, drinking boilermakers. When she set the foamy mug and a shot of whiskey in front of him, he looked her up and down as if she was standing there naked.

"What time you get done here?" he asked.

Sally put on her sexiest smile and answered, "Midnight."

"I can wait," he said and downed the whiskey.

That night Sally gave him the best sex she knew how to give and promised there was more where that came from. Three days later they were married, and she returned home claiming he was the daddy of her baby.

Otto had a stomach way bigger than hers ever would be and a bushy beard with crumbs of food stuck to it, but he was the best she could find on such short notice. It's possible that she'd have kept looking if she'd seen his meanness in those early days, but she didn't. All she saw was an ugly man looking for a pretty girl and a good time. She was willing to make the trade to avoid the wrath of a daddy who would have beat her black and blue for shaming the family.

**FIVE MONTHS LATER THE TWINS** were born, and both of those boys had Billy Crowder's pale gray eyes and coppery red hair. Otto was dark complexioned with coal black hair and eyes close to the same color. With Sally's hair and eyes being the color of dirt, there was no way of explaining the boys' appearance. In the end poor Sally was not only shamed, but she was also stuck with a husband who was bad natured on a good day and flat out abusive most of the time.

It was no wonder the boys grew up as they did. They had Billy Crowder's genes and Otto's penchant for drinking and violence.

When they were ten years old both of them quit going to school, and the teacher, Missus Boyle, didn't bother reporting it. Actually she was glad to have it be the last of them. They were a disturbance to the class, and there was no way of disciplining either one of those boys.

She'd tried once with Eddie. The following morning she found her cat lying on the doorstep, dead as a doornail with a rope tied around its fragile little neck.

Before their fourteenth birthday, both boys walked off the mountain and were never again heard from. There were rumors that they'd been seen in Charleston, then Huntington, and even as far away as Portsmouth, but nothing was ever known for sure.

**FOR A GOOD NUMBER OF** years the Coggan boys stuck together. They got by with petty thievery. A wallet here and there, a few snatch-and-runs, an occasional check lifted from a mailbox; nothing big enough to set the cops in search of them. They bounced around from place to place, never staying in one town long enough to become known or get caught.

They'd just turned eighteen when they left West Virginia and traveled south into Kentucky. There they met up with Willie Brice, a moonshiner who needed a distribution arm. Tom would have been content to stay there forever, running deliveries at night and sleeping it off during the day, but Eddie pushed Brice to the wall and demanded a cut of the action. That's when the whole deal went sour, and they both hightailed it south to Tennessee.

Tennessee is where Eddie met Cassidy.

Everything changed with Cassidy. She wanted more than getting by.

"You're capable of bigger things," she told Eddie, and being a bit like his mama he was gullible enough to believe her.

"I already checked out the big liquor store off the highway," Cassidy said. "After nine o'clock there's only one night clerk. You guys can take him, easy. I'll wait outside with the car running."

"I don't like it," Tom said. "What if they've got one of those silent alarms?"

Short on patience, Cassidy gave a snort of annoyance.

"So what if they do?" she said. "You'll be in and out before the cops have time to get there."

When Tom continued to argue against the plan, she rolled her eyes and called him a chicken shit.

That's when the rift between the boys started. Tom didn't like Cassidy, and the feeling was more than mutual. A dozen or more times she whispered in Eddie's ear that they ought to ditch Tom and move on, just the two of them.

In spite of the constant bickering, the three of them stayed together for another two years. They were passing through Alabama when the split finally happened.

It was two weeks before their thirtieth birthday on a day when it seemed the rain would never let up. Since the first of the month they'd been staying in a motel a few miles north of Route 20, and Cassidy was as agitated as a soaking wet cat. She pulled the rubbery curtain back and squinted out the window, watching rainwater drip from the eaves.

"This place gives me the willies," she said. "We oughtta go back to Tennessee."

"Fine by me," Eddie said.

Tom was staunchly against such a move. The cashier in that last convenience store had gotten a good look at Eddie, and with that red hair he'd be easy enough to pick out of a lineup.

"It's too soon," he said.

One word led to another, and before long the argument got out of control. Tom said nobody but an idiot would go back to where the police were sure to be looking for him, and Eddie then accused Tom of calling him an idiot. Once Cassidy had them going at each other, she simply stood by with a smirk on her face.

After a while the argument was no longer about going or staying; it was about who was in charge. Eddie grabbed Tom by the front of his shirt and screamed, "I say we go, and if you don't like it then get the hell out!"

Tom did. He counted out one third of the money they had left and stuck it in in his pocket. Then he walked out into the rain and didn't bother looking back.

**TOM DIDN'T HEAR FROM THEM** for nearly a year, and when he finally did get a call on his cell phone it was Cassidy telling him that Eddie was in the West Tennessee State Penitentiary.

"He got three years," she said unapologetically. "I ain't big on working alone, so I was thinking if maybe you changed your mind about coming to Tennessee we could hook up."

"Ain't you supposed to be waiting for Eddie?" he asked.

"For three whole years?" she replied.

For a moment Tom sat there waiting for such a thought to fade away or for her to perhaps offer more of an explanation. When neither one happened he pushed the button and disconnected the call.

"Piece of trash," he muttered.

That night he wrote a letter to Eddie saying he was still in Alabama and had settled in Clarksburg.

"When you get out, come look me up," he wrote. He gave Eddie the address of his apartment building. Then at the bottom of the letter he added a P.S., saying that if Cassidy was with him not to bother coming.

That was the last communication the Coggan twins had, because Albert Dunninger shot Tom to death five months before Eddie was released.

# The Text Thing

Two days after the meeting with Miss Abrams, Drew came up with a plan that he hoped would help him connect to Brooke. When he picked her up at school that afternoon there was a gift-wrapped package lying on the back seat of the car.

"What's this?" Brooke asked.

He turned, gave her a quick smile then pulled out of the pick-up line.

"It's a special present for you," he said.

"It's not my birthday, you know."

Drew glanced in the rear view mirror and saw her already starting to open the package.

"I know it's not," he said. "But I thought you deserved a present anyway."

When she lifted the lid from the box she scrunched her nose and frowned. "This isn't a present, it's your phone."

"Not my phone," Drew corrected. "Your phone."

The corners of her mouth curled slightly. "Mine?"

"Yep." He glanced into the rear view mirror again and gave her a grin. "I've already programmed it with my number, Grandma and Grandpa Green's number, and Grandpa Bishop's number. Now you can talk to the whole family anytime you want, and you'll never have to worry about being alone again."

"But Mama said I couldn't have a phone until I was twelve."

"Under the circumstances, I think she would want you to have it now."

Her smile broadened. "Really? And it's for keeps?"

"Absolutely."

He heard the seat belt snap open then felt the thump of her arm as she reached across the back of the seat to hug him.

"Hey, back in your seat," he said, laughing affectionately.

**THAT AFTERNOON THEY SAT SIDE** by side at the dining room table. He taught her how to answer calls, make calls and text.

"Use your thumbs," he said and placed the phone in her hands.

For the first time in months the side-slanted looks of anger were gone. He'd found something that didn't remind her of Jennifer. As he demonstrated the use of voice commands, she scooted her chair closer and asked questions. When he'd finished going through the how-to's he handed her the phone.

"Go ahead and try it," he said. "Send me a message."

With a look of determination, she tapped out her first message and hit Send. Seconds later his phone buzzed, and he tapped on the Message icon. Her message read, "I love you, Daddy." He smiled and hit Reply.

Her phone buzzed, and she grinned ear to ear. "I got a message."

She tapped the Message button and read his response. "I love you more."

Not wanting to let go of this moment, he told her the phone could also be used for a number of fun things then suggested they play a game. He set up an e-mail account for her then signed them up to play Words with Friends.

"It's like you and me playing Scrabble," he said. "Only you're on your phone and I'm on mine."

Drew started the game by feeding her spots where she could add a single letter and form some easy words to get started. "Do" became "dog," "or" became "ore" and "at" became "cat."

After they'd begun whizzing along she took the "m" in his word "team" and created the word "mother." The H landed on a triple letter spot and the R on double word. She scored thirty-seven points and laughed with delight.

"Ouch!" Drew said. "You're killing me!"

Again she laughed.

They continued playing until it was well after suppertime; then he suggested they go out for hamburgers.

"Sort of like a date," he said.

She grinned and gave an enthusiastic nod. "Okay, but let's go to Papa's Pizza! It's really, really good, and they give kids free ice cream."

Drew gave a half-hearted smile.

"Sure," he said, ruefully remembering the hundreds of times he and Jennifer had done the same thing, especially in the early years before he began to do so much traveling.

Brook pulled on her sweater then asked, "Can I bring my phone?"

"It's yours. You can bring it wherever you want. The only rule is you can't turn it on while you're in school."

"Can bring it to school if I leave it off during class?"

"Absolutely," he answered. "I want you to know you always have your family right there with you all the time."

Already thinking of how Ava would be green with envy, Brooke hiked her shoulders up around her ears and grinned.

**PAPA'S PIZZA WAS AT THE** other end of Commerce Street, a half block down from Dunninger's Drugstore. The drugstore had remained closed ever since the shooting, and according to the *Clarksburg Times* there was no knowing when it would reopen. Albert Dunninger was discovered dead in his own home a week after the incident. A heart attack, the newspaper said, and since there was no next of kin his entire estate including the drugstore had been turned over to an attorney.

This was the first time Drew had been downtown since the day it happened. For nearly three months he'd avoided passing by the store or even driving along Commerce Street. Now here he was, less than a block from where Jennifer had been killed. The weight of that memory settled in his chest as he parked the car on the side street next to Papa's Pizza.

Torn between the heartache of the memory and his desire to give Brooke some much-deserved happiness, he tried to remain upbeat but when they rounded the corner to Papa's entrance the glow of the green neon light smacked him in the eye. Although the drugstore was a distance away, Drew could see it was now open with the sign burning as brightly as ever.

It felt as if he had been punched in the chest. How could the damn drugstore be open again? Their life had been torn apart, and yet the drugstore was moving ahead as if nothing had ever happened.

*Where in God's name is the fairness in this?*

As they entered Papa's he saw a crowd of teenagers laughing in the back of the room. They had several tables pushed together just as he and Jennifer had done with their friends. He thought back on the time they'd come here with Molly and George Paley and that other couple whose names he could never remember.

The Paleys now lived crosstown. They'd come to the funeral, and Molly had stopped by once the week following. After that she'd called a few times and George had sent a text or two, but now it was well over two months since he'd heard from either of them.

Was that the way it was supposed to happen? Had he somehow gone from being part of a group of friends to being an outsider? Someone to be excluded from phone calls or gatherings? Now that he was a single parent, the Paleys apparently felt they no longer had anything in common with him. Through no fault of his own he'd become a reminder of what, God forbid, could happen to them.

The Paleys weren't the only ones. There were other friends he hadn't heard from, friends who no longer called. It was obvious; nobody wanted to face the reminder of such a tragedy so they stayed away.

Seeing the look of sorrow settle on his face, Brooke took hold of his hand and tugged him from his reverie.

"Daddy, are you sad because we came here?"

"No, sweetheart," he answered and forced a smile.

Luckily Papa's was a place where it was difficult to hold on to sorrow. It was a brightly-lit mix of chrome counters, tables with checkered tops and cherry red plastic booths. He and Brooke slid into a booth and sat across from one another.

Drew absently picked up the menu and looked at it, but the Dunninger's sign flickered back and forth in his mind.

*It had to happen. Sooner or later the drugstore would reopen, or something else would take its place.*

He stared at the menu for a moment then handed it to Brooke. "What would you like?"

"Daddy! You said we were going to get a pizza, don't you remember?"

Her voice was so like Jennifer's, a playful scolding. Even though they were sitting across from one another he'd lost himself to other thoughts, just as he'd so often done with Jennifer. Back then it had been thoughts of business; now it was simply a sorrow that refused to let go.

He tried to turn it off as a joke. "Pizza? I thought you wanted a hamburger."

She giggled. "You're not tricking me. You're the one who wanted a hamburger."

They both laughed. A few seconds later she pulled the phone from her pocket, pecked out another message and hit Send.

"Pizza w/ ice cream 4 dessert," it read.

He smiled at her use of the abbreviated words he'd taught her then tapped out an answer. Their exchange went back and forth several times. When the pizza was delivered to their table, she typed out one last message then stuck the phone back in her pocket.

"Daddy dates r fun!"

**LATER THAT EVENING AFTER HE** listened to prayers and tucked Brooke into bed, Drew wandered aimlessly through the house.

Every spot held a memory of Jennifer. In the kitchen he could see her cooking dinner with that funny-looking apron tied around her waist, and in the living room he pictured her curled up on the sofa with her nose in a book. He heard the sound of her laughter and caught the fragrance of the jasmine shower gel she used. No matter where he went her presence was close by, the way it would be if she was off in another room waiting for him to cross the threshold.

How could she be gone when she was still so alive in every room of the house?

He thought back to the phone call and remembered how Officer Scott had said it was no one's fault. An unforeseeable circumstance, he'd called it. But even then Drew knew the truth. It was someone's fault.

His.

When did he stop taking care of his family? When had he let business become the ruler of his life? If he had been here, at home with his wife and daughter instead of chasing after bigger and better clients, everything would have turned out differently.

They said Jennifer awoke with a headache that morning. If he'd been at home he would have lowered the blinds to darken the room and insisted she stay in bed. He would have driven Brooke to school himself. Then he would have stopped at the drugstore to pick up her prescription.

A flicker in time, one moment more or less might have made all the difference in the world. It's possible that he could have wrested the pistol from the perpetrator's hand and no one would have been killed. The gunman would have gone to prison, and Jennifer would still be alive.

Perhaps. Maybe. If only. All of it was useless conjecture. It changed nothing.

Drew sat on Jennifer's side of the bed and ran his hand across the sheet thinking of how it was when she'd been there. He closed his eyes, pictured the curve of her back and the spread of her hair billowed across the pillow. He remembered how on warm summer nights they'd raise the blinds and lie side by side, naked in the moonlight, belonging completely to one another.

The tears came, and he broke down.

"Why?" he sobbed. "Why didn't she stay home that morning?"

Even as he asked the question, he knew the answer would never be forthcoming.

He lowered his face into her pillow and cried for a long while. He cried because he'd done nothing to save her, and now he was left with a loneliness that was almost unbearable. After a long while, exhaustion overcame him and he fell asleep.

**JENNIFER WAS WEARING THE WHITE** cotton dress she'd worn on the Saturday they went to the fair. Her hair cascaded like a waterfall over her shoulders. A soft breeze ruffled the hem of her skirt and feathered her hair. A single strand fluttered across her cheek, and she brushed it back.

"You look so beautiful," he said.

She laughed. "I'm only a memory."

"A beautiful one." He took her hand in his, and it felt warm but without weight.

For a while they walked together, not speaking but somehow sharing thoughts. It was as if she knew and understood his sorrow.

She stopped and turned to face him.

"What happened is not your fault," she said. "You couldn't have stopped it."

"I wouldn't have lost you if I'd been there—"

She touched her finger to his mouth and stilled his words.

"You haven't lost me," she whispered. The tenderness in her voice was soft as a shadow. "You still have the best of me in Brooke."

He looked at her with a saddened smile. "She misses you as much as I do."

"I know. I've tasted the salt of her tears." Jennifer fixed her eyes on his, and they were filled with a silent plea. "Our daughter needs you to help her heal."

"Me? How can I—"

She again stilled his words. "Love her as you loved me. Speak not of sorrow but of a happy future."

"A happy future? How can there be such a thing when—"

"I have seen it and know it will happen," she said. Her voice grew softer still, and she lowered her eyes. "But only after you accept the past and move on."

He heaved a great sigh and reached out to touch her shoulder. Suddenly she became thin and wispy like a figure made of smoke.

He inhaled sharply. "Wait! Don't go!"

"I'm already gone," she said in a voice that was barely a whisper. "Know that I love you, and stay strong for Brooke."

He felt a rush of wind cross his brow, and then she disappeared from sight. The last thing he heard was a faraway voice saying, "If you're okay, she'll be okay."

"Don't go!" he screamed and bolted upright.

"Don't go where?" the childish voice said.

Drew opened his eyes and saw Brooke standing beside his bed.

"Don't go where?" she repeated.

# Finding Closure

The dream stayed with Drew for days afterward. He wanted to believe in the future Jennifer had spoken of, but it seemed impossible. How could he move ahead when so little of life even made sense? Simply moving through the routines of the day was exhausting.

Every day there seemed to be yet another thing needing his undivided attention. On Monday afternoon Brooke had dance class—not in town but over in Bellingham, which meant a forty-five minute drive each way. The class was one hour long, so he had no choice but to stay and watch the troupe of eight-year-old ballerinas struggle through their pitiful pirouettes. Once he tried calling a client while he waited, but the plink, plink, plunk of background music made the effort seem absurd.

Then on Wednesday it was the Brownie meeting. Twice he'd driven to the wrong house because Brooke was unsure about who was hosting the meeting that week. The second time he'd lost his patience and told her she should *know* these things. After only a few words it turned into a fiasco.

"Mama had a list telling the right place for the meeting," she said through her tears.

Such a declaration only served to make Drew feel more

incompetent than he already did. He finally promised to buy her a new Barbie if she'd stop crying.

On the days when he did manage to squeeze in a full afternoon of phone calls, the clients were less than thrilled to hear from him. Some didn't bother answering the call; they'd have their secretary say they were tied up or gone for the day. When he finally did talk to someone and asked about a job that had been promised him, they'd say it was delayed or cancelled. It had only been a little over three months, and already he'd lost four clients.

Robert Meecham was the largest. Drew had wined and dined Meecham for seven years. Then without a word of apology Meecham up and moved his summer catalogue to Pelham Printing.

"I'm no longer happy with the quality at Southfield Press," he said, but Drew knew that was nothing but an excuse. Printing was a one-on-one business. Clients expected to be pampered and paid attention to. They simply weren't interested in doing business over the phone.

Nothing was as it once was, not even Brooke. From time to time he'd get a glimpse of the happy little girl she used to be, but more often than not she was moody and fearful. At one time she'd wanted to ride the school bus with the other kids, but no more. Now she clung to him as if he was her one and only hope.

Each morning as she climbed from the car, she'd turn back and ask, "Do you promise to come back this afternoon?"

It wasn't just a question; it was a plea. He could see it in her eyes.

If he went to the store she wanted to go with him, even if it was for only a newspaper or quart of milk. If he carried the trash to the garage and was gone for more than a few minutes she came in search of him. And she slept with the light on, something she'd not done since the year she turned three.

On two different occasions she'd asked what would happen if

a robber shot him. At the time he'd turned it off with a lighthearted laugh, saying that like Superman he was indestructible. She'd given him a smile, but it was one that was only on her face and not in her heart.

It was as if life had suddenly divided itself into two eras: before and after that fateful day. They were now stuck in this new era, and Drew had no idea of how to break free.

**ON A TUESDAY MORNING IN** early June, Drew pulled out of the drop-off line and snapped on the talk radio station he listened to for the drive home. The interviews were generally with a local politician, a weight loss consultant or a sports figure, but on this particular morning Frank Lester had a new guest.

"Today we are talking with Margaret Hanson, noted psychologist and grief counselor," Lester said. He went on, listing her many credits, then asked a number of questions about overcoming the depression that often follows the death of a loved one.

Drew leaned forward and upped the volume.

"Grief is a natural reaction to death," she said, "but it can escalate into depression when a person fails to accept the reality of the situation and loses hope. An important part of the healing process is allowing one's self to experience and accept feelings of grief."

"That sounds logical," Lester replied. "But is there a right or wrong way to go about doing this?"

"Not really," she said. "Everyone grieves differently. Most people go through a stage we call denial or numbness before they're ready to start healing. Often they blame themselves for the loss, so instead of moving forward they dwell on what they could have done to prevent it."

"I would assume that could cause long-term problems."

"You're right. Closure is an important part of healing. Hanging on to guilt and anger inevitably leads to hopelessness, and that's when grief gives way to depression."

The questions and answers continued, and when Drew arrived back at the house he sat in the driveway listening to the end of the show.

"Well, folks, we're just about out of time," Lester finally said. "Doctor Hansen, before we go will you give our listeners one last word of advice about dealing with grief?"

She thanked him for having her as his guest then said, "Those who are grieving should not expect to forget their loved ones. It's an unrealistic expectation. But they do need to face the truth of what has happened. It's important for the person grieving to remember they are still alive. And as long as there is life, there is hope. Hope is the single most important building block to the future."

Drew snapped off the radio and thought back to the dream again. He remembered Jennifer's words.

*There is a better future, but it will only come after you accept the past and move on.*

He backed out of the driveway and turned toward Dunninger's Drugstore.

**DREW PARKED IN THE BACK** lot just as Jennifer had that morning, but he sat in the car for several minutes before he gathered enough courage to climb out and walk around to the front door. As soon as he turned the corner he saw the glow of the green neon sign.

Jennifer had also seen it, and it had no doubt worsened her headache. Her migraines were always like that; any kind of noise or brightness caused the pain to become unbearable. The last few minutes of her life were spent in agony.

He pushed through the door then stopped and looked around. It had been a year, maybe more, since the last time he'd been inside the store, and yet everything looked the same. Summer was just around the corner, but there was still an aisle of cold medications and cough syrups. Beyond that he could see a rack of sunglasses; that appeared to be new.

"Looking for anything in particular?" the young pharmacist behind the counter called out.

Drew shook his head. "Not really."

He walked toward the counter then looked back. Just above the shampoos and conditioners was a convex reflector. If Albert Dunninger was behind the counter, he had to have seen her walk in. Why then didn't he do something or shout out a warning?

"You new in town?" the pharmacist asked.

Again Drew shook his head. "My wife died, and I was hoping..."

"I'd like to help you out, but you've got to have a prescription for Xanax or any of the antidepressants. I could lose my license if—"

Drew gave a half-smile. "I'm not looking for anything like that. In February my wife, Jennifer, was in here when a robbery occurred—"

"Dear God, you're the husband..." The pharmacist came from behind the counter and walked toward Drew. "I heard about what happened and can't begin to imagine what you've gone through."

"Gone" implied it was in the past, something over and done with, but it wasn't. It was here and now. Drew gave a grimaced nod.

"It's damn hard," he said. "Not just on me, but our daughter. She's only eight and..."

He felt the sting of tears in his eyes, and there was no way he could stop them.

"I've got kids myself," the pharmacist said. "Two girls, five and six." He reached across, clasped a friendly hand on Drew's shoulder and said how sorry he was for such a loss.

"Thanks," Drew replied. Then he asked if the man was related to Dunninger.

The pharmacist shook his head. "Name's McIntyre. Peter. I bought this place from Dunninger's lawyer two months ago, and that's when I learned of what happened."

"It was all over the news," Drew said. "I thought everybody knew."

"We're not from this area," Peter replied. "We moved here from Chicago because my wife wanted to be near her mom."

They stood side by side and talked for a long time. Peter recounted all he knew of what happened that day and told how five days later Albert Dunninger had a heart attack and died.

"His lawyer was the one who handled the sale of the store."

Drew's expression took on a look of defeat. "You think if Dunninger hadn't pulled his gun, Jennifer might still be alive?"

"Not the way I heard it," Peter said. "My understanding is that Coggan shot her first, and then that's when Dunninger grabbed his gun."

That was it then. There was no one left to hate. Both of the men who had fired shots that day were now dead and buried. It was like a book of heartache slammed shut before coming to the end of the story.

They spoke for a short while longer; then Drew left the store and walked aimlessly along the boulevard. As he walked his thoughts drifted back to the times he and Jennifer had strolled this same street, his arm draped across her shoulder and hers wrapped around his waist, their steps evenly matched and hips brushing against one another.

Back then they couldn't afford to buy much of anything, so they window-shopped and built dreams of what they would do one day. In those early years he'd managed the print shop over on

Fairfax, and Jennifer worked for the lawyer three blocks down. Together they made enough to get by, to see a movie now and then and have an occasional dinner out. Sure, there were months when they'd barely scraped by, but he couldn't remember ever feeling poor.

The year after Brooke was born, he'd moved into sales. It seemed like a good idea at the time. In less than a year the commissions he earned more than doubled his salary, so naturally he'd jumped at the chance when Southfield Press offered him an expanded territory. It would be good for his family, he told himself. They could buy a house, and Jennifer could be a stay-at-home mom. Three years later, he'd been made vice president of sales with a substantial increase in salary and a hefty override on everything the salesmen in his division brought in.

Now he had to wonder: did he take that job because it drove him further up the success ladder, or did he truly believe it was best for his family?

He would leave for weeks at a time. What did Jennifer do in his absence? Did she walk this street alone and feel this same aching loneliness? Did she wish he'd not taken a job that kept him away from her for such long stretches? If so she'd kept her feelings hidden. She'd not once chastised him for being gone. Instead of being angry and sad, she'd spent her days raising a child who was happy and loving.

*Brooke.*

The thought of her settled in his mind, and Drew began to see them side by side. Mother and daughter. Alike in a thousand different ways. Until recently.

Brooke no longer had her mother's easy laugh. She seldom smiled. Like Jennifer, she kept her loneliness hidden away and said nothing. But it was there, behind the pretense of a smile and fearful questions.

*You still have the best of me in Brooke.*

# DREW

*Before today I thought I was handling things pretty well, but the truth is I wasn't. I was going through the motions of a day-to-day life almost as if Jennifer would be back. My brain knew she was gone, but my heart couldn't accept it.*

*Walking into that drugstore was the toughest thing I've ever done and it took all the courage I could muster to go through with it, but I'm glad I did. Talking with Peter McIntyre forced me to see the reality of what happened. All these months I've resented Albert Dunninger. I hated the store for being there, and I hated him for still being alive. Now I know I wasted all that energy on wishing death to a man who was already dead. I feel rather foolish.*

*Losing someone you love does that to you; it makes you bitter and angry at everything and everybody.*

*It's not just me; Brooke is carrying her fair share of anger also. There are times when I see her looking at me, and I know she's wishing God had taken me instead of Jennifer. I can't fault her for feeling that way. I've thought the same thing a thousand or more times myself. But the ugly truth is it didn't happen that way. I'm here and Jennifer isn't, so the only thing Brooke and I can do is pick up the broken pieces of our life and make the best of it.*

*For the past three months I've been just barely getting by. When*

*Brooke settled into her angry pouts, I let her stay there. I had my own problems, and they seemed way bigger than hers.*

*This afternoon as I was thinking about the way it used to be, I came to realize that the hardships Brooke and I face from day to day aren't my problems or her problems. They're* our *problems. Our life is what it is, and the only way we can make it better is by loving one another the way Jennifer loved both of us.*

# A Place to Start

By the time Drew pulled into the pickup line, he was determined to find a way to reach out to Brooke. Somehow, someway, he would remove the shroud of anger she was wearing and give her back the childhood she had before that fateful day. He didn't have Jennifer's ability to find the magic in the ordinary things of life, but he had a deep down love for his daughter and hopefully that would be enough.

As she climbed into the back seat he turned and smiled. "How was school today?"

She gave her usual shrug and answered, "Okay."

Up until now he'd accepted that answer, believing she needed space. This time he didn't.

"What did you study?" he asked.

"Fractions."

"Just fractions? A full day of fractions seems kind of boring."

"We did world history too."

"Oh? And was it better than fractions?"

She gave a funny little snort. "Anything's better than fractions."

Drew knew he had a dozen calls to make that afternoon, but he pushed them to the back of his mind and said, "I bet I have a fraction you'd like."

She leaned over and glared at him through the rear view mirror. "Daddy, there is not one single fraction that I like. None."

"How about this." He glanced at the mirror and saw her eyes still on his face. "I buy one ice cream soda for us to share. Then you get to choose what fraction of it you'll have and what the remainder is that I'll get."

She giggled. "What if I say I'll have the whole thing?"

"That's not the game. You have to choose a fraction."

"Okay, I'll have three quarters of it."

"Ha, you picked an easy one." He chuckled. "Well, if you have three quarters, how much will that leave me?"

She thought for a moment then grinned and said, "One quarter."

"Very good," he replied and turned toward Commerce Street. He parked in front of the Shake Shop, the same shop he'd passed earlier that afternoon.

Brooke looked at the place with a wistful smile. "I used to come here with Mama."

Not giving her time to slide into the sadness of those unspoken thoughts, Drew said, "I'll bet you've got some pretty good memories of this place then. Any you'd like to share?"

Again she shrugged. He could see her pulling back, hiding inside herself.

"Nothing, huh?"

They slid into the booth and sat across from one another. Drew plucked the menu from its holder and passed it over to her.

"While you decide if you want a snack to go with that three-quarter soda, I'll tell you something I remember about your mama. Her favorite flavor was vanilla, so I think we should have a vanilla soda."

Brooke scrunched her forehead into a puzzled frown. "No, it wasn't. It was strawberry."

"Vanilla," Drew repeated.

"Strawberry." Brooke's voice grew more adamant. "I know

because when we came here she used to order a strawberry milkshake or a strawberry sundae."

"Ah, so you do remember."

She looked across at him and gave a reluctant nod. "I remember Mama and me had a lot of fun." Her eyes grew teary, and she turned back to the menu.

"I know how much you miss your mama," he said. "I miss her too."

Brooke didn't answer and kept her focus on the menu.

"If you're missing Mama and I'm missing her too, maybe instead of each of us missing her by ourselves we could try missing her together."

"How can we do that?" she asked curiously.

"Well...I guess we could start by talking about her and thinking of all the nice things she did. That way we'd be remembering her but we wouldn't have to do it all by ourselves; we could be doing it together."

"Won't talking about Mama make you feel sadder?"

"I don't know." Drew gave a single shoulder shrug and smiled. "One thing I do know is that losing your mama has left us both with a whole lot of sadness and tears. If a person keeps all those tears inside, they'll drown in their own sorrow."

Brooke pushed back a loose curl that had fallen across her forehead and gave him a look of skepticism. "A person can't really drown in tears."

"Well, maybe not technically, but they sure can be miserable."

She gave a grim nod.

"I realize I haven't been a whole lot of fun these past few months," Drew said. "I guess it's partly because for so many years I was busy working and didn't take time to relax and have fun. Now I seem to have forgotten how."

"That's what Mama used to say." Brooke held back the grin tugging at one side of her mouth.

"Don't be a smarty pants," he replied jokingly. "I'm willing to admit I need help, but the question is are you ready to lend a hand?"

"I'm just a kid. What can I do?"

"Well, you already seem to know a bit about having fun, so I was thinking maybe you could teach me."

She hesitated for a few moments then finally said, "It wasn't me. Mama was the one who knew fun things to do."

"Oh. Well, then. I guess we've got a problem, don't we?"

She gave another solemn nod.

"Since neither of us knows much about having fun, I guess we'll have to try different things until we can figure out what's fun and what isn't."

"What kind of things?"

He cradled his chin in the valley between his thumb and index finger and sat there for a while acting as if he were pondering the thought.

"I suppose we could start with cleaning out the garage," he finally said.

She frowned. "That's not fun at all."

"Well, then what do you suggest?"

"Maybe make cookies."

He grinned. "I guess that might be a better idea."

On the way home they stopped at the Food Giant supermarket and bought three kinds of slice-and-bake cookie dough. That evening as they worked they spoke about Jennifer, not in terms of sorrow but in fond remembrances. Brooke told of the time they went to a Christmas party where everybody traded packets of homemade cookies. Drew shared the story of a time just after they were married.

"We were just out for a drive, and right there by the side of the road was a tree so full of apples some of them had already dropped to the ground. Your mama told me to stop the car; then she got out and gathered up all those loose apples. We brought them home, and she made the best apple pie I've ever tasted."

"Mama has a recipe for that pie," Brooke said brightly. "We could go back to the tree and get more apples."

Drew laughed. "The apples aren't ripe enough this early in the year, but if you can wait until fall we could give it a try."

"I can wait," she replied. She suggested that while they were waiting for the apples to ripen, they could practice by making some other dishes.

"Mama said anyone can learn to cook if they set their mind to it."

**THAT EVENING THEY PULLED THE** hand-painted box from the shelf of the pantry and poked through clipped-out recipes and handwritten notes until they came across one for crunchy mac and cheese.

"This looks easy enough," Drew said. "How about starting with this and working our way up to apple pie?"

"Good idea," she replied.

When the cookies were done Brooke said while they were not quite as good as the ones Mama made, they came close. She packed an assortment of cookies into a basket and headed for Marta and Walter Feldman's house next door. Since it was after dark, Drew trailed behind her.

"Daddy and I made these," she said and proudly handed Marta the basket.

At that moment Drew could almost see Jennifer standing there and doing the same thing. He smiled.

*You've still got the best of me in Brooke.*

**THAT EVENING BEFORE SHE WENT** to bed Brooke came to Drew.

"Thank you, Daddy." She wrapped her tiny arms around his

neck and squeezed her face up against his. "I'm glad we decided to miss Mama together."

He lifted her into his lap and said, "I'm glad too, baby."

They sat like that and talked for almost a half-hour, Brooke telling him all the things she'd thought of for them to do after next week when school was out for the summer. There was the beach, a trip to the zoo, a day of shopping for summer clothes, an afternoon at the park…

As she went on and on, Drew wondered how he was going to fit all of that in and still take care of business.

*One day at a time,* he thought. *Just one day at a time.*

**AFTER SHE'D GONE TO SLEEP** he walked through the house studying the bits and pieces Jennifer had left behind. Curtains stitched by hand, framed photographs of the three of them in happier days, a collection of *Southern Living* magazines that kept coming every month as if she was still there to read them. A thousand reminders of the precious moments that were now gone forever.

*Don't try to forget your loved one; it's an unrealistic expectation. Remember them, but understand these are now only memories and move forward with your life.*

He looked at the handwritten recipe clipped to the refrigerator door and again wished he'd been there to change the events of that day. There was no way he could alter the past, but hopefully he could do something about the future. The warmth of Brooke's hug meant he'd made a start. He would build on it. Take each day as it came and make his goal to make her life better. It's what Jennifer would have wanted.

When Drew fell asleep that night he was comforted by thoughts of a better future; he had no idea of the trouble that lay ahead.

# The Weight of Loss

The Keeper of the Scales saw the thoughts in Drew Bishop's mind and smiled. It was a good thing to see a father watching over his child, a thing that deserved to be rewarded. He took a large rose-colored stone from the pile and placed it on the happiness side of Drew's scale.

For a moment the scale found perfect balance, and then without a visible cause sorrow began to outweigh the new stone. Without lifting it from the scale, he rolled the stone over and examined it carefully. On the bottom, nearly hidden from his all-seeing eye, was a splattering of small dark spots. They appeared to be growing larger by the moment, spreading, connecting one to another and coloring the underside of the stone an ominous gray.

*How can this be?* the Keeper wondered.

His great eye traveled down the spire of the scale and found at the bottom a silver thread twined around the base.

He followed the delicate thread across the landscape. It traveled first one way and then the other, touching nothing until it came to a spot where it was caught beneath another scale. The scale of Eddie Coggan.

The Keeper gave an angry roar, and lightning snapped across the sky. In all his centuries of watching over the scales, he had never before encountered such an injustice. He railed at the power above him but was helpless to change the pathway of the thread.

For the first time since the dawn of mankind, the Keeper tried to remove the stone he had placed on the scale. It wouldn't budge. It had grown so heavy that not even his great power could lift it.

There was nothing he could do to change the course of events. Everything would happen as it had been destined.

# A Free Man

A week before Eddie Coggan was to be released, he stood in line and waited for a turn to use the prisoner telephone. Three times he dialed the number for Tom's cell phone, and three times his call slid into the same empty void. No ring, no wrong number, nothing.

That night he wrote a letter.

"I'm getting out July 13th," he wrote. "Come get me." He added a P.S., saying he hadn't heard from Cassidy for well over two years and wasn't planning to look her up. On the day of his release he expected Tom to be there, so when the guard asked if he wanted a lift into town he said no.

The first thing Eddie did when he stepped outside the gate was suck in a deep breath of air. It smelled differently on the outside. Fresher. Freedom had a good smell. It smelled like something he'd been missing.

For almost three hours Eddie stood in the hot sun waiting for his brother. He set his small duffle on the ground, swiped at the sweat on his brow and paced back and forth. Every so often he'd look up at the sun and wonder what time it was. In his letter he'd told Tom to be here at ten o'clock, but the sun had already crossed its high point.

It wasn't like him to be this late.

When Eddie's shadow grew longer he hoisted the duffle onto his shoulder, walked out to Green Chapel Road and tried to thumb a ride into town. He had no money, no car and no way of even making a phone call. After three years of working in the prison laundry, the only thing they'd given him was the address of a halfway house where he could supposedly stay.

*This is bullshit.*

When a car finally stopped, he jumped in. The driver was an elderly woman with white hair.

"It's a good thing I happened by," she said. "There's not a lot of traffic out this way, and a person could melt standing in the hot sun."

Eddie pulled a hankie from his pocket and wiped the sweat from his face. "Ain't it the truth."

She said her name was Margaret Elkins and asked his.

"Eddie Chapel," he replied.

The name of the road he'd been on was the first thing that came to mind. Avoiding the truth had always served Eddie well, and he saw no reason to do differently now. He said he was headed for Georgia to visit an ailing mama.

"I'm visiting family also," she told him. "My sister, Helen." She spit the sister's name out as if it were distasteful. "At my age I shouldn't be doing all this driving, but if I left it up to Helen we'd never see one another."

Eddie spotted the pocketbook on the back seat and wondered how much actual cash was in it.

"Helen don't drive?" he asked absently.

"Oh, she drives," Margaret snapped. "But since she moved into that assisted living place she sits on her rump and waits for jitney to take her everywhere." She gave a huff of annoyance. "That's the problem with those places. Once people move in they *expect* to be driven everywhere! Why, half the cars in that parking lot haven't moved since the day they arrived!"

"Really?" Eddie had to hold back the grin tugging at his face. "They just park the cars and leave them there?"

"Yes. Disgraceful, isn't it?"

Eddie nodded as he eyed the loose change in the well of the console.

For the next seventy-six miles, he let Margaret do most of the talking. He listened, and as she explained the faults of one thing and another he soaked up details of the Millpond Assisted Living Facility. By the time they arrived he knew that every resident was in the dining room between six and seven-thirty and before ten they were all in bed fast asleep.

"The crime of it all," Margaret said, "is that Helen is seven years younger than I am. She should be the one visiting me!"

Eddie again nodded his agreement.

Shortly before they hit Madison she dropped him on the corner of Route 72.

"Millpond is just a mile or so down the road," she said, "but outside of the assisted living place there's not another thing for miles around. At least here you'll be able to catch another ride."

He thanked her and waved goodbye as she drove off.

**THE WALK WAS SHORTER THAN** Eddie expected, and the sky was just beginning to turn dark when he arrived at the Millpond Assisted Living Facility. Keeping a good distance between himself and the building, he walked toward the back and eyed the parking lot. Even from a distance he could see what Margaret told him was most likely true. The cars sat like gray ghosts lined up across the lot, layers of dust and pollen covering whatever color was beneath. The front of the building was landscaped with small green bushes and flowering plants that bordered the walkways winding around and back again. Along the walkways were slatted benches for people to sit.

Eddie heard laughter and voices across the courtyard. He turned away. A face they might recognize but the back of a man, never. He waited until it was quiet then circled around to the far side of the building looking for an open window on the ground floor, hoping to find a wallet left lying about on a dresser within easy reach.

In the back he found places where he could look in and see the rooms, but these were not regular windows with a sash that could be raised or lowered. They were large panes of glass cemented into place. Peering into a long hallway he saw clusters of people talking and laughing together, the men dressed in suit jackets and the women with sweaters shrugged over their shoulders. Although a rivulet of sweat ran down his back, when he touched his hand to the window it was cold.

*Air conditioning.*

He circled the building but found not a single window that could be pushed open.

Lights began popping on in first one room and then another. The residents were now returning from dinner. He'd have to wait two, maybe three hours.

Beyond the parking lot there was a field of high grass, as good a place as any. He tromped through the grass and found a spot where he could see without being seen, then lowered himself to the ground. He was tired and hungry, but he couldn't afford to think of food right now.

First he had to get a car then some cash, at least enough to tide him over until he could get to Tom's place. Once he'd hooked up with his brother they'd do as they once did, and everything would work out just fine. It would be as it was before he'd met Cassidy.

As he sat in the tall grass listening to the call of the katydids and the growl of his stomach, he thought about Tom. He remembered the good times, the times when they'd rambled from place to place, grabbing a wallet here and there. It was always enough to get by, and they'd had fun doing it. Tom knew how to keep things in check; he knew when to stay and when to pack up and run. He'd said not to go back to Tennessee, but Eddie hadn't listened and that's how he ended up spending three years behind bars.

*No more. From now on it's gonna be me n' Tom, glued together like we always been.*

The darkness in the sky grew deeper, and one by one the lights of the building began to go out. After a while there was only the faint glow that came from the dimly-lit hallway. Eddie waited a while longer just to be certain; then he crept toward the parking lot.

The cars in the back of the lot were also covered with a thick layer of dust and pollen. It was obvious they had been sitting there for a long time; months, maybe even years. He walked along the row and tried the door handles. The first five doors were locked. Then the sixth, a Ford Fairlane, squeaked open. Hopefully it would start.

Sliding into the driver's seat, Eddie reached under the steering column and used his pocketknife to pop off the plastic panel covering the wiring. He pulled the bundle of wires out, but without a light it was impossible to distinguish color. He reached up and clicked the light switch. Nothing. He tried again. Still nothing.

"Friggin' battery's dead," he grumbled and got out.

After he searched the remainder of the back row and found door after door locked, he remembered how Tom had gotten the Buick they'd snatched in Kentucky. Eddie started working his way back down the row, feeling up under all four fenders of each car. Finally he found what he wanted stuck under the back fender of a Lincoln Town Car. He grinned and pulled out the small magnetic box that held a spare key.

Easy peasy. The key slid in the lock, and the overhead light came on as he opened the door. He slid into the driver's seat and twisted the key in the ignition. The engine coughed once or twice then came to life.

The dust and grime that covered the car also covered the windshield. Eddie pushed a button. Washer fluid squirted across the windshield, and the wipers swished back and forth. It was enough to see. The first thing he had to do was get out of here. After that he'd think about stopping to clean off the windows.

The Town Car was long and wide with a big squared-off grill in the front. Eddie inched back, cleared the parking space then turned toward the drive. He glanced across at the building. It was still dark, and he could see no movement. He moved slowly down the long driveway then turned onto the road that led back to Route 72. The car had over a half tank of gas, more than enough to get across the county line.

At the junction of Route 72, Eddie swung into the right-hand lane and headed west. He waited until he'd passed the sign that read Limestone County then pulled off the road. He popped the trunk open and found a bottle of washer fluid and some rags, so he cleaned the windows. Beneath the dust and grime he discovered the car was a metallic gray, black almost.

"Nice and forgettable," he said to himself and began searching the trunk for something else that might be of use. There was a baseball cap, a sweater and what looked to be the nozzle of a garden hose.

He put the cap on and pulled the brim low then stuck the nozzle in his pocket and climbed back into the car. After he crossed into Marion County, he left the highway and turned down a side road. It was less than a mile before he came to a brightly-lit roadhouse with the sound of music coming from it. He pulled in and circled around to the back parking lot. Now the only thing he could do was wait.

The clock on the dashboard ticked off twenty minutes before he saw a column of light fall across the lot. The door swung open, and two couples stumbled out laughing and falling into one another. Drunk was good, but even drunk he couldn't handle four of them.

Eddie slunk down into the leather seat so he was less visible and waited until they'd passed by. After that group there was a couple and then another couple. Still he waited. He was hoping for a loner, someone with half a bag on who'd be easy to take. The clock on the dashboard ticked on minute after minute, and before long it was nearing one o'clock. The place would be closing soon; he had to act now.

The door swung open again, and another couple came out. They stopped a few feet from the door, and the man pulled the woman into a passionate embrace.

*Too close to the door.*

Eddie eased himself out of the car and stood in the shadows. He waited, his fingers nervously clutching and then unclutching the nozzle. After what seemed like a ridiculously long time the couple broke apart. She turned toward the front parking lot and he moved toward the back. Even from this distance Eddie could tell the guy was soused.

*Perfect.*

He waited until the man walked past him without noticing. Then he came at him from behind. Eddie swung his right arm around the man's neck and with his left hand jabbed the nozzle into his back.

"Make a sound, and you're a dead man," Eddie hissed. "You hear me?"

The man gave a silent nod.

"Now put both hands on the back of your head. Nice and slow, don't try any funny business."

Eddie released his hold on the man's neck but kept the nozzle pressed tight against his back.

"No fast moves," he warned. "Keep one hand where it is. Use the other to reach into your pocket and pull out your wallet and car keys."

Following instructions, he pulled the wallet from his back pocket.

"Pass it back," Eddie said. "Now the car keys."

Without turning the man fished in his right pocket and pulled out the keys.

"Good boy," Eddie said. "Now walk to the far end of the lot and lie face down. If you even think about turning around, I'll blow your head off."

Again the man nodded.

"Go," Eddie said and gave his back another sharp jab.

Before the man reached the end of the black top Eddie was gone. About thirty miles later, Eddie opened the window and tossed the car keys into a wooded lot. There was no way the man from the roadhouse could follow him now. He kept the wallet and the nine hundred bucks in it.

It had been fifteen hours since he'd last eaten, and the lack of food was causing his head to hurt.

*Not yet.*

No more tossing caution to the wind like he did with Cassidy. This time he was playing it smart. He was going to do things the way Tom wanted. No violence. Go for smaller scores, nothing big enough to have the cops chasing him.

He drove until he'd crossed the line into Marengo County, and somewhere near Demopolis he stopped at a twenty-four-hour truck stop, ran the Lincoln through the car wash then went into Denny's and ordered the Grand Slam.

# The Search for Tom

It was after three in the morning when Eddie finally got to Clarksburg, and it took another twenty minutes to find Parson Street. He'd held on to the letter for almost three years knowing this is where it had come from. Now that he was here, he couldn't get through the damn door.

Eddie rattled it a second and then a third time, but the lock refused to budge.

Irena Polanski was in bed trying to get some sleep when she heard the noise. Figuring it to be another drunk looking for a hallway where he could sleep it off, she buried her head deeper into the pillow.

"Go away," she said with a moan then turned over to face the wall.

Parson Street was a crooked little strip of cement close to the edge of town. It was one block long, and the only things on it were two small apartment buildings and an empty lot covered with overgrown weeds. The end of Parson Street was smack up against the city dump, and on the far corner was the Mother of Mercy Church. It was the kind of street where even the church locked their doors at night.

After nearly twenty minutes of banging on the apartment

building door, Eddie gave up and returned to the car. He pushed the seat back and closed his eyes. He'd waited three years to see Tom; he could wait another few hours.

**THE SUN WAS WELL INTO** the sky when Eddie woke. He eyed the building across the street. The door was now propped open, and a bushy-haired woman was busily sweeping the front steps. He climbed from the car and started over.

"Hey there," he hollered.

Irena gave the broom another swoosh then glanced up. "What?"

Her tone reflected the annoyance she felt. The building was an albatross around her neck. She'd have sold it long ago if she had a buyer.

As Eddie drew closer he said, "I'm looking for Tom Coggan. You know his apartment number?"

Irena turned and leaned heavily on her broom. Getting involved in other people's troubles was something she didn't need. She had troubles enough of her own.

Skipping over the gory details she said, "He don't live here no more," and went back to sweeping.

"Where'd he go?"

She gave an offhanded shrug and continued swooshing the broom back and forth across the steps. Eddie reached out, grabbed hold of broom handle and held on to it.

Irena looked up and gave an angry glare. "Let go or—"

"Or what?" Eddie said, keeping his grip on the handle.

"Or I start yelling for the cops," she said, looking him square in the eye.

Clearly Irena wasn't a woman who was easily frightened. After staring her down for another minute, Eddie let go of the broom.

"I ain't looking for trouble," he said apologetically. "But Tom's my brother. He's all I got in this world, and I gotta find him." There was a sense of urgency in his words, a sound of neediness.

For a brief moment the thought of her own sister flashed through Irena's mind. More than two years had gone by since Helga's death, but the thought of it was still raw and painful.

*Dead, the policeman said. A hit-and-run driver who didn't bother stopping.*

Irena leaned the broom against the porch rail and turned back to Eddie.

"I'm sorry I gotta be the one to tell you this," she said, "but your brother died some five months ago."

Eddie stood there looking like he'd been struck by lightning. "But...how..."

She glanced at the car he'd gotten out of. It was clean, conservative, responsible-looking. He was not the type of man she usually got in here.

Trying to soften the blow she said, "Some sort of an accident; he got caught up in a robbery gone bad."

"Tom?"

She nodded. "Look, I'm not sure what happened. All I know is that the police came banging on the door, and when I let them in they carried a bunch of stuff out of his place. Evidence, supposedly."

"You sure it was Tom?"

"He had the same color hair you got. Ain't too many with that color."

It seemed almost inconceivable. Tom was careful; he was always in and out. Quick. No violence. Tears welled in Eddie's eyes, and he brushed them away with the heel of his hand.

"They didn't tell you nothing about what happened?"

Irena shook her head. "Sorry. Seeing as how you're family, you could try asking them. The stationhouse is down on Branch

Street." She went on to say the remainder of Tom's things was packed away in a box she'd stored in the basement.

"You can take them if you want."

"Yeah, I'll take them," Eddie said.

He stood and waited while she went to fetch the box. When she returned he took it from her. It was small and surprisingly light.

"What about Tom's apartment?" he asked. "Is it still avail—"

"We ain't got no apartments here," she said. "Just furnished rooms, and all of them's rented right now."

Saying it she sounded believable enough, but in truth there was an empty room on the fourth floor and another one on the second. Something about the way he looked had made Irena lie.

"Sorry," she said again.

Eddie carried the box back to the car, placed it in the trunk and drove off. Going to the police wasn't an option for him. He'd have to find another way to learn what happened.

**FOR THE REST OF THE** afternoon he drove around town, looking for something but of what he was unsure. He and Tom were twins, and twins had a thing about them. A sixth sense, something that connected them to one another. There had been any number of times when he'd been able to reach out and grab hold of Tom's thoughts. He was hoping he could still do it.

He drove up and down Commerce Street several times, but nothing jumped out at him. It was like any other business street, one shop pushed up against the next with nothing but a neon sign to tell them apart. Whatever sense of knowing he'd hoped for was not here.

Turning off of Commerce, he drove through one side of town and then the other. Nothing. No feel of Tom ever being there.

*Impossible,* he thought as he drove past small houses with bicycles left in the driveways and front doors painted a rainbow of colors. Eddie knew he was missing something. But what?

When darkness settled over the town he turned back to Route 20. Less than three miles down the road he came across The Hungry Eye, a roadhouse with only a handful of cars in the parking lot. He eased his foot down on the brake and turned into the driveway. He needed something to eat and time to think.

Under other circumstances, Eddie would have bellied up to the bar. He'd done enough drinking to know they poured heavier there. Tonight he had other things on his mind. If the drink came watered down, he'd tell them to take it back and make it a double. With nine hundred bucks in his pocket, he could afford it. He passed by the bar and slid into a back booth that was away from the crowd.

He didn't notice the brunette on the far side, but she noticed him. She noticed him the minute he came through the door. There was no mistaking that hair.

Alisha watched for almost fifteen minutes; then when she couldn't stand it any longer she walked over and slid into the booth across from him.

She leaned forward and whispered, "I thought you were dead."

Eddie looked at her the way one eyes a crazy person. "I know you?"

She pinched her face into an angry looking snit. "So that's the way it is? You don't want to talk to me, fine, Tommy, but don't think—"

"Tom? You knew Tom?"

She glared at him with the same look he'd given her seconds earlier.

"Forget it," she snapped. "I'm not up for some asshole game where—"

"Tom was my twin brother."

"Brother, huh?" She eyed him suspiciously. "Funny, when you was Tommy you never said nothing about having a brother."

"I been away." Eddie pulled Tom's letter from his pocket and handed it to Alisha. "Tom wrote me that letter and said come stay with him when I can."

She did a quick read through of the letter then raised an eyebrow. "Tommy said come see him when you get out. Was you in jail?"

"Yeah; so what?"

"Don't get snippy with me. I was just asking." Alisha slid to the end of seat and started to stand.

Eddie grabbed hold of her wrist. "Hold up. Sit. Have a drink."

"You buying?"

He nodded and signaled the waitress over. Alisha ordered a Jack Daniels on the rocks. Eddie said, "Make it two," and drained the last of his beer.

Once they were settled with their drinks, he asked how much she knew about what happened with Tom.

She gave an almost cynical laugh. "Nobody knew nothing about Tommy; he mostly kept to himself. He'd come here, we'd spend a few days together, then he'd take off and I wouldn't see him for another month or two."

Eddie shook his head sorrowfully. "Man, that sure doesn't sound like Tom."

"It got worse. For a while he was just dealing. Then he got hooked on the stuff. Real bad. That monkey on Tommy's back wasn't about to let go."

A look of doubt crawled across Eddie's face. "The landlady said Tom got killed in a robbery gone bad. You got anything to say about that?"

"When that happened I hadn't seen Tommy for two, maybe three months. All I know is what they said in the papers. Two people were shot, Tommy and some woman. It was all over the news, even on TV."

"You keep any of those newspapers?"

She shook her head. "Nah. That was five months ago. They probably got 'em at the library. They keep stuff on file."

Alisha and Eddie sat across from one another knocking back one Jack Daniels after another until the bartender hollered, "Last call."

When Alisha asked if Eddie wanted to come home with her he was tempted for a moment, but after he remembered how things turned out with Cassidy he shook his head.

"Some other time," he said.

For the second time, Eddie spent the night in his newly-acquired car. He didn't get much sleep, but that was mostly because he was still thinking about how he was going to find out the truth of what happened to Tom. Alisha claimed the library kept old newspapers, but he'd never once even been inside of a library and wasn't sure he was up to doing it now.

Tomorrow he'd go back to Clarksburg and hopefully this time he'd find a clue, some thought or memory Tom had left behind. There had to be something. He'd simply missed it that first time around.

# Coming of Summer

Drew thought once Brooke was out of school his life would be a bit easier, that there would be less hurrying from place to place and he could focus on the clients he'd been neglecting. It turned out to be just the opposite.

Without the distraction of school Brooke's moods went up and down like a yo-yo. One moment she would be the happy little girl she once was, and then without warning she'd turn sullen. Or clingy. And on occasion there were temper tantrums that erupted over some bit of silliness not worth worrying about.

Such an episode happened on the Tuesday morning Drew had a conference call with Ed Mathews, the client he'd been trying to get for three years. Mathews was the owner of a chain of discount stores that stretched across Alabama, Georgia and South Carolina and did over two million mailers each month. Landing an account like that would more than make up for the business he'd lost.

They were less than ten minutes into the conversation when Drew heard crashing and banging from upstairs. Hoping Mathews wouldn't hear it, he slid his hand over the mouthpiece and tried to focus on what Matthews was saying. The noise continued, so with the phone in his hand Drew started upstairs.

When he opened the door to Brooke's room, she was sitting on the floor sobbing and the big dollhouse was in pieces.

He stepped back into the hall and said to Mathews, "I've got a bit of an emergency going on here. Can I call you back in a few minutes?"

Matthews was a short man with a Napoleon complex and an even shorter fuse. What he lacked in stature he more than made up for in aggressiveness, and the one thing he could not tolerate was being pushed aside for someone else.

"What kind of emergency?" he demanded.

With his back to the wall, Drew explained what had happened to Jennifer.

"It's only been four months," he said, "and Brooke is having difficulty adjusting."

For a moment Mathews said nothing, and Drew could almost picture him giving an intolerant glare over the half-size glasses he wore.

"Yeah," Mathews said. "Call me back. But this better not be an ongoing problem."

More hopeful than certain, Drew assured him it wouldn't be.

"Don't worry," he said. "Once we start the print runs I'll be right there, on top of every last detail."

"You'd better be," Mathews said and hung up.

**WHEN DREW RETURNED TO BROOKE'S** room she was still sobbing. He lifted her from the floor and sat on the bed with her in his lap.

"What's the matter?" he asked.

For a few minutes she kept sobbing even as he held her head to his chest and kept a firm grip on her back. In time the sobbing slowed to sniffles and he again asked what happened.

"The garage door on my Barbie house was stuck so I tried to fix it, and it broke."

Drew eyed the pieces of plastic scattered across the floor. "It looks like more than the garage door is broken."

She nodded and sniffled through her words. "They got broke when I was trying to fix it."

"Did you maybe knock the Barbie house over because you were angry?"

Brooke sat there with her face tilted to the floor and said nothing.

"Didn't we talk about this?" Drew's voice was soft, gentle and understanding. "Didn't we talk about how sometimes when things don't go the way we want, we have to be patient?"

Without taking her eyes from the floor she gave a barely perceptible nod.

"Now that you've made this big mess, what do you think you should do?"

With her chin tucked into her chest she mumbled, "Pick everything up and put it back where it belongs."

"Okay then." Drew eased her off his lap and stood. "Get to it."

"Will you help me?"

"Not right now. I'm busy working."

"You're always busy working," she replied bitterly.

DREW KNEW THAT WAS THE crux of the problem. He was her security blanket. With him right there beside her she was fine, but when he turned away to work she became needy.

He'd tried a dozen different strategies to overcome the problem, and so far none of them had worked. When he suggested she sit across from him and color or read as he worked, she'd talk, hum, sing or swing her legs back and forth banging her feet against the table while he was on the phone.

"Can't you be quieter?" he asked, but that only resulted in pouting and more tears.

Inviting her little friends, Ava and Emily, over for a playdate was somewhat helpful, but even then there were constant interruptions because they needed help with one thing or another. Or they were hungry for snacks or it was time to get ready for parent pickups.

The one advantage was that after he'd had her friends to the house for a playdate, the moms would call and invite Brooke to spend the afternoon at their house. On afternoons like that Drew could get in four, sometimes five hours of work with no interruptions.

And there were a few other occasions when Marta would take Brooke shopping or invited her over to bake cookies. Marta would have been happy to have her there every afternoon, but Brooke wouldn't hear of it. In her mind she associated poor Marta with the loss of her mama. Although Drew had explained a dozen or more times that one thing had nothing to do with the other, Brooke persisted in saying, "When I stayed with Miss Marta, Mama got killed."

In early July Drew was searching the Internet for a weekly cleaning service when he spotted an ad for a day camp. He clicked on it and watched the video of happy little campers scrambling on and off a bus that was painted with a jungle theme. There was video of rainy-day lunches with a clown entertaining the kids, craft classes, games, story time, sing-alongs and even a small pond for swimming and canoeing. At the end of the video he clicked on "More Information" and learned that it was a door-to-door service with kids picked up between seven-thirty and eight AM and returned home between four-thirty and five.

The price was $300 a week. It would be a stretch for his budget, but he could more than make up for it by beefing up his clientele.

He called for Brooke to come and see the video. With her standing beside him, he clicked Start and allowed it to play through. He noticed the smile on her face and said, "Doesn't this look like fun?"

She gave an apprehensive nod.

With each new scene he had a comment. The pond was lovely, the crafts looked like such fun, the kids seemed to be enjoying story time. When the video ended he turned to Brooke.

"Well, what do you think?"

In the past few months she had developed a manner of pulling her features together into a tight little knot expressing doubt, concern or displeasure. With her face arranged in just such a manner, she asked, "Are we going there?"

"This isn't a camp for grownups. It's just for kids. You get picked up in the morning and brought back home in time for supper. That sounds good, doesn't it?"

The expression on her face tightened a bit more.

"I thought maybe you'd like to go there this summer."

"By myself?" she exclaimed.

"You wouldn't be by yourself. You'd be with all the other kids."

"They're strangers."

"Well, they wouldn't be for long. Once you got to know them—"

Drew saw the tears welling in Brooke's eyes.

"You don't have to go if you don't want to. I just thought it would be—"

Before he could get to the word "fun," she said she didn't want to go. He heaved a weighted sigh and said she didn't have to do it if she didn't want to, but by then she was already on her way back to her room.

# Rethinking Alisha

After two nights of sleeping in the Lincoln, Eddie decided he needed to get a room. He wasn't anxious to stay in the town where Tom had been killed, but neither was he ready to leave it behind. He couldn't shake the feeling there was something more to the story, something that he hadn't yet heard.

This need to know what happened was like an ache that kept growing inside of him. Maybe it would have been smart to set it aside, but he couldn't. It was the same feeling of needing another cigarette or another drink but a hundred times worse.

That afternoon he drove through Clarksburg again. He slowed the car to a near crawl, inching along streets that might offer up the feeling he sought, but there was nothing. After one last run down Commerce Street, he turned back toward the highway. On Route 20 he made a quick stop at the liquor store, grabbed some snacks and a half-gallon of Jim Beam, then started looking for a motel.

The Sleepway Inn was eighteen miles from Clarksburg, and it looked like a place where they didn't ask a whole lot of questions. Trying to err on the side of caution he wore the baseball cap and sunglasses then checked in as Bruce Kersey, the owner of the

Lincoln Town Car. His signature on the register was scribbled in such a way that it would have been unrecognizable anyway.

The room was only marginally better than the cell he'd occupied for the past three years. The bed, although wider, was just as lumpy, and the lamp gave less light than the jailhouse overheads. He unwrapped one of the disposable plastic cups, poured himself a shot then snapped on the television. One station came in clearly; the rest were mostly snow.

The news was on, and a reporter was telling how the Martinsville Zoo was scheduled to get a new zebra.

"Exciting news for Martinsville," the newscaster said with a wide grin.

"A friggin' zebra?" Eddie grumbled. "You got news about a zebra and nothing about my brother getting killed?"

He poured himself another drink and watched while they showed clips from the Independence Day parade. Each new segment was another source of agitation. Although Tom's death had supposedly taken place over four months ago, it felt recent to Eddie, still new, still raw. The more he drank, the more the feeling of anger and resentment swelled inside of him.

It was near eleven when he picked up the phone and dialed the number Alisha had given him.

"I'm gonna need your help," he said.

"Who is this?" Alisha's voice was thick and groggy.

"Eddie. Tom's brother."

"Oh. Ain't it kinda late?" she asked.

Eddie had planned to come right out and say he needed her to help him find the story of Tom's death in the newspapers at the library, but she didn't seem all that glad to hear from him so he figured he'd better go at it easy.

"I got a room and a bottle of Jimmy B," he said. "I was thinking maybe you'd like to come over for a drink."

"I don't know," she drawled. "Seems kind of funny you

weren't too interested in me yesterday, and now you're wanting me to come over."

"I had to get warmed up to the idea," Eddie replied. "You know, with you being Tom's girlfriend and all."

"Whoa there," Alisha cut in. "I wasn't never Tommy's girlfriend. We was friends with benefits. We hung out and had some laughs. Tommy never had no expectations from me, and I never had none from him."

There was a bit of back and forth kibitzing about what Eddie might or might not expect from her, but in the end she agreed to come.

"Park in the back," he said, "and just come to room one twenty-seven. Don't bother stopping at the desk."

**FORTY-FIVE MINUTES LATER THERE WAS** a knock on the door, and when Eddie opened it Alisha was standing there in a thong and lacy bra. Her skirt and tee shirt were dangling from her fingertip.

Eddie grabbed her by the arm and yanked her inside. "Are you crazy or something?"

She gave a husky laugh. "I figured I'd go ahead and get you started."

"Idiot! That ain't what I wanted you here for—"

"Hey, watch what you're saying. I don't gotta—"

"Sorry." Eddie tried to sound apologetic. "It's just that I'm keeping a low profile until I find what I'm looking for."

"So if it ain't a roll in the sheets, what do you want from me?"

Eddie caught the curtness in her tone and held back from speaking his mind. Alisha was a bit like Cassidy, the kind of woman who'd walk off unless there was something in it for her. He grinned and slid his fingers along her neck and down toward her bosom.

"I figured we could have a few drinks, get to know one another."

"Yeah, I bet." This time she gave him a look that reeked of skepticism.

"I think you're misjudging me." Eddie unwrapped the second plastic glass, poured two inches of bourbon into both glasses and handed one to her. He gave her what he hoped was his most charming smile then said, "Cheers" and gulped down a sizeable swallow. She did the same.

Once Alisha got started drinking, it didn't take a whole lot of convincing to get her to stay. By the time the bottle was down to the halfway mark she was ready to either make love or go dancing, but Eddie, who was never a happy drunk to begin with, had started getting teary eyed over thoughts of his brother.

"We was twins," he said as he cried. "Twins, that's the same as two halves of the same person."

Alisha rolled her eyes. "You gonna keep this crap up all night? I come here for a good time and ain't interested in listening to you moan and cry."

Drunk as he was, Eddie had enough presence of mind to know it would be a lot easier if he had her help.

"Looks like you'd be interested in helping me find what happened to Tom, 'specially since he had all that money hidden away."

Alisha, who had a good tolerance for liquor, wasn't nearly as drunk as Eddie. She raised an eyebrow and asked, "What money?"

"Money from the bank job we did back in Tennessee. Tom stashed it 'cause we planned to split it once I got out."

Eddie considered this a mere stretch of the truth. In actuality it was a convenience store not a bank, and they'd split the money the night he and Tom parted ways.

She still had that doubtful look stuck to her face. "That don't sound right. Last time I saw Tommy he was hurting for money. If he had all that money why wouldn't he dip into it?"

"I told you. 'Cause we're twins we got this special—"

"Yeah, yeah. I know. Connection."

Eddie nodded. "So you in or out?"

She hesitated then gave a huge yawn and fell back onto the bed. "In, I guess. But I better not find out you're just screwing with my head."

**EDDIE SPENT ANOTHER HOUR TRYING** to pry something new from Alisha, but there was nothing. She said again that Tommy was doing drugs, but she had no idea who his dealer was.

"Someone big up the line," she said. "Someone Tommy was afraid of."

When it came to his murder, she could only remember parts of what she'd read in the newspaper.

"Tomorrow we'll go to the library and look it up," she said. "I told you, they keep newspapers like forever."

"Yeah, but from four or five months ago, they'd still have them?"

"The library's got papers a hundred years back, maybe longer."

"They got room for that much shit?"

"Don't be a dummy," Alisha said. "They don't keep the real newspaper, they keep copies of it on microfiche." She explained how they took pictures of each page of the newspaper and stored the film.

"You look at the film through a viewing machine and once you find what you're looking for click print and bingo, you get a copy of it. Looking at the film is free, but if you print something you gotta pay for it."

This whole set up was new to Eddie. There had been a library in the West Tennessee jail but it contained nothing but books, and a good number of them had some of the pages torn out.

"Sounds good," he said and snapped off the lamp.

As they lay there side by side in the darkness, there was not an iota of passion between them. Alisha was wondering just how much money there might be, and Eddie was thinking of Tom lying dead in his grave with no one else caring.

*I care. I'll make sure somebody pays.*

# The Trip

After nearly six months of calling Ed Mathews, Drew finally got him to agree to a test run. He had cut his commission to the bone and given Mathews rock bottom pricing, but if the test run went well Southfield would get the printing contract for a year. That meant twenty-four thousand full-color flyers plus bounce-back cards and scratch-offs. It was an account that would dwarf the Meecham account he'd lost and one that would put things right between him and Brian Carson, Southfield's CEO.

The run for 500,000 magazine insert cards was set to go to press on the last Thursday of July.

"Let's schedule this for an early morning press run," Mathews said. "I'll fly in the night before so we can have dinner and talk details of the contract."

"I think that's doable," Drew said, although he had no idea how he was going to manage it from his end. Although Marta would have been more than happy to keep the child overnight, Brooke would have panicked at the thought. Desperate to find a solution, Drew called Lara Stone, Ava's mom.

"I'm kind of stuck," he said and explained the situation. "The printing plant is in Troy. It's only a four-hour drive, so I'd be back by early afternoon."

"I'd be more than happy to take her," Lara said, "and I know Ava will be thrilled to have her here for a sleepover."

"Brooke worries about me going anywhere without her," Drew said, "so if you wouldn't mind, can you have Ava call and invite her?"

Laura laughed. "I know what you mean. Our little ladies like to think they're the ones in charge."

"Exactly," he replied.

That same afternoon the phone jingled and Drew called upstairs, "Brooke, it's your friend, Ava."

He handed her the phone and watched as she chatted with Ava. There were a few whispered secrets and a peal of laughter. Then Brooke said, "Wait a minute, I'll ask my dad."

She turned to Drew, "Daddy, can I go to Ava's house for a sleepover?"

He knew if he made it too easy she'd be wary, so he hesitated then asked, "Is this something you really, really want to do?"

She nodded and gave a happy-looking grin. "Please?"

"Okay," he said, returning her smile. And that was it.

**ON WEDNESDAY AFTERNOON HE HELPED** her pack a small overnight case, which along with the toothbrush and pajamas included two candy bars, a package of cookies and Sammy the Sleepy Bear. Sammy had one button eye missing and a small hole in his right ear, but he'd been Brooke's nighttime companion since she was two and he went wherever she went.

When they arrived at Ava's house Drew went in with her, and to make it look as though he had nowhere else to go he stayed long enough to sit down and enjoy a glass of wine with Lara. By the time he left Brooke had disappeared up the stairs with Ava, and there were shrieks of laughter coming from the room.

"See?" Lara said. "Nothing to worry about."

He answered with an apprehensive smile. "Well, just in case, you have my cell phone number."

**IT WAS ALMOST SEVEN WHEN** Drew arrived in Troy, so he went directly to the restaurant rather than check into the motel. When he walked in, he saw Ed Mathews sitting at the bar. Mathews was a big man who liked to eat and drink. He was on his second martini when Drew joined him.

"You're late," Mathews said.

Drew glanced at his watch; it was barely five minutes after seven.

"Heavy traffic," he said, giving it the sound of an apology. He swung himself onto the stool alongside Mathews and ordered a Dewar's on the rocks.

"Hit me again too," Mathews told the bartender. "And bring us an order of hot wings." He turned to Drew. "That okay with you?"

"Yeah, sure. Sounds good."

For over an hour there was no mention of business. Mathews polished off the wings, ordered some fried cheese sticks and went item by item through the menu deciding what he was going to have for dinner.

"The missus worries about my blood pressure, so she watches everything I eat," Mathews said with a smirk. "That's why I've gotta enjoy myself when she's not here."

Although Drew thought the wife was justified in worrying, he gave an amicable nod. Trying to move on to the subject of business he said, "I spoke to the press foreman, and it looks like the inserts will be up and running by seven-thirty tomorrow morning."

Mathews tapped the rim of his empty glass and signaled the bartender for a refill.

"That sounds good," he said. "I'm not much of an early riser, but I can be there by nine."

When Mathews ordered some loaded potato skins and a fifth martini, Drew excused himself and slipped away to call Brooke. He cupped his hand around the phone to muffle the noise of the restaurant.

"I just wanted to make sure that you're okay and having a good time," he said.

She giggled. "We're having a very good time. Missus Stone let us make our own s'mores."

After an exchange about playing dress-up with real jewelry, Brooke asked, "What time are you coming to get me?"

"I figure you girls will want to have lunch together, so I'm thinking sometime in the early afternoon. Two, maybe three."

There was a lengthy moment of silence; then Brooke said, "I don't want to stay for lunch. Can't you come earlier?"

*One day at a time,* Drew reminded himself.

"If you're having fun you might change your mind," he said. "Why don't I call you in the morning, and we can see how you feel then?"

"Okay," she replied, but there was a hint of reticence in her voice.

After saying he loved her, he hung up and returned to the bar.

It was almost ten by the time they left the bar and moved to the table for dinner. By then, in addition to the five martinis, Mathews had downed two beers and devoured three platters of appetizers. His laugh had gotten considerably more boisterous and his words slightly slurred.

At least a half-dozen times Drew started to say something about the business—that he appreciated the opportunity, that Mathews could be assured of Southfield's commitment to quality, that he could expect a solid commitment to service and that Southfield was looking forward to a long and mutually rewarding relationship between the two firms. Each time Mathews nodded with a "Yeah, yeah" and moved on to a totally different subject. He talked about going fishing in the Florida Keys and buying a bigger plane.

"The Piper Warrior I flew down in is a four-seater," he said. "I'm thinking a Cessna 206. More room, and that baby can land almost anywhere."

Every now and again he asked a question of Drew, but it was generally something that required a simple yes or no answer. Then he'd swing back to telling whatever story he'd moved on to.

"What about deep sea fishing?" Mathews asked. "Your ever do that?"

Drew shook his head.

"Afraid not," he said, but before he could go any further Mathews had moved on to telling of his own experience.

"Yep, there's nothing like deep sea fishing. Now that's a man's sport." He licked his lips and said, "Once you get a mouthful of fresh-caught tuna, you can't go back to that frozen crap they sell in the supermarket."

It was one o'clock when they finally left the restaurant.

"Want me to drop you off at the hotel?" Drew asked.

Mathews gave a wiggly shake of his head. "Nah, I got a rental car."

Seeing him list first to one side and then the other, Drew asked, "Are you okay to drive?"

"Yeah, sure," Mathews said and slid behind the wheel of the car. He stuck his arm out the window gave a wave and hollered, "See you in the morning!"

**IT HAD BEEN A LONG** day, and Drew was exhausted. He checked into the motel and went straight to his room. He set the cell phone alarm for seven o'clock figuring he'd be at Southfield by eight to make sure everything looked good before Mathews arrived at nine. Hopefully they'd be out of there before ten, and he'd be back in Clarksburg by two.

*Brooke will be okay until then,* he told himself. *Once the girls get to playing again, the morning will have flown before she even thinks about it.*

He snapped off the light and closed his eyes.

**HE WAS SOUND ASLEEP WHEN** the sharp sound of the phone woke him.

*Seven o'clock already?*

He fumbled his hand across the nightstand and grabbed the phone. That's when he realized it wasn't the alarm, it was an incoming phone call. The caller was Lara Stone.

A rush of fear swept through his head as he swiped the screen to answer.

"Is Brooke okay?" he asked, sounding apprehensive.

"Yes and no," Lara answered. With concern tucked in between each word, she went on to say that apparently Brooke had a bad dream and she had awakened screaming.

"She wants you to come and get her."

Drew could hear the sound of sobbing in the background. "Put her on the phone."

With ragged sobs squeezed into every breath, Brooke said, "I want to come home, Daddy..."

Trying to hide the dread he felt he asked, "What's the matter, baby? Did you have a bad dream?"

"Uh-huh. I dreamed you were dead like Mama." She sniffled.

"That was just a dream, Brooke. It wasn't real. I'm alive. I'm right here talking to you on the phone."

"I wanna come home," she said, sobbing again.

"It's the middle of the night, honey. I was in bed fast asleep.

Don't you think now that you know it was just a scary old dream maybe you could go back to bed and enjoy your sleepover with Ava?"

"No, I wanna come home!"

Drew gave a labored sigh. "Okay, I'll come and get you, but it's going to take me a while because I have to get dressed and drive over there. Do you think you could stop crying until I get there?"

"I'll try," she said tearfully.

Seconds later Lara came back on the phone. "I'm sorry to have to drag you back like this. I tried to calm Brooke down, but she wasn't having any part of it. She's obviously very attached to you."

"I know," Drew answered wearily. By then he'd already pulled his trousers on and thrown his toiletries back in the bag. "It's a four-hour drive, but at this time of night I think I can make it in three."

"Drive carefully," Lara said and hung up.

Once Drew was on the road, he began thinking about what he was going to say to Mathews.

# Dog Days

The print run was a fiasco. The job was on press at seven, and at seven-thirty they started running the inserts. At eleven Mathews finally showed up with eyes so bloodshot it was a wonder he could see where he was going, never mind distinguishing whether the green was an exact match to the proof he'd received.

"Where the hell is Bishop?" he roared.

"He had a family emergency," the shop foreman explained. "We video chatted with him at seven-thirty this morning, and he gave us an approval to go ahead."

"What is he, blind? The green is off! You can't see that?"

The foreman held the proof and press sample next to one another then said the green looked like a match to him.

"Get Bishop on the phone!" Mathews stormed.

The next twenty minutes were spent with Drew apologizing for having to leave so suddenly and Mathews screaming about a poor color match and perforations that didn't break away cleanly.

"That's it!" Mathews finally said. "I'm done with you. I'm not paying for this job, and you're never getting another one!" He slammed the phone down before Drew could say anything more.

Hearing the conversation, the foreman spoke up.

"We've got three hundred and fifty thousand of these off press," he said. "What am I supposed to do with them?"

"Stick 'em up your ass," Mathews said and stormed out.

At that point they pulled the job off press, and the foreman called Herbert Glass, the plant manager.

**TWO DAYS LATER, DREW RECEIVED** a call from Brian Carson.

"I guess you've heard about what happened with Mathews," he said.

Drew acknowledged he had and explained that a family emergency had called him home.

"It was the first time I've been away since Brooke's mom died, and she got a little panicky," he explained. "It won't happen again."

"See that it doesn't. Your sales are way off, and while I'm sympathetic to your situation I've got a responsibility to the company..."

His words trailed off. Coming out with a flat hard statement was not necessary. The implication was clear enough.

When he hung up from the call, Drew knew he was in jeopardy of losing his job if he didn't make some changes.

That evening he sat Brooke down and had a long talk with her.

"I know losing your mama has been hard on you," he said, "but it's been hard on me too."

He explained the conversation he'd had with Brian Carson, and the whole while he spoke Brooke sat there teary-eyed and stone-faced.

"I didn't mean to make your boss mad," she said. "But I dreamed the bad man who killed Mama was coming to kill me too, and I was afraid."

Despite Drew's efforts to keep the newspaper sensationalism away from Brooke, she'd seen it splashed across the front page—a picture of her mama and next to it one of a fiery-haired Tom Coggan. She'd had nightmares for nearly a month, but then they'd stopped. He'd thought she'd moved past it but evidently not.

"That man is dead," he said. "Remember we saw it in the newspapers?"

Brook gave a reluctant nod. "Yes, but—"

"There are no buts. He's dead. He can't ever hurt anybody again, so there's no need to be afraid."

"What about if I'm missing Mama? You said we could miss her together."

"We can, just not while I'm in the middle of working."

Drew held his arms open. She moved into them and laid her head against his chest, and for a long while neither of them said anything more.

It was Drew who finally spoke.

"I know this is really, really hard, but how about this. I'll get you your own notebook, a secret diary like big kids have. Then when you're lonely or scared you can write it down in your diary, and if you want to we can talk about it that evening."

"Okay," she answered, but the word was weak and non-committal.

The next day he and Brooke took a trip to Justice, the shop where she'd seen a collection of diaries. She selected one that had a lock and key then picked a matching ballpoint pen that wrote with purple ink. She seemed enthused with the idea, and Drew was hopeful it would give him some uninterrupted time for making business calls.

**IN THE WEEK THAT FOLLOWED** Brooke took to sitting on the front steps of the house, writing in her diary and making calls to tell people about the diary she now had. Both the cell phone and the diary were a novelty to be explored. She called her grandma in California and then wrote about the call in her diary.

"Grandma was very glad to hear from me," she wrote, "but said it would be better if I call her in the evening when she is not at work."

After that she called her friend, Ava, and her other friend, Kelly, then wrote about those calls. Once she even called Marta. It seemed that everyone else was doing something she could write about, but she herself had nothing. Just thoughts of not interrupting her father and missing her mama.

During that week there were no interruptions, and Drew began to think they'd solved the problem. But the newness of it wore off quickly, and the following Tuesday when he was in the middle of a video conference with Joe Wilkes, the advertising manager of Bradley's Department Store, Brooke came running into the room with a fluffy white dog in her arms.

"Daddy, I found a puppy!" she yelled with excitement. "Can I keep him?"

Drew looked over and glared at her.

"We'll discuss this later," he said and turned his attention back to the screen.

"Please, Daddy, just say yes."

Joe Wilkes laughed. "Looks like you've got a problem on your hands."

Since there was little else he could do, Drew laughed also. He turned to Brooke and said, "I don't think that's a lost puppy. He's got a tag on him. Take him out front and wait in case his owner is out looking for him."

Although Drew could feel the agitation swelling inside of him, he finished the pitch he'd been making for Bradley's then told Joe Wilkes he'd be in touch again the following week. When he disconnected the call he knew it hadn't been his best effort. It had been going well but the interruption threw him off base, made him feel awkward and unprofessional. He sat there in front of a blank screen waiting for his irritation to dissipate before he spoke to Brooke, but it didn't.

When he walked outside she was sitting on the porch with the dog in her lap. He sat down beside her.

"I thought you said you weren't going to keep interrupting me in the middle of my work day."

"I didn't *keep interrupting,*" she said petulantly. "I did it one time, and it was an emergency."

"Finding a dog is not an emergency." Drew lifted the tag hanging from the dog's collar. "The owner's phone number is right here. You can't keep a dog that belongs to somebody else."

Brooke's lip began to quiver. "I already named him Buddy."

"That's not his name. His name is Rocky. It says so right here."

"When I called him Buddy he licked my face."

"That's because he likes you, but it still doesn't mean you can keep him."

Tears welled in Brooke's eyes. "Maybe his owner didn't want him anymore."

"I doubt that," Drew said. He took the cell phone lying beside her and placed it in her hand. "You have to call the owner and tell them you have their dog."

With her chin dropped onto her chest Brooke punched in the number on the tag. When a young man answered she asked, "I found Rocky. Do you not want him anymore?"

"Thank heaven you found him!" The lad went on to say that somebody had left the back gate open and Rocky had wandered off. He asked for Brooke's address and said he'd be there in five minutes. When the call ended, Brooke turned to her daddy.

"You should've just let me keep him," she said. There was a note of bitterness in her voice.

"Keeping something that belongs to somebody else is stealing.

Just like you miss your mama, don't you think Rocky's family would miss him?"

The spark of anger made Brooke's eyes turn green; the pale blue that softened the color was all but gone.

"Nobody cares if I miss Mama, so why should I care if they miss Rocky?"

Drew wrapped his arm around her shoulder and nudged her close.

"I care," he said. "I care about you the same as I cared about your mama."

Although he already had more than he could handle, he said that if having a dog was what would make her happy they would get one.

"It won't be the same as having Buddy," she said, but the bitterness seemed to be gone from her voice.

# DREW

*Brooke is lonely; I get it. I'm lonely too. This is a pretty shitty life for both of us. I'm trying to make it better, but it seems like I take one step forward and then get knocked back two. Nothing goes right anymore.*

*It used to be that my showing up at a press run was little more than a goodwill gesture. Things ran smoothly without me. I was just there to glad-hand the client and maybe take them to dinner. Now when I really need for things to go well without me, the bottom falls out.*

*Brian doesn't have to tell me I've got problems. I know I do. Last month's commission check was a third of what I used to make. I made more than that when I managed the little print shop over on Fairfax.*

*At first I thought I could do this—be both a mother and father to Brooke—but the truth is I'm failing miserably. I can see how unhappy and frightened she is, but the simple truth is I don't know how to fix it.*

*Yes, she wants a dog. But obviously I'm doing a rotten job of taking care of her, so how am I supposed to take care of a dog too?*

*Maybe if I tell her the dog is her responsibility. I could say she has to walk it, feed it and work at getting it trained. Maybe that would keep her busy enough so that I can get some work done.*

*Oh, who am I kidding? When she goes back to school in the fall, the dog will end up my responsibility again. That's how it goes lately, a step forward, two backward.*

*But if it makes Brooke happy, I guess we'll get a dog.*

# The Library

After Eddie and Alisha consumed a sizeable amount of Jim Beam, morning came hard. It was nearly noon when they finally crawled out of bed. Despite the pounding in his head, Eddie immediately suggested they get started for the library.

"I ain't going nowhere 'til I get something to eat," Alisha said.

Eddie had little choice but to humor her. "Okay, but let's make it quick."

Alisha didn't know the meaning of quick, and when he complained for the third time she said if he didn't pipe down he could go by himself. After hearing about the microfiche and viewing machine procedure Eddie was reluctant to go it alone, so for the better part of an hour he waited. He tapped his foot and gave an impatient huff every so often; Alisha didn't pay one bit of attention to either.

When they finally got to Denny's the lunch crowd had already settled in, and they had to wait twenty minutes before getting a table. With Alisha having three cups of coffee and a second order of pancakes, they didn't get to the Clarksburg Library until almost three o'clock. By then Eddie was as edgy as a scalded cat.

"Let's get what we came for and get out of here," he whispered in her ear.

"You don't just get it!" she said with an air of annoyance. "We have to have an exact date or search 'til we come across something."

Again Eddie gave an exasperated huff. "I thought you said this was easy."

"It would be easy if you'd get off my back."

She walked over to the desk and asked the librarian to point the way to the *Clarksburg Tribune* microfiche section.

"Are you searching for something prior to nineteen-eighty?" the librarian asked.

"No, more like four or five months ago."

"The microfiche files only go up to nineteen-eighty," the librarian replied. "You can use the online newspaper source for anything more recent than that."

"Shit," Eddie grumbled.

The librarian glared across at him then turned back to talking with Alisha as if he weren't there.

"If you have a library card, you can use any of the computers at the center console."

Of course Alisha didn't have a library card, and it took another twenty minutes for her to fill out the forms and obtain one. The whole time Eddie stood there huffing and puffing like an overheated steam engine.

It was after four by the time Alisha sat down at the computer and began searching. She typed in "Clarksburg robbery and murder."

Five results came back. The first was a listing of crime statistics for Clarke County. It listed everything from bicycle thefts to murder, but it was nothing more than a list of month-by-month numbers. The second was a newspaper article saying that robberies in Clarke County were up by 9 percent over the preceding year. The third article described a father and son murder that took place in 2009.

The fourth article with the headline "Innocent Bystander Killed" told about the attempted robbery of Dunninger's Drugstore. Two faces flashed on the screen. Eddie recognized his brother even though his name was not mentioned in the article. Sitting side by side with Alisha he read a little over two paragraphs about what happened that day, but in the middle of a sentence it stopped and a window popped up saying for the full context of the article the viewer would need to log in with their subscription number. Beneath the message were two boxes. The first was to log in, the second was to subscribe.

"I don't have a subscription," Alisha said.

"Get one," Eddie replied.

"No. It's forty-eight bucks. I don't even read this dumb-ass newspaper."

"I'll pay you back."

She just sat there, looking at the screen and doing nothing.

"Get it," he said. "Forty-eight bucks is nothing compared to the money Tom's got set aside."

She turned and looked him square in the eye. "How can I be sure there even is any money? For all I know this could be—"

"There's money," Eddie said, "big money, and if you ain't willing to help..."

He left the remainder of that thought hanging in the air, a carrot for her to chase.

"If I put this on my credit card, you gonna pay me back today?"

"Yeah, yeah. Just hurry it up."

After she subscribed to the newspaper she didn't want nine more articles came up, eight about the robbery and one about Albert Dunninger's sudden death. Eddie was in the process of reading through them when the librarian breezed by and said the library would be closing in ten minutes.

"Quick, print everything," he told Alisha.

"That's another nine bucks!"

Eddie smacked his hand to his forehead.

"I don't know what Tom saw in a dumb dame like you. I'm talking about big money, and you're yanking my chain over nine measly bucks. I already said I'd pay you back."

Alisha gave a disgruntled snort and hit Print.

Less than five minutes later they picked up the printed pages at the front desk, paid for them and left the library. As Eddie pulled away from the parking lot, Alisha read the printed pages aloud. The first story told about the events of the day, called Tom an as-yet-unidentified gunman and referred to the incident as a bungled robbery.

*Bungled? Tom? Not likely.* Now more than ever Eddie was certain there was something more. Something still unsaid. A hidden truth to the events of that day.

On the drive back to the motel he listened as Alisha read through page after page of articles retelling the same story. One article included an interview with Albert Dunninger, the pharmacist who'd shot Tom. It quoted Dunninger as saying, "I'm no hero. If it wasn't for Jennifer Bishop distracting the gunman I might be dead, and he would have walked away with whatever was in the register."

That thought got stuck in Eddie's head, and he couldn't shake it loose.

*Tom always preached no violence, so why would he start shooting? The woman must have threatened him. That had to be it. She was the cause of what happened. If not for her Tom would be alive.*

He was deep in his own thoughts and barely listening when Alisha read how according to the police report, Tom shot first and Dunninger fired after the gunman shot Jennifer Bishop.

After she'd read through each of the articles Alisha said, "I don't see how you're gonna find any money from this crap. There's nothing much here."

"I'll find it," Eddie said. "I just gotta study them stories a bit more."

"Fine. You can study them tonight, 'cause I gotta go home and get dressed for work."

"Work?"

"Yeah, I gotta work for a living. You know, just in case this big payday you're promising don't come through."

"What time you get done?"

"The bar don't close 'til one, so maybe one-thirty, two."

Eddie turned into the motel parking, circled around to the back and pulled up next to Alisha's Pontiac. "How about you come back here later tonight?"

She slid him a sideways look and scrunched her nose. "No, thanks. This place is a dump." She popped the car door open then looked back and grinned. "But you can come by my place if you want."

When Eddie gave an eager nod, she rattled off the address and told him the key was under the mat.

"Maybe by the time I get home, you'll have figured out where that big payday is hiding."

"Yeah, maybe," Eddie replied.

**ONCE HE WAS BACK IN** the room, Eddie took the articles and started going through them word by word. For nearly two hours he sat there reading the same eight pages over and over again. He tried to picture the events of that day, but the image of it just wouldn't come. He had bits and pieces of information, but nothing fit. As he studied each word, looking for another meaning, a truth he'd missed the time before, Eddie felt a great weight settle in his heart.

For three years he'd sat in that prison cell, and the thing he'd held on to was the thought of him and Tom being together again.

That was how it was supposed to be. Twins, each one a half of the other, only now one half was gone. Eddie felt the ache of it the way one feels the phantom pain of a missing leg or arm. Losing Tom was an injustice far greater than Cassidy's betrayal.

After a long while Eddie decided the truth of what happened couldn't be found in these papers. The truth was back there in the store where Tom was killed.

He folded the printed pages, slid them into his back pocket and headed out to his car. It was only eight-thirty; Dunninger's Drugstore would still be open.

**WHEN EDDIE PARKED IN BACK** of the store he could already feel the pull of Tom trying to tell him something. He was almost certain of it. He pushed through the front door then stood there for several moments letting the feel of the place settle in.

Peter McIntyre was behind the counter.

"Can I help you with something?" he called out.

The sound of a voice interrupted Eddie's thoughts and startled him. After a few moments he remembered the pounding in his head and said, "Tylenol. I need a bottle of Tylenol."

"Aisle two," Peter called back. "Want me to get it for you?"

Eddie shook his head. "I'm okay."

He walked slowly down the first aisle and across to the next. Here he could feel Tom. He could picture him dead, lying on the floor in a pool of blood. Now it was more than just words; it was the actual ripping away of one twin from the other. He listened for Tom's voice knowing that in time it would come to him.

He plucked a bottle of Tylenol from the shelf and walked to the back counter.

Peter's days of working behind the counter were long and monotonous. He welcomed the diversion of talking to customers. He smiled and asked if Eddie was new in town.

"Just visiting," Eddie replied then in turn he asked if Peter was a Dunninger.

Peter shook his head. "No relation. I bought the store from his lawyer. Mister Dunninger died shortly after that terrible incident they had in here."

"Incident?" Eddie replied as if he'd never heard of it.

Happy to have someone to chat with, Peter retold the story as he'd heard it.

"Two people were killed, the gunman and a woman from the neighborhood."

"From the neighborhood?"

Peter nodded. "Jennifer Bishop. Her husband was in here a few months ago. Luckily, him and their little girl are getting along okay."

It didn't take much to keep Peter talking, and before Eddie left he knew that Drew was a successful salesman for a printing firm, had a good-sized house over on Greenhaven Drive and an eight-year-old daughter. He also knew Tom wanted revenge.

Eddie had heard his brother's voice—not clearly, but clearly enough to know he had to do something.

# THE DOG

Despite his misgivings about adding something else that could conceivably be another disruption to his workday, Drew agreed to get a dog. He told Brooke that on Saturday they would go to the Clarke County Animal Shelter and find a puppy that needed a home.

Brooke's eyes lit up. "Like Buddy."

"Well, not exactly like Buddy, because Buddy's real name was Rocky and he had a home."

Without acknowledging that fact Brooke started listing the things they would need: toys, a food bowl, a leash, a collar.

"Buddy won't need a bed," she said. "He can sleep with me."

In the beginning Drew hoped that by putting it off until Saturday there might be a chance Brooke would forget about the dog and move on to something else, but she didn't. She talked about it from morning until night. Several times a day she would peer into the kitchen and listen long enough to know he was not on a phone call. Then she'd come charging into the room with another new thought or question.

On Wednesday it was a desperate need to go to the library and get a book on dog training.

"Can't you wait until you actually have the dog?" Drew asked.

"No," she insisted. "I need it now!"

Marta, who'd breezed in with a tuna casserole, heard the request and volunteered to take Brooke.

Knowing how skittish his daughter had become about going anywhere with anyone but him, Drew looked over to her and asked, "Do you want Marta to take you?"

Without any hesitation, she nodded.

As he watched her trot off hand in hand with Marta, Drew thought maybe getting the dog wasn't such a bad idea after all.

**THE SKY WAS JUST STARTING** to turn light when Drew felt her small hand push against his shoulder.

"Daddy, it's Saturday."

"Already?" He peeked at the bedside clock. "It's not seven o'clock yet. The shelter doesn't open until nine-thirty. Go back to sleep for a little while."

"I'm too excited to sleep."

"Okay."

Drew swung his legs to the floor, and when his eyes were fully open he noticed the smile on Brooke's face. This was the happiest she'd been in months, and he couldn't help but be happy for her.

**WHEN THE CLARKE COUNTY ANIMAL** Shelter attendant arrived, Brooke was waiting at the door.

The silver-haired woman laughed. "You must be very anxious to adopt a pet. Dog or cat?"

"A white puppy," Brooke answered. "I'm going to name him Buddy."

The woman unlocked the door, and they followed her into the reception area.

"I don't think we have any white puppies right now," she said. "How about a cute little gray schnauzer?"

Brooke didn't answer; she just stood there with her lower lip quivering. The woman noticed.

"On second thought, let me check in the back. While I'm looking would you mind playing with one of the other pups? They get awfully homesick being away from their mama."

"Okay," Brooke said in a small voice.

"Wait here, I'll get one."

The woman disappeared into the back and returned with a squirming ball of light tan fur. She led the father and daughter to a side room with glass windows and a bench seat.

"You can play with her in here while I go look for that white puppy, okay?"

"Okay," Brooke said as she nodded. "What's her name?"

The woman feigned a look of sadness. "She doesn't have one yet. She's an orphan puppy who came in yesterday."

She started to leave and then turned back as if she'd had an afterthought.

"If you want to give her a name while you're playing, that would be very nice."

"Okay," Brooke said again, but this time a smile lit her face.

It was all Drew could do to hold back the grin playing at the corners of his mouth. In an odd way this woman reminded him of Jennifer; not in appearance, but in the clever way she turned a potential problem into a satisfying solution. He knew that by the time she returned to the room, his daughter would have given the puppy a name and her heart as well.

As the woman turned to leave he mouthed the words, "Thank you."

Brooke sat on the floor and the dog wriggled itself into her lap.

"I think he likes me," she said with a grin.

"He's a she," Drew replied. "This is a girl puppy."

"A girl?"

Drew nodded. "You might want to think up another name. Buddy doesn't work so well for a girl, does it?"

Brooke wrinkled her nose and shook her head. She hesitated a second or two then looked up with a twinkle in her eye.

"I'm going to name her Lucy," she said definitively.

"Why Lucy?"

"Because when Mama was a little girl she had a brown dog named Lucy."

Brooke leaned down with her face close to the dog's snout. "Little puppy, would you like to be named Lucy?"

The pup licked her face, and Brooke squealed with delight. "Daddy, she really, really likes her name!"

"I think maybe she likes you playing with her," he said.

A good twenty minutes passed before the woman came back to the room.

"I'm terribly sorry," she said, "but I've looked all over the back room and we don't have a white puppy right now." Although there was obviously no need for it, she volunteered to take an order and call Brooke when one came in.

"No, thank you," Brooke said, sounding very grown up. "I've decided to take Lucy."

"Lucy?" the woman echoed. "So that's what you've named her?"

"Yes. And she really likes her name. When I say it she kisses me. Watch. Lucy!"

Brooke again tilted her face to the dog and was again covered in doggie kisses.

On the way home they stopped at the pet shop and bought a pink rhinestone collar, a pink leash and two pink bowls, plus all the other things Brooke had on her list. As they browsed through the treats aisle, she lifted Lucy into her arms and held her up to sniff the selection.

That afternoon instead of sitting on the front steps like a lost soul, Brooke walked Lucy up and down the street. With the kitchen window open Drew could hear her issuing commands such as "heel" and "stay." He peeked out the window and watched her tugging at the leash as the puppy scrambled from one lawn to another.

How was it, he wondered, that he never knew Jennifer once had a dog named Lucy? He didn't even recall her ever suggesting they get a dog. There was that one time when she'd picked up a stray in the park, but that was back when they were living in the apartment building. It was a third floor walk-up smaller than a broom closet. She'd hinted at keeping the dog but never really said she wanted to.

A sad thought picked at Drew's mind.

*Brooke was closer to Jennifer than I was. She would have known Jennifer wanted to keep the dog.*

He gave a sigh that was weighted with regret then returned to his laptop and finished the e-mail he'd been working on.

# An Unfair Life

After he left the drugstore, Eddie couldn't get Tom's voice out of his mind. It was trying to tell him something, but what? Knowing the way Tom didn't take any bullshit from anybody, Eddie had to believe it was something about the people responsible for his murder.

Drew Bishop's address wasn't hard to find. Neither was the one for Albert Dunninger. Both were listed in the phone book. Dunninger's house was closer to the store, so Eddie went there first.

He turned onto Cambridge Street and drove slowly counting off the numbers until he came to 1271. The house was dark inside, lit only by the glow of a walkway lantern. He parked the car two doors down then got out and walked back. Circling the house he found an empty garbage can, upturned it and climbed up to peek inside the window. The rooms were empty; no furniture, no sign of anyone living there. As he headed back toward his car, he noticed the realtor's lockbox hanging on the front door handle.

"Shit," he grumbled then turned the car around and headed crosstown toward Bishop's place. Hopefully he'd have better luck there.

**THE HOUSES WERE BIGGER IN** this area of town, the lawns manicured with rows of flowers bordering the walkways. Finding Bishop's house was easy; it was a large two-story with oversized windows and bright gold numbers on the door. Eddie parked the car across the street and watched. Inside he saw a young girl, a kid really, and the man who was obviously her father. They sat side by side on the sofa, and in the distance there was the flickering of a television screen. They seemed peaceful, happy even, talking, laughing, enjoying a life with no problems.

Why was it, Eddie wondered, that people like this got all the good stuff and he got shit? He couldn't remember one time when his daddy had wrapped an arm around him the way this man was doing with his kid. The only good thing he ever had in his life was Tom, and now Tom was gone. Shot dead because of some stupid woman.

Why wasn't her family suffering like he was? Why did they get to go right on enjoying life, being happy and living in their fancy house? He thought about the crappy hotel room where he was staying, and the anger inside of him started to simmer. What justice was there in a situation such as this?

A short while later the television was turned off, and Eddie watched as the girl disappeared up the staircase. Moments later a light in the side window of the second floor clicked on.

He got out of the car and walked around to where he could see what was going on. Hidden in the shadow of an oak, he watched as the girl moved about changing from her shorts and tee shirt into pajamas. She lifted a small dog into her arms then climbed into bed. Before long the kid's daddy came into the room. He bent and kissed her forehead, then said something and snapped off the light. After that there was only the soft glow of a nightlight.

The stillness of the evening settled around Eddie as he stood there in the shadows. Crickets chirped, the wind sighed and he continued watching as the downstairs lights went off one by one until the house was lost to darkness.

As he drove back to the Sleepway Inn, his thoughts bounced up and down as if they were on a trampoline. One moment he'd be remembering the good times he and Tom had when they caroused around the country. The next he'd switch to thinking of what lay before him.

A life of being poor and alone.

By the time he arrived at the motel, he'd made a decision. Alisha wasn't the same as having Cassidy or Tom, but she was better than being alone. He packed up the few things he had, got back into the car and headed for her place. On the way he stopped and bought another bottle of Jim Beam. A good stiff drink would make him feel better.

**EDDIE FISHED THE KEY FROM** beneath the doormat and let himself into Alisha's apartment. The place was nice, better than he'd expected. He set the bottle of Jim Beam on the kitchen counter, searched the cabinets for a glass then poured himself a drink and went into the living room.

He clicked on the television, pushed some throw pillows aside and settled down on the sofa. He wanted it to feel the same as what he'd seen at Drew Bishop's house, but it didn't. The furniture was nice enough and the TV got all the channels, but alone was alone. That was the thing bothering Eddie the most. He swallowed a swig of bourbon then closed his eyes and leaned his head back against the sofa.

From somewhere far away he could hear Tom's voice. The sound was familiar, but the words were scrambled and falling one on top of the other. He tried to call to mind the image of himself and Tom together, standing side by side, joking, him with his arm hooked around Tom's neck and Tom elbowing his ribs. He could picture bits and pieces of it: arms locked together, feet next to one another, a peal of laughter, part of a grin, but the complete picture of two brothers who looked exactly alike never materialized.

With Tom gone it was as if he'd lost part of himself as well.

**IT WAS ALMOST TWO O'CLOCK** when he finally heard Alisha's key in the lock.

She smiled when she saw him sitting there. "Glad you could make it." She dropped her tote bag on the floor then came and sat beside him. "So, did you find out anything else?"

Eddie had already downed four, maybe five, drinks, and his brain was feeling fuzzy.

"About what?" he asked.

"The money!" With an annoyed look stretched across her face she said, "Tommy had this big pile of money set aside for you, remember?"

"I ain't stupid, 'course I remember." *That's why she invited me here. 'Cause of the money.*

"Well, what about it?"

"I ain't got it yet, but I got a plan."

"What kind of plan?"

"I ain't ready to talk about it yet. You'll find out when it's time."

Alisha gave him her "liar, liar, pants on fire" look.

"Is this for real, or are you just bullshitting me?"

"You'll see," Eddie said with an air of false bravado.

**AFTER A FEW MORE DRINKS** Eddie and Alisha headed for the bedroom. She expected way more than he could deliver, and after a half hour of fumbling she said she was too tired for such nonsense and turned on her side.

Eddie was left naked and feeling extremely inept. This was yet another thing he'd failed at. He'd never had a problem performing when he and Tom had worked jobs together. After Tom left he'd had a few such episodes with Cassidy, but it wasn't this bad. At least, he couldn't remember it being this bad.

For a long while he lay awake, looking up at the ceiling and wondering where he could go from here. As far as he could see there wasn't anywhere else. He had less than six hundred dollars and a twenty-year-old car that could be reported as stolen any day now. Sooner or later someone would notice the empty parking space and ask good old Bruce Kersey what he'd done with his car.

For a second or two he thought of Cassidy, but he knew there was no going back to her. The whole time he was in jail she'd sent one letter, and that was filled with words like "stupid" and "loser." Instead of signing it with Xs and Os, she had written that if he ever came near her again she'd shoot his head off.

Now he had Alisha. Well, he didn't really have Alisha, he just had the possibility of having her. He couldn't afford to blow this.

Alisha expected him to divvy up the money with her, but there was no money. There never had been. He'd said it because he figured it was the kind of thing Tom would say.

Every thought he had circled around and came back to Tom. If Tom were here, he'd know what to do. If Tom were here, he'd have a place to stay. If Tom were here, he wouldn't be alone.

This time the picture came to him, but it wasn't of the two brothers standing side by side. What he saw was Tom stretched out on the floor of the drugstore with a part of his skull blown away. Tears overflowed Eddie's eyes and rolled down his cheeks, falling silently onto the pillow.

*It ain't fair,* his brain screamed. *It just ain't fair!*

# The Plan

After a mostly sleepless night, Eddie had come up with a plan. He was all but certain the idea was the message Tom had been trying to send him. He could feel it in his bones. Even with Tom gone their connection was as powerful as ever.

As he sat across the breakfast table from Alisha, he talked about having things to do that day. He made no mention of what it was he'd be doing, and she didn't bother asking.

"That's fine," she said. "I'm on the early shift today."

On the early shift Alisha worked from three in the afternoon until ten at night. She told Eddie she'd be home by ten-thirty.

"You coming back here tonight?" she asked.

He nodded even though it should have seemed obvious with his duffle stored in the bedroom closet.

Alisha was still putting on her makeup when Eddie left.

"See you tonight," he called out. Then he scooted out the door and headed for the parking lot.

**Eddie felt good this morning.** He could feel a surge of confidence swelling in his chest. It was the same kind of confidence he felt when he and Tom started out on a job. He was on the right track, he was sure of it.

This time he was doing things the way Tom would have done. The first step was to scope out the place, look for any possible snags and take care of them ahead of time. The kid was small; she'd be easy to carry. But before he thought about that he had to watch the house, make sure everything was as he thought, make sure there'd be no last-minute changes in their routine, no foul-ups or interruptions.

When he turned onto Greenhaven Drive he was already wearing his baseball cap and sunglasses.

At the far end of the street, he spotted a kid walking a dog. It looked like the girl he'd seen last night, but he couldn't be sure. When he'd seen her through the window she'd seemed smaller and her hair darker. He parked half a block back and watched. If this were the right kid, she'd turn into the Bishop house when she finished walking the dog.

Brooke walked Lucy to one end of Greenhaven. Then she turned and walked back to the other end. Every so often she'd stop and issue commands such as "stay" or "sit," but the puppy paid little attention.

Eddie watched for almost an hour; then he spotted a frizzy-haired blonde coming out of the house next door to Bishop's. The woman stood at the end of her walkway looking up and down the street. If she were to turn in his direction, Eddie feared she might see him. He pulled the baseball cap lower on his forehead and peered from beneath the bill as he slunk lower in the seat.

After a few moments she spotted the girl and called to her.

"Brooke!" she yelled. "Come have some cookies."

The girl turned back, and both she and the dog followed the woman inside the house.

"Rat shit," Eddie muttered.

This turn of events neither proved nor disproved anything. He had no alternative but to sit and wait for whatever happened later.

Another hour rolled by before the girl reappeared, but instead of going back to the Bishop house she started walking the blasted dog up and down the street again.

JIM MORRISSEY LIVED FOUR DOORS down from the Bishops. He was the youngest of four boys and rumored to be the most incorrigible of them all, which was saying something since Alvin, the eldest of the lot, had been arrested three times for miscellaneous mischief. Jim wasn't afraid of the devil himself, but he had a healthy dose of respect for his daddy who could pack quite a wallop when he'd a mind to.

At fifteen years old Jim was a full year away from getting his learner's permit and two years out from legally obtaining a driver's license. But the lad had a love of cars, and to him two years seemed an eternity.

Twice before Big Joe, Jim's daddy, had caught the boy taking the family Oldsmobile out for a spin, and both times there'd been hell to pay. When Big Joe took to cussing that boy out, the neighbors could hear it five blocks away. The fisticuffs escalated to such a point that Emma Paulson, who lived directly across the street, called the police because she feared one of them might kill the other.

On a day when Jim knew his daddy wouldn't get home from work until four-thirty, he took the Oldsmobile out again. Two days earlier he'd bragged to Stephanie Wilkins about driving his daddy's car, and she'd goaded him into promising to take her for a spin. He hadn't counted on Stephanie being as amorous as she was, and when he came up for air he saw the dashboard clock read four-twelve.

"Holy crap!" he bellowed. "I gotta get this car home, or my daddy's gonna kill me."

He dropped Stephanie off and went flying down Pine Street. He was rounding the corner onto Greenhaven when he hit the UPS truck. It was a head-on collision, and the sound of it could be heard nine blocks away. When the two vehicles finally ground to a stop, the UPS truck was missing the right fender and the front end of the Oldsmobile was folded up like an accordion.

Looking out her front window and seeing what had happened, Emma Paulson knew it was time to call the police. By then almost everyone on the block had rushed outside to see what happened.

**EDDIE COGGAN HEARD THE SCREECH** of sirens in the distance and knew it was time for him to get going. With one end of the street blocked by the UPS truck and the crumpled up Oldsmobile, he made a three-point turn and headed in the opposite direction. As he passed by the gathering crowd he saw Drew Bishop holding onto the kid with the dog, and a great sense of satisfaction settled over him.

It had been a good day.

**BY THE TIME ALISHA ARRIVED** home that night, Eddie was pumped and he'd lost count of the number of bourbons he'd downed. But it wasn't just the bourbon that was giving him this euphoric feeling; it was the adrenaline rush of knowing he'd stood on the edge of danger and walked away whole. He had driven right past the police car, and they'd not so much as turned their heads.

This feeling was the same kind of feeling he'd gotten after he and Tom had pulled a job together. It was the thrill of tempting danger, the power of knowing they'd outsmarted their opponents, the confidence of realizing they could take what they wanted and nobody could stop them.

"You seem to be in a pretty good mood," Alisha said. "You find where Tommy hid the money?"

Eddie gave a lusty grin. "Pretty much. Now all I gotta do is figure out when and how to take it."

That statement got Alisha's attention, and she began wheedling him for more information. One question led to another, and before long Eddie began enjoying the game. It was almost like foreplay.

She tugged at her lower lip and suggestively ran her finger along the inside, pretending to be thinking up the next question.

"Is the money all in cash?"

He laughed. "Not ready cash, but she's worth a hundred grand."

"She?" Alisha repeated curiously.

Eddie hadn't anticipated telling her about the plan. Something like this was always better kept under wraps—Tom taught him that early on—but it slipped out one juicy little piece at a time.

Once it was out in the open Alisha looked at him as if he were stark raving mad.

"You're going to kidnap this kid?" she echoed. "Are you friggin' nuts?"

Such an implication took a chip out of Eddie's confidence.

"No, I ain't nuts!" he replied. "I'm doing what Tom wants me to do."

"Tom's dead!"

"Dead or alive don't matter; we got this—"

She rolled her eyes. "Yeah, I know, connection."

"That's right." He went on to say it was the search for Tom that led him to the drugstore and ultimately to Drew Bishop's house.

"It's just the two of them," he said. "The father and the kid. She goes to bed at ten o'clock, and he goes to bed on the other side of the house fifteen, twenty minutes later."

"And, Mister Genius, once you nab this kid, what are you gonna do with her?"

Eddie hadn't thought that part through yet. He hesitated a minute then smiled and said, "I'm gonna bring her back here and keep her in the pantry closet until I get the ransom money."

Alisha saw the smile on his face and began laughing uproariously.

"You had me going there," she said, clutching her sides from laughing so hard. "For a while I thought you were actually serious."

The smile faded from Eddie's face. "I *am* serious."

Then she laughed even harder. "Yeah, and after that we could do a bunch of bank heists, maybe be this century's Bonnie and Clyde."

As she stood there laughing Eddie began to feel smaller, less sure of himself. The confidence he'd felt that afternoon vanished, and he was left with the same feeling he'd had back in the West Tennessee jail when he read Cassidy's letter telling him that he was and always would be a stupid good-for-nothing loser.

Earlier he'd had thoughts of making love to Alisha, thoughts of hot sweaty sex that would make up for his impotence of the previous night. Now such a thing was all but impossible.

Despite the friction in the air, they polished off the bottle of bourbon. When they climbed into the bed, he turned on his side facing away from her.

"Aw, come on," she said. "Don't start pouting just because I laughed at your sorry-ass idea."

"I'm not pouting," he grumbled. He let another minute of silence hang in the air then said, "And it's not a sorry-ass idea. It's a plan, a good plan. You'll see."

By then Alisha was too tired and too drunk to argue. She knew by the next morning she'd forget about it and so would he.

"Whatever," she said.

Long into the night Eddie lay there thinking of his plan, laying it out piece by piece. When he finally closed his eyes, he could see Tom giving him a proud wink of approval.

# THE CHECK LIST

With the plan bristling through his head, Eddie found it almost impossible to sleep. As soon as slivers of daylight began filtering through the blinds Alisha kept drawn tight, he reached across and nudged her shoulder.

"I've gotta get going," he whispered. "I've got a lot to do."

"Mummph." She brushed his hand away and pulled the lightweight blanket over her shoulder.

When Eddie left the building, his step was jaunty and he was whistling *Two Pina Coladas.* He'd already decided that once he had the money, he was taking off for Mexico. A person could get lost easily enough in Mexico. The hundred grand would last two years, maybe three. Good living was cheap in Mexico. When the money ran low, he'd head back to the States. Not Alabama and certainly not Tennessee. Maybe somewhere in the northeast; Philadelphia or New York.

*No more small-town shit,* he thought. People became invisible in big cities. They could pick a pocket or rob a bodega then disappear into the crowd.

He turned onto the highway and headed west. It was fifty, maybe sixty miles to the Mississippi border. He planned to cross over then start looking for a Home Depot. He could buy what he needed without leaving any traceable tracks.

Eddie grinned. The ingenuity of this plan was a new high for him. His brother would be proud. He could almost imagine Tom saying, "Now you're thinking with your head."

Over the past few days he'd grown to like Alisha. She was easy to be with and less bossy than Cassidy. Okay, she'd laughed at his plan, but that was only because she didn't know what he was capable of doing. Once he proved himself, she'd change her tune. Money impressed women like Alisha, and once she saw the hundred grand she'd be happy to quit that crappy job and tag along to Mexico.

Eddie imagined the two of them living in a place alongside the beach. They'd start the day at noon and drink pina coladas or margaritas for breakfast. She'd be all over him, and any performance issues he'd once had would be long forgotten.

**AFTER HE'D CROSSED OVER INTO** Jones County, Eddie began driving through the small towns and keeping his eye peeled for a Home Depot. He found it in Marston. Acting as if he were any ordinary homeowner shopping for fix-up supplies, he grabbed a cart and started through the aisles.

In the paint aisle he tossed a package of plastic gloves into the basket then moved on to the next row and added a roll of duct tape. Finding the right ladder was a bit trickier. Most of the ladders long enough to reach the second-floor window were too long to fit into the car. He finally found one he could get into the trunk; it had three sections that slid one on top of the other. The Werner Compact ladder was $149, more than he'd planned to spend, but what the hell. By tomorrow afternoon he'd be looking at that amount of money as small change.

His last stop was the aisle where Home Depot had camping

supplies. He added a good sized folding knife to the basket then headed for the checkout register. The woman at the register slid the items across the scanner one by one and never even glanced at Eddie. So far everything was going along exactly as planned.

Eddie wheeled the basket out to the parking lot, and that was when a sudden storm came up. In seconds the gray cloud that had been hovering overhead turned black, and thunder boomed. The car was parked at the far edge of the lot, so Eddie began to hurry. With the ladder bouncing up and down in the basket he could only go so fast, and before he made it to the car the sky burst open. In the few minutes it took to load the trunk, his shirt and hat were soaked through.

He pulled the wet baseball cap off and laid it on the seat beside him then used his handkerchief to sop up some of the water from his arms and tee shirt.

**SHORTLY AFTER NOON, HE ARRIVED** back in Clarksburg. Figuring there was no such thing as being too careful, he headed for Greenhaven Drive. While he had daylight and could see, he needed to check that there were no bushes to block placement of the ladder and make sure there were no neighboring windows from which he could be seen. He also had to know if he was dealing with a storm window or screen. Once he started the job, it had to be quick. In and out in less than three minutes. Any unforeseen challenges could slow him and lead to way more trouble than he could handle.

He turned onto Greenhaven and drove past the house, but the way it sat angled to the street he couldn't get a clear picture. Three times he circled the block then finally came to a stop and parked the car across from Marta's house.

The kid was at the far end of the street, still tugging on the leash while the dog scrambled from one spot of grass to the next. Eddie looked around, saw no one else in sight and climbed out of the car. He could walk over there, check what he needed and be back in the car in less than thirty seconds.

He moved quickly, darting across the street then cutting over to the grassy area that ran between Bishop's house and that of the next-door neighbor. Once he had a clear view, he could see that the kid's window would be no problem. It was a simple up and down sash. The worst that could happen would be if the lock was on, and even then a few twists of the steel blade and he'd have it open. Ten, maybe fifteen seconds at the most.

He eyed the house next door. No downstairs windows on this side, but upstairs there was a single window about three feet back from the kid's room. A bit risky but not as bad as something directly across the way. He'd just have to make certain there was no noise.

**BROOKE WAS HALFWAY BACK TO** the house when Lucy tugged the leash from her hand and took off running.

"Stop!" she yelled, but the dog didn't.

Eddie was two-thirds of the way across the street when the dog darted out after him. Brooke had her eye on Lucy and didn't look up until she ran smack into him. There was an instant when she bent down and scooped up the dog, but the second she lifted her face his wild coppery hair came into view and she started screaming.

Eddie panicked. He jumped into the car and took off, but Brooke stood there in the middle of the street screaming like a banshee. Emma Paulson heard the screams and figured the Morrisseys were at it again, so she called the police. Marta also heard the screams, as did Drew. Before either of them got to the door Eddie had rounded the corner of Greenhaven and was halfway down Pine.

Marta was the first to reach Brooke. She pulled the child into her arms and asked, "What on earth is the matter?"

Drew got there seconds later. He squatted down beside Brooke and asked the same question. Brooke tried to answer, but with the words sandwiched in between sobs they sounded like gibberish. Drew picked her up and held her in his arms, still not knowing the reason for her screams.

"Did you fall down?" he asked. "Did you hurt yourself?"

She shook her head and kept sobbing. Finally her crying slowed to the point where her words were understandable, and between whimpers she said, "The man who killed Mama is going to kill me too."

Drew hugged her to his chest.

"Honey, that's not possible," he said. "That man is dead. Remember, we saw his picture in the newspaper?"

"He's not dead anymore. I saw him."

"You must have made a mistake, Brooke. Maybe you just thought you saw him."

She pushed back and looked him square in the face. "I did see him! He tried to steal Lucy, but I saved her."

Drew glanced up at Marta. "Did you see anybody?"

She shook her head. "Just Brooke."

Drew again held her close. "Maybe you just saw shadows or imagined something like when you have a bad dream and it seems real, but it's not. Do you think it could be something like that?"

Brooke shook her head adamantly. "I saw him. He had red hair just like in the newspaper picture."

In the distance they could hear the sound of a siren. When the patrol car pulled up Sergeant Rodriguez was the first one out.

"What's the problem?" he asked.

"I think it's nothing," Drew said. He began explaining about Jennifer's death and how Brooke had thought she'd seen the same man coming after her.

Officer Lutz stepped out of the car and joined the group. "Got anything?"

Rodriguez shook his head. "I don't think so." He suggested they go inside and let Brooke calm down while he wrote up a report. He grabbed a clipboard from the car and followed Drew as they started back to the house. Marta tagged along. Once inside the five of them gathered around the dining room table. Rodriguez turned to Brooke.

"I'm going to need you to answer a few questions," he said. "Is that okay?"

Brooke gave a silent and rather somber nod.

"This man you saw, can you describe him? What he looked like? What he was wearing?"

"He looked like the man who shot Mama."

"Was he tall or short?"

Brooke sat there with a blank look.

Rodriguez had Drew and Officer Lutz stand side by side. Drew was over six feet, and even with his shoes on Lutz barely made 5′6″.

"Was the man you saw the size of your daddy or more like the size of Officer Lutz?"

Brooke sat there looking puzzled for a few moments then said, "I didn't see his size, just his red hair."

They went through question after question, but there were few if any answers. Brooke did recall he drove off in a car that was big and maybe black.

"Did this man try to grab hold of you or push you into his car?" Rodriguez asked. "Did he call your name or say anything to you?"

The answers were no and no.

Once Rodriguez ascertained the only thing Brooke had to say was that the perpetrator had red hair and looked like the man who killed her mama, he asked Drew if they might have a private word and they stepped into the kitchen. Rodriguez's face was drawn and unsmiling when he spoke.

"It seems as though Brooke may have had a flashback of what happened to her mother. She honestly believes she saw the man, but there's no indication anyone was ever there."

"How can that be?" Drew asked.

"It's not all that unusual. Obviously Brooke was very close to her mother, and when a child loses a parent in such a violent way it can cause the same kind of trauma as if it actually happened to her."

"But why now? She was fine earlier, playing with the dog and—"

Rodriguez gave a saddened nod. "There's no way of knowing what triggered it. A flash of red light, the backfire of a car. Maybe seeing the dog run into the street frightened her into reliving the terror of what happened to her mother."

"Is there anything I can do to prevent—"

Rodriguez shook his head. "Time is usually the great healer, but for now you might want to have her talk to a psychologist. Sometimes that helps."

Drew gave a labored sigh. "I may do that."

Rodriguez, himself a father of four, gave an understanding nod.

"Tough being a single dad," he said. "Real tough."

He said he would file a report on the off chance Brooke had actually seen someone stalking her.

"Keep a close eye on her for the next few days," Rodriguez said, "and if you see anything that looks even remotely suspicious, give us a call."

**ONCE THE OFFICERS LEFT BROOKE** asked, "Are they going to arrest him, Daddy?"

Drew was at a loss for what to say. After a long moment of hesitation he said, "They know for certain the man who killed Mama is dead, but they're going to keep an eye out for anyone who looks like him."

# Drew

*I can't help thinking back on how Miss Abrams suggested I have Brooke talk to a psychologist. I scoffed at the idea then, but now I'm beginning to wonder if maybe she was right. Given what happened today, I have to believe Brooke is suffering way more than I realized.*

*You'd never know it looking at her. On the outside she seems like a happy little girl. Yesterday when I stood at the window and watched her playing with the dog, I thanked God she was settling into this relatively haphazard life. I know it's nothing like the life she had with Jennifer, but I wanted to believe that for her it had become a new normal.*

*Kids need that kind of stability. They need to know that from one day to the next, the life they know is not going to change. They need to know they're safe and that no harm can come to them.*

*It breaks my heart to know Brooke doesn't feel safe. She's worried that the man who murdered her mama is now after her. When it happened I kept the newspapers hidden away, but the story was all over the place and somehow she saw it. I guess having an image like that in her head made it real. Real enough for her to be fearful it could happen again.*

*I won't lie; this is scary. I would know what to do for a runny nose or a broken leg, but those things are on the outside. They're things I can see and do something to fix. How do you fix a hurt you can't even see?*

*Brooke's pain is on the inside, buried so deep she doesn't even know it's there. Dealing with a problem like this is like walking into a blind alley. The danger is hidden, and when it does jump out you have no idea of how to fight it.*

*I've been trying to give her as much attention as possible and I thought getting the dog would help, but I guess it's just not enough. Tomorrow I'll start looking for a psychologist. Hopefully I can find one who will give Brooke the reassurance I've failed to give her.*

*I can only pray they will, because carrying such fear in your heart is a terrible burden.*

# A Time to Wait

The kid had seen him and she knew. There had been a brief moment when he could have grabbed her and shoved her into the car, but he'd bungled it. He'd panicked and ran off. Tom's face flickered in front of him, and Eddie could almost see the look of disgust tugging at the side of his mouth.

"I wasn't ready," he said, speaking to the brother who was dead and buried.

Eddie hoped the expression he saw on Tom's face would change, but it didn't. That's when he decided he'd have to move faster than he'd originally planned. It would have to be tonight.

It was only one-thirty now. He had all afternoon to kill, and it was probably better to stay out of sight. He turned back toward Route 20. Alisha's place was as good as any to waste some time. A few blocks before he turned onto Kettering Street, he pulled the still-wet cap on and stopped at Walmart. He bought a pair of black pants, a black long sleeve tee shirt, a new baseball cap and pocket-sized flashlight.

**BACK AT THE APARTMENT, ALISHA** was sitting at the kitchen table smoking a cigarette and nursing her second cup of coffee.

"Where'd you go?" she asked.

"I had errands to run." After Alisha had laughed at his plan, he decided to tell her nothing more until it was over and the money was in his hand. That way he'd be the one to have the last laugh.

"What shift you working today?" he asked.

"I'm off." She stubbed out her cigarette and downed a swig of coffee. "I thought since I ain't charging you for room and board, maybe you'd want to take me out for some fun. We could do dinner and a movie then stop by the Hungry Eye for a nightcap."

Eddie sat there for a moment saying nothing. He would have enjoyed that; it could've been the way it was with Cassidy but better. Only right now the timing was wrong. He'd missed his chance this afternoon and couldn't afford to do it again.

"Tonight's no good," he said.

"Whaddya mean no good? I told you, I'm not working."

"Yeah, but I got something I gotta take care of."

A look of annoyance slid across her face. "Whatever."

"Don't be mad." He crossed over behind her and kissed the back of her neck. "I really do have a man I gotta see about business." He rolled his tongue around the edge of her ear and curled his arm across her chest. "How about I make it up by taking you on a nice vacation to Mexico?"

"Mexico? Really?"

He nodded. "You'd like that, wouldn't you?"

She turned and kissed him full on the mouth then pulled back. "Yeah, I'd like that."

A short while later Alisha mentioned that since Eddie was busy she might invite her friend Luella over to play cards and have a few drinks. That was the last thing in the world he wanted.

"Don't do that," he snapped.

She turned to him her face knotted into one giant look of mad. "You trying to tell me I can't have friends in my own apartment?"

"Of course not," Eddie answered. "I was just gonna say let's go have lunch at that pancake place you like. I ain't gonna be gone that long, and when I get back we can have ourselves some fun." He gave her a sexy wink. "You know, the kinda fun where you don't want nobody else around."

After two nights of lying side by side in the bed with him keeping whatever he had to himself, the suggestion came as kind of a surprise to Alisha.

"Okay," she said, but her voice had a hint of suspicion threaded through it.

**IT WAS ALMOST SIX WHEN** they got back from the pancake place and Alisha expected Eddie to leave, but he dropped down on the sofa and clicked the television on.

"Don't you have to get going?" she asked.

"Not yet." He click-click-clicked through the channels without giving any one station time to settle into the program.

"Don't do that," she said. "You'll ruin the TV."

He snapped the television off and pushed back against the sofa, but his back was stiff as a ramrod and he kept drumming his fingers on his thighs.

"Is something wrong?" she asked.

"Wrong?" he echoed. "Nothing's wrong. Why would you think—"

"It's just that you seem kind of edgy."

"Indigestion," Eddie said and rubbed his hand across his chest.

She smiled. "Well, you should've said something. I got Tums." She dug through her purse then handed him two pink tablets. "Chew these, you'll feel better."

As he chomped down on the tablets, she snuggled up to him on the sofa looping her arm through his then giving a satisfied sigh.

"So tell me about this trip to Mexico," she said.

Eddie didn't want to talk; he wanted to think. He wanted to picture the way it would happen and make sure he'd covered all the bases. He wanted to have some quiet time, time to think it through the way Tom would have thought it through.

"There ain't much to tell," he said. "We'll get in the car and start driving. Maybe stop somewhere in Texas and see what kind of nightlife they got."

It seemed that everything he said led to her having another question, something more she wanted to talk about. When he couldn't stand it anymore, Eddie said he had to get dressed for his meeting. He went into the bedroom, but she trailed along.

"You think I ought to get something new to wear? Something like a dressy dress for when we go out clubbing?"

Tired of all her prattle, Eddie gave a haphazard shrug as he ripped the tags off of the pants and shirt he'd bought at Walmart. She kept talking about what she might or might not need to buy. When Eddie pulled on the long sleeve black shirt, she stopped talking and looked at him strangely.

"It's ninety degrees outside. Ain't you gonna be awful hot in that?"

He shook his head.

"They got air conditioning," he said and pulled on the new black baseball cap. He glanced over at the clock: 8:05. Too early, he thought, but it was either that or sit around listening to Alisha yak while he was trying to think.

"I gotta get going," he said.

"Okay." Alisha thought perhaps he would take her in his arms and kiss her goodbye. When he didn't she reached up and kissed his cheek.

"Good luck with the deal," she said and smiled.

**ONCE EDDIE WAS GONE ALISHA** started going through her closet, looking for outfits for Mexico. She tried on dresses that were a decade old and wondered if maybe they could somehow be spruced up.

*A scarf maybe? Or a brooch?*

After almost two hours the bed was covered with cast off dresses, jeans that had been a bit too tight and tops in colors that made her skin look sallow. Noticing that it was close to ten o'clock, she started scooping things up and hanging them back in the closet. When she picked up the jeans Eddie had been wearing, a receipt from Home Depot fell out of the pocket.

Without thinking anything one way or the other, she picked it up and glanced at it. At first there didn't seem to be anything special about the items listed, but the $149 for a folding ladder jumped out at her. She read down the list item by item. A knife. Duct tape. Plastic gloves.

"Holy shit!" she exclaimed. "He really is gonna kidnap that girl!"

Alisha felt as if her legs were going to collapse beneath her. This was way more than she'd bargained for. She was okay with partying and sex. She was even willing to look the other way if somebody lifted a wallet that didn't belong to him. But she was not okay with this.

Kidnapping was a federal offense. It was a crime that could have someone locked up for the rest of their life. It was something she wanted no part of.

She walked back into the kitchen, picked up the phone and asked the operator to connect her to the Clarksburg police station.

# In Clarksburg

Detective Hilbert rarely worked nights and was none too happy about working this one. He was sitting at the desk talking to Melanie Parks on his cell when the call came in.

"Aw, crap," he said. "We've got an incoming, can you hold on?"

"Hold on to what?" Melanie tittered.

Hilbert laughed.

"Hold on to that thought," he said and set the cell phone aside.

He'd been dating Melanie for three months and was ready to take it to the next level. Tonight it was beginning to sound as if she might be interested in doing the same thing. He answered the stationhouse phone determined to make quick work of the caller and get back to Melanie.

The first words out of Alisha's mouth were, "I need to report a kidnapping."

Hilbert was in no mood for crank calls.

"Who is this?" he asked sharply.

"I'd prefer not to give my name," she said. "I don't want to get involved."

"Involved in what?"

"I told you, the kidnapping."

"Why don't you start over," Hilbert said. "Who's kidnapping who?"

"Eddie Coggan, Tom's brother, is planning to kidnap the little girl whose mother was killed in the drugstore holdup last February."

"What's the girl's name?"

"I don't remember her name. But I know it was her mother who was killed in that holdup."

"How exactly did you get this information?" Hilbert asked suspiciously.

"I found the receipt where Eddie purchased a ladder and duct tape."

"That's it?"

"He also started talking about going to Mexico."

Hilbert was starting to think the woman on the phone was nothing more than a busybody with an overactive imagination.

"Things like that could be nothing more than coincidence," he said. "It doesn't necessarily suggest a kidnapping."

Alisha gave a huff of impatience. "Eddie's brother was killed in that robbery, and Eddie's got it in for the family." Her voice became heavy and grim. "If he hasn't already grabbed that girl, he's gonna do it tonight!"

"So you know this Eddie Coggan is going to kidnap somebody tonight, but you have no idea who?"

"I know who, I just don't know her name," Alisha said angrily. "But I do know that if something happens to that kid and you do nothing to stop it, the blame is gonna be on you!" With her heart banging against her chest, she slammed the phone down.

Hilbert hung up and sat there feeling bewildered. Because Tony Niles was out with a sprained back, Lutz was working a double shift. Hilbert turned to Lutz.

"You remember the name of that woman who was killed at Dunninger's last February?"

"Jennifer Bishop," Lutz replied. "Funny you should ask, Rodriguez and I had a call out to her house this afternoon."

"What for?" Hilbert asked.

"Turned out to be nothing. Rodriguez figured it to be some kind of post-traumatic memory flash, the kind his nephew had after Vietnam."

Forgetting about Melanie, Hilbert leaned forward and asked, "What exactly happened?"

"The kid thought she'd seen the guy who killed her mama. Said he was coming to—"

Hilbert didn't wait for Lutz to finish.

"Grab that address," he said. "We've got to get out there."

**GREENHAVEN WAS THE KIND OF** street where people parked their cars in garages and went to bed early. When Eddie pulled up a few feet in back of the Bishop house, his was the only car on the street. He parked in the shadow of a large oak, a place where even if someone peeked out the window it would be difficult to see. Dressed all in black, he himself would appear little more than a shadow.

Moving slowly and with great stealth, he climbed from the car and gently eased the door shut. He circled around to the back, lifted the trunk and removed the ladder. The knife he stuck in his pocket and the roll of duct tape he slid onto his arm like a bracelet. He then tugged on a pair of the plastic gloves and pulled the lid of the trunk down, not allowing it to click shut. This way he'd be able to yank it open quickly when he returned with his package.

For a brief moment he hesitated, looking up and down the street, checking that everything was as it should be. The glow of the nightlight came from the kid's room, and downstairs a light was on in the back of the house. The kitchen maybe. He would have preferred the father to be in bed, but there on the far side of the house he'd be unlikely to hear anything anyway. The lights in the house next door were off, which was good. Three doors down a few lights were still on, but the remainder of the neighborhood was dark.

Eddie picked up the ladder and eased his way along the shadowy side of the house, moving into position. He knew this was the right time; even the moon was cooperating. It was little more than a sliver, which gave him the ability to see without being seen. Section by section he slid the ladder open, and when each section clicked into the locked position he waited and gave the sound time to die away before moving on.

Once the ladder was ready he steadied it against the house and started up the rungs. He climbed slowly, stopping every so often to cast an eye over his shoulder and make certain he was the only thing moving. When he was even with the window he could see the girl asleep. She was turned on her side with her back to the window.

Without needing the penlight in his pocket, he could see the lock was slid over but only partway. He quietly slid the blade of the knife in between the upper and lower frame. Bracing his arm against the siding, he pushed against the knife until little by little the latch slid open. Then he eased the window up.

Eddie was partway in the room when the dog started barking, and that forced his hand. Being silent was no longer his biggest worry. He bolted across the room and whacked the pup so hard it sailed across the floor and hit the wall. Then there was only whimpering.

The barking woke Brooke, but it was a few seconds until she opened her eyes. When she finally did she saw the figure hovering over her and let out an agonizing scream before the strip of duct tape slapped over her mouth silenced her.

Drew heard her scream and thought she was having a nightmare. He ran from the kitchen and charged up the stairs.

When he burst into the room, he saw the black clad figure trying to subdue Brooke.

Charging to her defense, he leapt across the room and rammed his shoulder into the intruder. The knife flew out of Eddie's hand and slid across the floor. For a moment Drew had Eddie pinned down.

He looked over to Brooke and yelled, "Run, get out of here!"

That brief lapse in the struggle enabled Eddie to push off, and they both scrambled for the knife. Instead of running as her daddy said, Brooke pulled the tape from her mouth and screamed again.

This time Marta heard it, and the upstairs light in her home blinked on immediately. She looked out the window, saw the ladder and called 911.

By then Hilbert and Lutz were already in the squad car headed crosstown. They were on Pine Street when the radio crackled and the dispatcher said they had a report of screams coming from the upstairs bedroom of 910 Greenhaven.

"The caller said there's a ladder on the east side of the house."

That's when Hilbert turned on the siren. Seconds later the car careened around the corner of Greenhaven and screeched to a stop in front of Bishop's house. The lights of the Feldman house were on, and Walter was standing on the lawn with a shotgun in his hand. Marta was on Drew's front porch with the door already opened.

"Upstairs," she said as she waved an arm in that direction. There was no mistaking the sounds of a fight and screams of a frightened child.

"Police!" Hilbert yelled and took the stairs two at a time. Lutz was right behind. Both had their guns drawn.

Eddie heard them on the staircase. He'd already sliced Drew's chest and given time he might have been able to take him, but now there was no more time. He knocked Drew to the floor and scrambled back out the window.

Hilbert burst into the room and found Drew lying on the floor with Brooke clinging to him and crying hysterically. Lutz recognized Drew from earlier in the afternoon.

"That's the kid's father!" he yelled.

Hilbert bent over Drew, but before he could ask what happened two shots rang out and the sound of breaking glass filled the air.

"What the hell was that?" Hilbert said.

He looked out the window and spotted Eddie lying on the lawn. Walter was standing over him with the shotgun still in his hand.

"Sorry about the window," Walter hollered up. "My eye's not nearly as good as it used to be."

Although Walter had been aiming for the intruder's chest, he'd taken out the dining room window with the first shot and nailed Eddie in the leg with the second.

While they waited for the ambulance to arrive, Lutz cuffed Eddie and recited his Miranda rights to him. It was unlikely Eddie heard much of what was said, because he was doubled over and howling about the pain in his leg. Lutz took the shotgun from Walter and said for the time being they had to hold on to it as evidence.

"Anyway," he added, "I think you've done enough shooting for tonight."

Hilbert remained inside with Drew. He assured Brooke the danger was over, but she continued to sob hysterically. He picked Lucy up and put her in the girl's arms.

"I think your puppy is more frightened than you," he said.

Still pushed up against her daddy, Brooke cuddled the dog in her arms and then sniffled, "Don't be afraid Lucy, the bad man can't hurt us now."

**DREW AND EDDIE WERE TAKEN** to the hospital in separate

ambulances. Drew's injuries were not life threatening but bad enough to require twenty-six stitches and a night's stay at the hospital. Although she still had the dog in her arms, Brooke refused to leave her daddy and Marta refused to leave Brooke. Once Drew was settled in a room, two reclining chairs were brought in and everyone spent the night there.

Although the hospital had a strict no pets policy, when Brooke came through the hallway carrying Lucy all three night nurses looked the other way.

**AS IT TURNED OUT, EDDIE** had a shattered femur in his right thigh and would likely walk with a limp for the rest of his life. After the surgery he was placed in a room with a policeman standing outside the door. There were no visitors allowed, which wasn't a problem because no one came anyway.

**REALIZING WHAT A VENGEFUL NATURE** Eddie had, Alisha became frightened he'd come back looking for her. That same night she called her married sister in Secaucus, New Jersey, and said she was coming home to stay. Before leaving she wrote a letter to her property management company stating that she'd been called out of town and would no longer need the apartment. She apologized for giving such short notice and then dropped her key into an envelope along with the letter. On the way out she slid the envelope under the apartment door of the building superintendent.

# The End of Halfway

Drew was released from the hospital the next day, but neither he nor Brooke could face going back to the house. The thought of what had happened there was still fresh in their minds and too painful a memory. Although it was over, it wasn't really over. There were questions to be answered, statements to be taken.

"Had you ever met either of the brothers before?" the detectives asked. "What about your wife, was there a chance that she knew one of them, from years ago maybe?"

Until they'd explored every avenue, swept the corners clean and poked into forgotten memories, Drew was asked not to leave town. So he and Brooke checked into the Marriott Suites where, with a small upcharge, dogs were welcomed. The suite had two separate bedrooms with a living room in between and a small efficiency kitchen tucked in the corner. For now it was home. Drew made a few trips back to the house to get the things they needed: some clothes, his laptop, Lucy's bowls and leash.

The morning after they checked in, he dashed off several e-mails explaining that there had been a family emergency and he would be unavailable for the next few days. In the afternoon, he and Brooke went to the pool together. At first she just sat on the steps and dangled her legs in the water. Then Drew carried her in and held his hand beneath her tummy as he taught her how to swim.

Even after she'd learned to stay afloat with no trouble she remained by his side. If he walked back to the lounge for a glass of iced tea or to pick up their sandwiches she watched him with hooded eyes, never letting him go beyond her range of sight.

That evening after Brooke had gone to bed, Drew placed a call to Jennifer's parents in California and told them of everything that had happened. With Jennifer's mother on one extension and her dad on the other, it became a three-way conversation.

"I think you and Brooke should come to California and live with us," she said.

"Absolutely," the father agreed. "I'm certain I could find some sort of job for you here in our firm."

"A law firm?" Drew replied. "I don't think that's a place where I'd fit in."

"No matter," Daddy Green said. "If I tell them to hire you they'll hire you, even if you do nothing but sit around and drink coffee."

Drew took a deep breath and held back from speaking his thoughts.

*Hire me as a useless hanger-on? No, thanks.*

"We have plenty of room," Sylvia added. "You and Brooke would each have your own room, and I could hire a full-time housekeeper to watch over her."

"I think right now Brooke needs more than a housekeeper to watch over her," Drew said. "She's frightened, and she needs to be with people who she believes will love her and protect her."

"Are you suggesting a bodyguard?" Daddy Green asked.

"No," Drew answered. "I'm asking if her grandparents would have time to spend with her. Do things like occasionally driving her to school or taking her to ballet lessons. Brooke needs to realize that she is not alone and doesn't have to be frightened if she's out of my sight."

There were a few moments of silence. Then Sylvia said, "Well, I suppose Edgar and I could take a week or two off, but with the case load I've got two weeks would be sort of stretching it."

"I understand," Drew said, but the truth was he didn't understand. These people were nothing like Jennifer. They were absorbed in their careers and worried more about the imposition he and Brooke might be, whereas Jennifer had been the most generous person he'd ever known.

Drew closed his eyes and tried to imagine Sylvia Green bringing the next-door neighbor a box of taffy as a thank you for watering a few geraniums. The picture never came. Even imagining it was a total impossibility.

"You know how much we love you and Brooke," Sylvia said. "We'd be delighted to have you live here, but realistically speaking I do think we'd need full-time domestic help to take care of—"

"No problem," Drew cut in before she could say it again. "But I think it would be better if we just wait and come for a vacation. Next summer maybe. By then Brooke will hopefully be feeling more secure."

"That's probably best," Sylvia said. "If you let us know ahead of time when you're coming, I can arrange a few days off while you're here."

"What about money?" Daddy Green asked. "Are you okay, or do you need me to send you a check?"

"I'm okay," Drew said. If Daddy Green didn't have love to give, then Drew flat out didn't want his money either.

**ON THE THIRD DAY MARTA** and Walter came to visit.

Drew ordered sandwiches and tall glasses of iced tea, and they all gathered around one of the poolside tables with an umbrella shading them from the sun.

As they sat and talked, Marta saw the toll this past year had taken on Drew. There was now a bit of graying at his temples and a dullness in his eyes. He looked tired—not the kind of tired that comes from missing a night's sleep, but the kind of tired that is soul-weary. The kind that comes from carrying the heartaches of life on your shoulders.

When Brooke clicked the leash on Lucy and walked her across to the grassy area designated for dogs, Marta seized the opportunity to broach the subject on her mind.

"What's going to happen now?" she asked.

Drew shrugged. "Well, they've booked Eddie Coggan, and he's being held without bail. Hilbert told me this is his second offense and they've got him for parole violation, car theft and attempted kidnapping, so the likelihood is that he'll be in jail for a long time."

One thought remained unspoken. *A long time is not the same as forever.*

"That's good," Marta said. "Has Brooke accepted that he won't be able to come after her again, or is she still frightened?"

"Still frightened. I doubt that she'll ever want to go back to the house to live, but I haven't made any other plans yet." Drew gave a weighted sigh. "I think what I'll do is cash in my IRA and take some time off. Brooke needs to get away. Maybe a month of traveling, being in places where there are no bad memories..."

He left the end of that thought unsaid. Brooke forgetting wasn't a given; it was, at best, only a hope.

"Where would you go?" Walter asked.

"Not California," Drew said absently. "And not a place crowded with tourists."

"We have a summer cottage in Magnolia Springs," Marta offered. "You'd be welcome to use that."

Drew thanked her and said he'd keep it in mind but that he still had a lot of thinking to do before he decided on anything.

"Right now my main concern is just spending time with Brooke. I want her to realize that no matter where we go or what we do, I'm here for her."

**THE THOUGHT OF GOING SOMEWHERE** else and starting over remained in Drew's mind long after he'd tucked Brooke in bed for the night. He sat in the living room with the television flickering and the sound turned so low it was impossible to hear what was being said. Long after Jimmy Fallon had signed off and Seth Meyers had given up poking fun at politicians, Drew reached a decision.

He was going to quit his job.

For the past six months he'd lived a halfway life. One half of him always thought about the job, the other half always worried about Brooke. Neither of the two things he loved ever got his full attention. Whenever he sat with Brooke and tried to focus on their conversation, he was thinking about the next sale, or a job on press, or mulling over the fact that next month's commission check would be smaller than the current month's check. It was unfair to Brooke and unfair to Southfield Press.

His thoughts flickered over to Eddie Coggan. Sooner or later Coggan would get out of jail. Five years? Ten years, maybe? Then what? Would he come back? And if he did what would happen?

It was near dawn when Drew finally decided the answer was to sell the house and move away. Start over again. A smaller house in a quiet neighborhood. A place where Brooke would feel safe again. A place where Eddie Coggan would never find them. He had no idea where that place was but they'd travel around until they found it, and when they did they'd settle down and stay. He'd find some kind of work, and they'd live a quiet peaceful life.

Drew decided to call a realtor and put the house up for sale. After that he would call Brian Carson and tell him that he was leaving the job.

# High Above the Earth

The Keeper of the Scales saw the sadness in Drew's face, the heavy ridges of worry creasing his brow and the way his shoulders now slumped. Drew Bishop was a good man, a man undeserving of such a life. He had lost his wife, almost lost his daughter, and now he would lose his home and the job he loved.

The Keeper's power was such that he could only balance the happiness and sorrow of a man's life. He could not reverse or change what had been ordained. The injustice of such a destiny caused a fire to blaze in his great heart.

"This cannot remain so!" he roared.

He lifted the blue stone of benevolence and dropped it onto Brian Carson's scale. Then, in what to a mortal would be a single heartbeat, his majestic eye scanned the silver threads crisscrossing the heavenly landscape. He selected one that passed near Bishop's scale.

At that moment the moon moved from behind a cloud and lit the sky with a brightness that rivaled day. The Keeper smiled then lifted a large stone that glittered with the color of rose quartz. He placed that stone on the happiness side of Elizabeth Cunningham's scale and watched as the weight of it caused the silver thread beneath her scale to grow taut. As it tightened the thread began to move, and when it finally came to rest it was lying across Drew Bishop's scale. Just as the Keeper had foreseen.

That morning the sun rose with a seldom-seen brilliance and the Keeper, pleased with his work, settled back to watch what would happen.

# The Offer

Drew's first call was to Marta. He told her of his plan and asked if she would show the realtor through the house.

"Of course," she replied, hiding the sadness she felt. Much as Marta hated to see them leave, she knew it was for the best. Sooner or later she and Walter would also leave, downsize or possibly go live in the Magnolia Springs cottage.

"I hope wherever you go, you'll stay in touch," she said.

"Of course we will," Drew replied. "We consider you family."

The words "wherever you go" settled on Drew's ear uncomfortably. He needed to think it through, find a place that was right for them.

*Tomorrow. Or the day after. Or maybe a week from now. But soon.*

**Drew's second call was to** Brian Carson. Before he tapped in the number, he thought through all the things he would say. He would tell him what an honor it had been to work for the company and how he'd enjoyed the years of their association. He would explain that with being unable to travel, he wasn't giving Southfield Press the full measure of loyalty they deserved. He would volunteer to provide a comprehensive list of his account activity to make training a replacement easier. And lastly he would explain how he had no other choice. His daughter had to be his first priority, and he needed to be there for her.

Brian was a no-nonsense businessman. He would appreciate a man owning up to the fact that his performance was less than it should be. Although Drew was saddened by the thought of leaving, he knew they would part ways on an amicable basis and that was of some small comfort.

Drew dialed, and Brian answered on the first ring.

"I don't know if you've seen the story in the newspaper," Drew said. He'd planned to go on and detail what had happened, but Brian cut in.

"Yes, I read it," Brian said. "Helluva thing to go though, that's for sure."

Drew told him that they'd moved out of the house and were living at the Marriott Suites.

"This is just temporary," he said. "But Brooke will never feel safe in that house again, so we're planning to move."

"I figured," Brian said.

"Not just from the house but away from here. Maybe downsize, find a small place in a quiet little town—"

Brian gave a muffled snort. "Did Wilcox tell you?"

Such a response puzzled Drew. "Tell me what?"

"About the job in Burnsville. Wilcox already clued you in, right?"

Still confused, Drew said, "I'm not sure what you mean."

"He didn't tell you I was going to offer you the job as plant manager for the Burnsville Offset Shop?"

"Plant manager?" Drew echoed. "Me?"

"Yeah, Wilcox has already given notice. He's retiring as of September first. The job's a good fit. You're familiar with the company, understand the ups and downs of offset, and there's no travel."

Drew knew Fred Wilcox. He'd known him for years, and he

was also familiar with Burnsville, Virginia. He'd been there for press runs a half dozen times or more. The town was exactly the type of place he'd envisioned raising Brooke, but the thought of it came at him so quickly he had to pause for a breath.

"I don't know—"

He was going to say "I don't know how to thank you," but Carson interrupted before he finished.

"Think about it before you say no," he said, assuming Drew's hesitation was a prelude to declining the offer. "Southfield is willing to match your previous year's income and pay all relocation costs including a buyout of your current home at fair market price."

This time Drew didn't hesitate.

"It's a deal," he said.

**LATER THAT AFTERNOON AS HE** and Brooke sat by the pool he told her about the job.

"It means we'll have to move away," he said. "Are you okay with that?"

"What about Marta? And my friend, Ava?"

"They'll stay here in Clarksburg. But I'll fix it so you can Skype with them like I do with my customers."

"What about my ballet class? Missus Thomson said I was going to be a fairy in the next recital."

"We can find you a new ballet class, but I can't promise you a fairy role. You'll have to work real hard and earn that yourself."

"Oh." A look of disappointment settled on Brooke's face.

"What I can promise you is that you'll be safe. I'll be working right there in the same town where you go to school." Remembering how more than once he'd seen one of Wilcox's kids in the office, he added, "And there will even be days when you can come to work with me."

"Really?"

He gave a nod. "Really. I'll give you a tour of the plant and explain how all those printing presses work."

Of course Brooke had a dozen other questions about school and the house they'd live in. Would she have her own room? Would there be kids for her to play with? Was there a doghouse for Lucy? Would Lucy still be allowed to sleep in her bed?

"Lucy saved my life," she said, as if he needed a reminder.

"I know," he replied.

As they sat there side by side with legs dangling in the pool, the questions continued. In time they would all be answered, but for now there was only the sadness of saying goodbye.

**IN THE DAYS THAT FOLLOWED** Drew went back to the house several times. He packed boxes with things they would carry in the car and filled suitcases with the clothes they would need. He chose the most precious things to carry with them: the photo albums Jennifer treasured, the potted plants she'd loved, a set of silverware that once belonged to his mama, Brooke's favorite books and toys.

On those days, Marta came to the Marriott and sat with Brooke alongside the pool.

"I'm going to miss you and your daddy," she said, trying to hide the sound of her sorrow.

"I'm going to miss you too," Brooke replied. "But I can call you from the computer, and we can still see each other. Daddy said so."

Marta laughed. "I'm afraid you're going to have to teach me how to do that."

"No problem," Brooke said, repeating what she'd heard her daddy say.

**ON THE DAY BEFORE THEY** were to leave Clarksburg and begin the trek to Burnsville, Drew called Fred Wilcox. They spoke for a long time about the plant operations, the people working there and the town itself.

"It's a nice place to live," Wilcox said. "I think you're going to like it here."

"After what we've gone through here, any place will be a welcome change," Drew replied. He asked if there was a Marriott Suites or other chain hotel nearby.

"We'll need a place to stay for the first week or two," he said. "At least until I can find a more permanent place."

Thinking back twenty-five years to when he'd first arrived in Burnsville, Wilcox said, "No Marriott, but we've got the Memory House Bed and Breakfast Inn."

Remembering how Ophelia had served a breakfast of homemade muffins and eggs so light they could almost float away, he added, "Mildred and I stayed there when we first came to town, and she still goes there to buy the tea and remedies they sell at the apothecary shop."

"Is it nearby?" Drew asked.

"Yep, just a mile or so from the plant," Wilcox replied. "The place has a new owner now, but Mildred claims she's pleasant as Ophelia was."

"Sounds like a good place to stay. I'll call the reservation desk. Do you have the phone number?"

Wilcox chuckled. "They don't have a reservation desk, but I'll have Mildred tell Annie to expect you."

Before they hung up Drew asked for the address of Memory House, and although Fred didn't have the address handy he claimed it was a place you couldn't miss.

"It's the white house at the end of Haber Street. You'll see a sign that reads Memory House Bed and Breakfast right before you turn into the drive."

**After he'd hung up the** phone Fred Wilcox sat there thinking back on the weeks they'd spent at Memory House. This past year he'd grown increasingly forgetful, but he forgot little things like dentist appointments and the dry cleaning Mildred asked him to pick up on his way home. He could easily enough think back twenty-five years and remember Memory House with its fluffy comforter, pots of dandelion tea and ducks splashing about on the pond.

Months ago Mildred told him that with the twins toddling about Annie Doyle had closed the bed and breakfast part of the house. The rooms were still there, but now it was simply Oliver and Annie's home with a small apothecary shop in the front of the house. That was one of the things Fred forgot.

That evening as they settled down to supper, Fred got to talking about the fishing trip planned for Saturday, and thoughts of Drew wanting a room at Memory House were gone from his mind.

When Mildred asked, "How was your day?"

He answered, "Same old, same old. Nothing new."

# A Sad Goodbye

Marta Feldman set her alarm clock for five-thirty, but she was awake long before it started to ring. Today was the day. Brooke and her daddy were leaving for Virginia, and Marta knew this was probably the last time she would see the child. Yes, they'd talk on the phone and send letters, but it would never be the same as hugging Brooke to her chest and feeling the rhythm of her tiny heartbeat.

Marta hurried down to the kitchen and began her preparations. This was going to be a very special breakfast. She set the table with the china and crystal used for holidays, then scooped the inside of the melon into tiny round balls and placed them in a silver dish. She set skillets of ham and eggs on the stove and a tray of biscuits in the oven, then poured herself a cup of coffee and waited for the doorbell to ring.

Drew and Brooke pulled into the Feldman driveway at seven-thirty, and as he walked from the car he turned to take one last look at the house he'd lived in.

It was the place he'd called home for almost ten years. Brooke had been conceived in that house. It held a million memories both good and bad. Now they were leaving it behind.

A new family would move in. Strangers. People he didn't even know. In an odd way he wished they could have stayed long enough to sell the house himself, perhaps get to know the people who would be living there. Tell them how in the early morning they could see the sunrise from the master bedroom and how on a stormy night they could listen to the slush of rainwater rolling across the roof without ever having to worry that it might leak.

When she opened the door Marta saw the weariness in Drew's face. She pulled him into her arms.

"I know this is hard," she said. "It's hard for me also, but we both know it's the best thing for Brooke."

Drew gave a solemn nod.

Although the table was laden with food, it seemed no one but Walter had much of an appetite. Marta scooped a pile of eggs onto her plate then drank a second cup of coffee and left the eggs untouched. Drew picked at a single sausage. Brooke ate one biscuit and asked if instead of eggs she could have a cookie.

"I have a whole bag of cookies for you and your daddy to take in the car," Marta replied.

They talked about the trip, the anticipated weather and what they might expect in the new town, but beneath the words there was an underlying layer of sorrow.

At eight-thirty Drew said it was time for them to get on the road. Marta walked them to the car, hugged Brooke to her chest one last time then turned away before they could see her tears.

Drew pressed his foot to the gas pedal and pulled away from the curb. In the rear view mirror he could see Brooke turn for one last look at Marta. A cascade of tears rolled down her cheeks.

**HE PULLED ONTO ROUTE 20** and drove east until they circled around Atlanta. Then he continued on Route 85 North. It was almost all highway driving so there was little to see, and Brooke found a dozen different reasons to stop. She had to go to the bathroom, then she needed a soda. After that Lucy had to have a walk, then it was time for lunch.

Although Drew had loaded three new games on her phone thinking it would be enough to keep her busy, that too was a problem. "Catch the Berry" was too hard. "Hungry Guppy" was too much like doing math. She'd already read the first two stories in the *Secret Keeper Series* he'd selected for her. And sometimes for miles at a stretch there was no data signal at all.

"When I went for a ride in the car with Mama we used to sing," she said petulantly.

"And what exactly did you sing?"

"Whatever was on the radio."

Drew snapped on the radio. "Let's see what we can find."

He jumped from station to station, pausing at each one long enough to glance into the rear view mirror and catch Brooke's grimace. When the radio didn't work out too well, Brooke unbuckled her seat belt and began playing with Lucy. Drew spotted this in the mirror.

"Back in the seat," he said. "And buckle up!"

In Spartanburg, South Carolina, he finally pulled off the road, and they stopped for the night. He had hoped to make it to Charlotte or possibly even Greensboro so they'd have a shorter drive the second day, but with all the stops and delays it was an impossibility. They had already been on the road for over nine hours.

**THE SECOND DAY WAS NO** better than the first. Each time Drew thought he'd have a chance to make up some of the lost time, Brooke found another need to stop. It was almost four o'clock when they finally crossed into Virginia, which meant he wasn't going to make it to Burnsville before seven.

With another two stops, it turned out to be almost eight when they finally reached Burnsville. Drew stopped at the gas station and asked for directions to Haber Street.

"I'm looking for Memory House," he said.

The attendant nodded. "Yep, that's sure enough on Haber Street." He waggled his finger, pointing to a road that ran off to the side. "Take Chestnut for as far as you can go then make a left. Haber is about three blocks down on the right."

Drew thanked him and started off.

When he made the right onto Haber Street, the sun was low on the horizon and the glare made it difficult to see. Drew spotted the sign that read Memory House but failed to notice that it said nothing about a bed and breakfast.

He pulled into the driveway and clicked off the engine. Turning back to look at Brooke face to face rather than in the mirror, he smiled and said, "Well, we're here."

Cramming a Barbie and her phone into the backpack she carried everywhere, Brooke unbuckled her seat belt and scrambled out. Looking up at the house, its window boxes filled with red geraniums, she said, "This doesn't look like a hotel."

"It's not," Drew replied. "It's a bed and breakfast inn."

"What about dinner?"

"Just breakfast, no dinner." Drew pulled their overnight case from the trunk and turned toward the house. "Once we get settled in our room, we'll go out and look for a place to eat."

Drew reached for the brass knocker and rapped it.

**THURSDAY EVENING WAS WHEN OLIVER** held night court, so Annie was busy in the apothecary. When she heard the knocker her head popped up from behind the counter and she called out, "Come on in."

Drew eased the door open and stepped inside. "Hello?"

"I'm in the apothecary," Annie hollered.

Following the sound of her voice, he turned right. Carrying Lucy in her arms, Brooke followed along. Once they were inside the apothecary, her eyes grew big and sparkly. She tugged on Drew's sleeve and in a very loud whisper said, "Daddy, this is a magic shop!"

Annie laughed. "Sometimes it feels like that to me too but it's not magic, just some roots, herbs and spices." She looked over at Drew and asked, "Were you looking for something special?"

"We're the Bishops. Fred Wilcox said you'd be expecting us?"

"Oh." Annie thought about the orders she was preparing that evening and didn't remember having one for Mildred or Fred Wilcox.

"Were you supposed to pick up something?" she asked.

"Not from the apothecary," Drew said. "We'll be staying with you for a week or so until we can find a more permanent place."

Annie was just about to say this was no longer a bed and breakfast when she noticed the memories clinging to both the father and the little girl. They were like icicles hanging from a wintery pine, stiff and frozen in place. She felt the heartache of those memories just as she'd felt the power of the locket she once wore.

She thought back to the night she'd come here with no reservation and very little hope for the future. She'd been heartsick and weary. Ophelia saw that and brought her in. She'd given her a warm welcome and renewed hope. If Ophelia did that for her, wasn't it only right that she should do the same for this father and daughter?

"I only have one guest room available," she said. "But it has twin beds and a lovely view of the pond."

Drew smiled. "That sounds perfect."

As she led them through the hallway toward the back room where she'd first stayed, Drew asked if she could recommend a nearby place for dinner.

"We're kind of off the beaten path out here," Annie said. "You'd have to drive back to the highway for the closest restaurant."

When they got to the room she pushed the door open and stepped aside so they could enter. Brooke was first through the door and Drew followed. Just inside the room he stopped and turned back to Annie.

"You weren't really expecting us, were you?"

Annie smiled and shook her head. "Fred Wilcox has gotten very forgetful this past year. Mildred brews periwinkle and ginseng tea for him, and while it helps it doesn't actually cure a failing memory."

Drew gave a sheepish shrug.

"Sorry," he said. "I hope we're not putting you out too much."

"Not at all," Annie replied. "In fact I was just going to ask if you'd like to join us for dinner. It's beef stew, nothing fancy."

Before he could answer Brooke said, "Oh, boy, I love beef stew!"

It was all Annie could do to hold back the grin tugging at her mouth.

"I take it that's a yes."

Drew nodded. "It's a yes."

# Dinner and a Dream

It was close to nine o'clock when Oliver arrived home, but once they sat down to dinner time was all but forgotten. Drew and Oliver immediately segued into talking about the town and the growth potential for any business located in or around Burnsville.

"Just this year we've added two new radio stations, a cell phone tower and eight retail shops," Oliver said.

Drew was adequately impressed and said he was looking forward to being part of such a thriving community. He explained that he was going to be the new plant manager at Southfield and would be looking for a house to rent or buy in the area.

"Someplace fairly close to the plant," he said.

Oliver in turn suggested that he stop by the courthouse the next afternoon.

"I know a few realtors who I think might be able to help you."

**As the men talked, Annie** told Brooke about the twins who were now fifteen months old.

"They'd love to have someone as grown up as you play with them," she said. "Maybe once in a while you could babysit them for me. Not that I'd go off and leave you but, say, for instance, if I was busy working in the apothecary."

Brooke's eyes were fixed on Annie's face as she leaned in listening.

"I never babysat little kids before," she said, "but I know I could do it because my friend, Ava, has a baby brother, and I helped watch him."

"Well, then, you've got experience. For a girl with experience, I'd be willing to pay a dollar an hour."

Brooke's eyes popped open. "A dollar? Just for playing?"

"Well, sure," Annie said, "because that would give me time to straighten up the house and do some work in the apothecary."

"Can I babysit them tomorrow?" Brooke asked.

"You sure can. Your daddy said he has to go visit the Southfield office tomorrow. You can babysit the twins while he's gone."

"You mean stay here by myself?"

"You wouldn't be by yourself. I'd be here and the twins would be here."

She saw the gray cloud of concern covering the girl's face and added, "Maybe we could make cookies in the afternoon and have ourselves a tea party."

Brooke turned to her father. "Daddy, how far away is the office where you're going?"

"Not far," he answered. "Maybe a mile or two."

Annie saw fear creeping up on the girl, and she was determined not to give it room to move in.

"I'm thinking chocolate chip," she said. "How about you? Should we do chocolate chip or rainbow sprinkle cookies?"

"Chocolate chip," Brooke replied tentatively.

"Okay, then, chocolate chip it is."

A look of apprehension remained on Brooke's face.

**WHEN THE EVENING ENDED AND** everyone went off to bed, Annie couldn't let go of the memories she'd seen in the father and daughter's faces. Although the details were fuzzy, as they always were, she knew something horrific had happened to the child's mother.

"I can feel their heartache," she told Oliver. "I wish there were some way I could do something to help them."

"You *are* helping," he answered. "You're giving them a place to stay, food to eat and an ear to listen. Sometimes those things are all a person needs to heal."

He kissed her cheek, mumbled, "Goodnight, sweetheart," then turned on his side and closed his eyes.

Annie remained awake for a long while. Through the skylight she could see a sprinkling of stars in the sky and couldn't help wondering if the child's mother was up there. Perhaps she was looking down at the sorrow she'd left behind. Perhaps she also was wondering what she could do to help heal their broken hearts.

This was the last thought Annie had before she closed her eyes and drifted off to sleep.

**IN THE DREAM SHE SAW** Ophelia as she was years earlier, not a young woman but with hair that had not yet turned silver. She was standing at the threshold of Memory House with the door flung open. One by one the people came, many with saddened faces and slumped shoulders.

Some were missing an arm, a leg, a foot or part of their face.

They all had a look of weariness about them, as if they'd carried a heavy bundle on their back until they could no longer stand straight. In a short while the house was filled.

Oddly enough there seemed to be a seat for everyone. Some sat in the cushioned chairs of the parlor, others at the kitchen table and a few were perched on the staircase leading to the loft. Inside the sound of laughter could be heard, and the melancholy of their faces was no longer visible.

Annie saw herself standing next to Ophelia and asked, *What now? All of these people have burdens too heavy to bear. If they leave them here, won't it change Memory House?*

Ophelia laughed.

*People don't change Memory House,* she said. *Memory House changes people.*

*But there are too many of them. Surely this is an impossible task.*

Ophelia gave a soft smile. *This didn't happen all at once. Look around; you'll see these are the people who came over the years, one at a time. Each of them was missing something, but here at Memory House they found the thing that made them whole.*

Annie looked around the room. The man who'd come with a foot missing was standing whole. The woman with part of her face gone was now wearing a broad smile. They were all that way. Whatever brokenness they'd arrived with had somehow vanished.

*I don't understand…*

*You will,* Ophelia said. *In time you will.* As she spoke her image began to fade away as did the other figures that had filled the house.

*Wait!* Annie shouted. *Don't go! I need you to explain!*

Oliver gently shook her shoulder.

"Explain what?" he asked.

Annie blinked several times before her eyes were fully open. The stars were no longer visible in the skylight. They had been replaced by the rose-colored dawn of a new day.

She pulled on a pair of jeans and hurried down to the kitchen. They had guests, so there was a special breakfast to be made and two toddlers to be fed. Even as Annie slid the tray of biscuits into the oven and sliced pieces of fresh melon, the dream stayed in her head. It meant something, she was certain of it...but what?

**LATER THAT MORNING WHEN DREW** mentioned that he was going to drive over to meet with the team at Southfield, a look of dread settled on Brooke's face.

"Can I go?" she asked.

"Not this time," he said. "We'll be talking business, and you'd just be bored."

"No, I won't. I like to listen to business talking."

By then the twins had just about finished their breakfast. Ethan was still pushing a few Cheerios around the tray of his high chair, but Starr was squirming to get down.

"I'd like it if you could stay and play with the twins for a while," Annie said as she lifted Starr from the chair and set her on the floor.

With her brows pinched together so tight they were nearly touching, Brook asked, "By myself?"

"I'll be here," Annie reassured her. Seeing the apprehension in the child's face she kneeled in front of Brooke and whispered, "You were right yesterday when you said this is a magic place. I don't tell everyone, because if word got around I wouldn't have a minute to myself. But I figure if you're going to babysit the twins, then you should know."

Like most kids, Brooke loved nothing more than a secret. Now mesmerized, her face lit up and she asked, "Know what?"

"How Memory House got its name." Annie's face was aglow with a magic of its own. "It began years ago, when a woman named Ophelia moved into the house..."

As she spoke Drew quietly slipped out the door.

# Annie Doyle

*I thought about that dream with Ophelia all morning long. I knew there was a message in it, but for the love of me I couldn't figure out what it was. Then I saw Brooke playing with the twins and laughing at their antics.*

*She had taken her Barbie doll out and was trying to teach Starr to say Barbie. Starr has a tendency to lop off the first letter of every word, so I knew such an effort was fruitless. Every time Brooke told her to say "Barbie," Starr repeated "Arbie."*

*Ethan doesn't do that. He looked up from the blocks he was playing with, said "Barbie" then went right back to building a tower.*

*"See," Brooke said, using Ethan as an example. "Barbie."*

*"Arbie," Starr repeated again.*

*Brooke laughed like I didn't think she was capable of. That laughter had the sound of happiness in it. She certainly didn't have that same fearful look she had when her daddy told her he was going to the plant. I thought,* She seems like a different girl, *and that's when I started to understand the dream.*

*This past year I've been busy with the twins and haven't given much thought to Memory House as it was when Ophelia gave it to me. I've been seeing it as a wonderful old house to live in, but I'd forgotten the sweet memories stuck in every corner. Memories from the people who came here and stayed until they found the piece of themselves that they'd lost.*

*It's selfish to keep a place as special as this for just my own family. There are so many others that need the healing this house has to give.*

*It's funny how fate works. Had Drew Bishop not showed up here with memories looking as painful as boils, I might never have seen the truth. Memory House isn't just a house, it's a starting point for new lives. We've got plenty of room, so I'm going to reopen the bed and breakfast.*

*Last year when Oliver painted the new apothecary sign for me, I took the old sign and put it in the basement. It was a sentimental thing. I never dreamed I'd one day use it again, but I'm going to.*

*Tomorrow I'll take the sign that says* Memory House Bed and Breakfast, *polish it up and put it right back where it belongs—out by the weeping willow.*

# House Hunting

On Saturday Drew had appointments with all three of the realtors Oliver had given him. This time Brooke got to go along, as did Lucy.

Their first appointment was with Frank Elgin, a man with gray whiskers and a low tolerance of both children and animals. Right off he indicated his listings were mostly apartments and a good number of those specified no pets.

"I've got a two-bedroom in Dorchester, but it's a thirty-minute drive," he said.

He turned the computer around and showed Drew a picture of the apartment. The living room had an oversized sectional and a coffee table that seemed to be made from a door. With two club chairs and a desk squeezed into the room, it appeared overcrowded and way too small.

Drew shook his head. "Too cramped."

The only other thing Elgin had at the moment was a working farm on the outskirts of Langley.

"A farm," he said, "now that's a good place for kids and animals."

Brooke's face brightened for a moment, but Drew shook his head.

"I'll be managing the Southfield plant, so working a farm would be impossible."

**THEY MOVED ON TO THE** second realtor, Emma Jean Burns.

"No relationship to the founder of the town," she said laughingly. Emma Jean had several houses in Drew's price range, but all of them were a half-hour or an hour from the plant.

"We can take a look," Drew said, "but I'd hoped to find something closer."

"I've got one on Beacon Street." Emma Jean replied. "That one is just ten minutes from the plant, but it's higher than you wanted to go."

Emma Jean made several calls asking if they could see the houses that day. They spent the remainder of the afternoon going from place to place. The first house was spacious enough, but it was at the far end of a street with a wooded lot next to it. Drew saw how Brooke eyed the woods and said the location wasn't right for them.

The second house needed work—lots of work. Termites had gotten to the front porch, so that needed to be torn down and replaced. Plus, the pipes rattled when the tap was turned on. And the owner said there might or might not be a problem with the furnace.

The third house they looked at was the one closest to the plant, a ten-minute drive at most. It was a large brick colonial with four bedrooms upstairs and two downstairs.

"Plus there's the maid's quarters off the kitchen," Emma Jean said.

The kitchen was immaculate with a large stainless steel Sub-Zero refrigerator and an island that featured a built-in Jenn-Air grill.

Brooke looked around then tugged on Drew's sleeve. "This looks like a princess house, Daddy."

He smiled. "Yes, it does, but it's way more room than we need." He looked across to Emma Jean and added, "And twice as much as I want to spend."

They left the house and drove back to Emma Jean's office where he'd parked the car. It was easy to see the disappointment in Drew's face but almost impossible to know whether it was because of the houses that were unsuitable or the last one that was more than he could afford.

By then it was late in the afternoon. Drew swung by the third realtor's office and filled out the application with specifics as to what he was looking for.

Crystal Mayer had only been in the real estate business for one year, but she had a knack for reading people. It was said that she could look into the face of a homebuyer and know exactly what the person was looking for.

"I'll bet you've been out looking at houses all day," she said. Her voice was soft, velvety almost.

Drew gave a weary nod. "Does it show?"

She chuckled. "Sort of. Why don't we sit here, have a cup of coffee and talk instead of running around town to look at more houses you probably won't like?"

"Sounds good," Drew said.

"Me too?" Brooke asked hopefully.

"For little girls I suggest a drop of coffee with a whole lot of milk. How's that?" She glanced at Drew looking for approval.

He smiled and nodded.

Crystal disappeared into the back room and returned with a bowl of water for the dog and three mugs. She set the water on the floor and handed Brooke the mug with milky pale coffee.

As she settled back into her chair she said, "So, would you like to tell me a bit about yourself?"

It had the sound of an invitation as opposed to a prod, and Drew felt comfortable with it. He began by telling bits and pieces of their life in Clarksburg then said they'd lost Brooke's mama but gave none of the particulars. He also left out the story of Eddie Coggan. Some things were better pushed to the back of the closet and forgotten. He said with Jennifer gone he wanted to live somewhere fairly close to the plant because Brooke needed him.

As they spoke she jotted notes on the tablet at the side of her desk. She wrote without looking down and never took her eyes from Drew. It was as if her hand operated independently of her mind and moved of its own accord. As she listened she began to visualize him in a three-bedroom Cape Cod, not small, but not too large either. White, probably, with blue shutters at the windows and flowerboxes filled with greenery. By the time he stood to leave she knew exactly what he needed.

The problem was she didn't have a property of that sort available.

"I believe I know what you want," she said. "Let me ask around, and I'll call if I can come up with something. Is there a number where I can reach you?"

"We're staying at Memory House," he said, "but it's best if you call my cell."

After they left the office Drew drove back to Memory House. Realizing they'd shown up unexpected and the Doyles had been kind enough to give them a room, his thought was to take everyone out to dinner. It was early enough that the drive back to the highway restaurant wouldn't matter.

When they arrived back at the house Drew again stepped to the porch and rapped the brass knocker. Annie was back in the kitchen, so Oliver answered the door.

"There's no need to knock," he said. "The door's almost always open."

"Well, I thought since it's your home and not really a bed and breakfast—"

Oliver laughed. "Apparently you inspired Annie, because she's decided to reopen the bed and breakfast."

Trailing behind Oliver, Drew asked, "Is that a good or bad thing?"

Oliver turned with a smile. "Good. Doing things for other people makes Annie happy and when she's happy, I'm happy."

The comment made Drew think of Jennifer.

"I'll bet she's the type to give someone a gift for doing something as simple as watering her geraniums, right?" he said.

"Absolutely."

When they got back to the kitchen the twins were already in their high chairs. Starr spotted Brooke and squealed, "Ook."

Brooke laughed. "It's Brooke. Try it. Say buh, buh, buh…"

"Buh, buh, buh," Starr repeated.

"Okay, now say Brooke."

"Ook."

**THE WEEKEND CAME AND WENT** uneventfully. Drew and his daughter remained at Memory House, and Annie refused his offer to take everyone out to dinner.

"It's enough that Brooke is helping with the twins," she said.

Drew received three calls from Fred Wilcox going over things he thought he might have forgotten to tell him and another call from Brian Carson checking that they'd arrived safely and his meeting with Wilcox had gone well. Unfortunately, there were no calls from any of the realtors.

# Across the Pond

Drew was still living at Memory House the Monday he took over management of the Southfield Printing plant. That week almost flew by as he settled into familiarizing himself with the nuances of the operation and the people working there. In what seemed little more than the blink of an eye Monday became Friday, and not just any Friday but the Friday before Labor Day.

In five days the kids started back to school.

He'd held off registering Brooke because the way things stood he wasn't certain whether they'd be living in the Burnsville district or not. So far the only affordable houses he'd seen were in Langley or Dorchester. Frank Elgin had shown him a tiny apartment in downtown Burnsville, but it was a one-bedroom on the third floor of a stodgy-looking apartment building. Granted, it had an alcove that would accommodate a single bed, but Drew simply couldn't imagine Brooke being happy in a place such as that.

In the time they'd been at Memory House Brooke had once again become herself. She was slowly but surely turning back into the happy child she'd been before Jennifer was killed. Drew knew it was because of Annie and the twins. Brooke acted like a little mama to those babies, and Annie treated Brooke as one of her own. She was always right there, keeping one eye on the three kids while she went about her work. Yes, Brooke was happy here, but living at a bed and breakfast wasn't something that could last forever.

On Saturday morning Drew woke filled with resolve.

"This weekend we have to find a place to live," he told Brooke.

"Why?" she asked. "I like it here."

"I know you do. But even though the Doyles have been nice enough to let us stay this long, we've got to move on. If we're underfoot much longer they'll—"

Brooke thumped her hands on hips the way she'd seen Marta do.

"I'm not underfoot," she said with an air of indignation. "I'm babysitting!"

It was all Drew could do not to laugh. "Well, Annie doesn't need a live-in babysitter, so we still have to find a place of our own."

With that he turned and headed for the bathroom to shower and shave. When he returned to the bedroom, he saw there was a message on his cell phone. He half-expected it to be Brooke having one last word as she sometimes did, but when he checked his voicemail it was a message from Crystal Mayer. With all the new people he'd met that week it took a few seconds for him to place the name. He selected "Listen to message."

"Hi, Drew. This is Crystal Mayer from Corner Realty. I have a property I think you'll like. It's a two-year rental, probably with an option to buy, but you'll have to act fast because this one is gonna go like hotcakes. Don't bother coming to the office. It's closer if I pick you up at Memory House. Nine-thirty. Be ready and bring your checkbook. Bye."

After so many disappointments, Drew was almost afraid to believe this was the real thing. He replayed the message twice, each time listening for some telltale sign or secret message tucked between the words. There was nothing; just the friendly sound of Crystal's voice.

He thought back on the day he'd met with her. Unlike the other realtors, she'd not tried to shuttle them around town looking at everything from a pup tent to a penthouse. She said only that she'd call if she could find something right for him.

Drew glanced at his watch then told Brooke to get ready. They'd be leaving in twenty minutes.

AT PRECISELY NINE-THIRTY CRYSTAL PULLED into the driveway and beeped the horn. Drew shoed Brooke out the door, and they climbed into the car. Crystal shot him a bright-eyed smile.

"You're going to love this," she said. "Three bedrooms, two-and-a-half baths, mint condition and..."

She backed out of the driveway, drove half a block, then turned into the small street that circled around to the far side of the pond.

"It's right here in this neighborhood!"

"A rental in this neighborhood?"

"Yep!" She gave a self-satisfied nod. "A stroke of luck if I've ever seen one!"

It was no more than five minutes before she turned into the driveway of a charming two-story Victorian with a large bay window in the front and a gingerbread trimmed wrap-around porch.

Drew eyed the flowering azalea bushes and manicured lawn. "You sure this is a rental?"

"With a two-year lease," Crystal reminded him.

He followed her up the walkway then stepped back as she rang the bell. Brooke stood behind him, craning her neck to see inside.

The woman who opened the door was neither young nor old but was impeccably dressed. Crystal stepped forward and wrapped her arms around the woman.

"Congratulations, Francine," she said. "Gerald must be thrilled."

"Very much so," Francine answered. "Although it's only for two years, he's all but certain it will become permanent."

Crystal turned back to Drew and explained. "Francine's husband Gerald has been offered a teaching position at the Sorbonne."

Drew gave an appreciative nod.

Turning back to Francine she said, "And this is the lovely family I told you about. Drew Bishop and his daughter, Brooke. Drew is the new plant manager over at Southfield."

After the round of introductions, Francine began to show them through the house. To the right of the foyer was a cozy study with bookcases lining one wall and a padded seat circling the bay window. Beyond the staircase leading to the upstairs bedrooms there was a living room on the right and dining room on the left.

Before they started upstairs Francine excused herself, saying she had a thousand errands to run and was confident leaving them in Crystal's capable hands. Brooke scrambled up the stairs ahead of everyone, and before they reached the top landing Drew heard her give a gasp of delight.

"Daddy," she called. "You're not going to believe this!"

Following the sound of her voice, they found her in the back bedroom with the French doors open to the Juliet balcony. She raised her arm and pointed almost directly across the pond.

"That's Memory House!" Looking up at Drew with her eyes sparkling she asked, "Can I have this room, Daddy? Please?"

Although Drew knew in his heart he'd already decided, he said, "I haven't rented the house yet." Catching the crestfallen look on her face, he added, "But as soon as I do, yes, this can be your room."

A squeal of delight was followed by a very enthusiastic hug.

"Thank you, thank you, thank you a bazillion times!"

Drew turned to Crystal.

"I guess we officially like the house." He mimicked a wince then asked. "What's the rental?"

"Not bad for this area. Fifteen-hundred unfurnished, Sixteen-hundred furnished. Two months' security and a two-year lease."

Drew gave a thoughtful nod then turned to Brooke who was now pushing back and forth in an enameled rocking chair.

"What do you think, this furniture or the furniture from back home?"

"This!"

Drew laughingly turned back to Crystal. "The young mistress says she would prefer the house furnished."

After they left the house, they walked out to the backyard and down the slope to the pond. Pulled up onto the grassy edge of the bank was a weathered canoe and paddle. Brooke saw it and grinned.

"Does this come with the house?"

"Do not even think about it," Drew said. "You are *not* allowed near this pond unless I am with you. Is that understood?"

The grin faded. "Yes, sir."

# A Changing Life

Two weeks later Francine and Gerald flew off to Paris, and Drew moved into 1220 Lakeside Drive. He had the moving company store the furniture they'd taken from the Clarksburg house and deliver the fifteen cartons of personal belongings to the Lakeside house.

It took nearly a month before all the cartons were unpacked and the right place found for each small reminder of their past life. When most everything had been put away, Drew ordered a print of the photo he'd taken with his phone the weekend before Jennifer died. It was a snapshot of her and Brooke laughing at something he'd said. It was odd how he couldn't remember what it was he'd said, but he could remember them laughing.

It was a moment frozen in time, part of what was and would never again be. He'd looked at the picture a thousand times since that day. Now it would also be part of their new life. He slid the photograph into a simple silver frame and placed it on the mantle in the living room.

Piece by piece father and daughter settled into their new life, and before Thanksgiving rolled around Drew had once again begun to enjoy getting up early and going off to work. He was never more than a phone call away from Brooke, but as weeks turned into months she seemed to find less and less of a need to call him. That was in part due to Hannah, the girlfriend she'd discovered two doors down. After a few weeks they were almost inseparable. Wherever one went, Drew knew, the other was close by.

On the afternoons he found Brooke without Hannah, she was babysitting Annie's twins. For most of that fall when the school bus stopped in front of Annie's house, Brooke jumped off and hurried in calling for the toddlers. At the end of the day when Drew left the plant he'd pull into the drive at Memory House, beep his horn and wait for Brooke to run out and jump into the car. Then they'd go home together.

As he and his daughter established themselves in this new life, Drew discovered he could hold on to the good memories and not buckle beneath the pain of losing Jennifer.

**JUST AS SHE'D PLANNED, ANNIE** hauled the old Memory House Bed and Breakfast sign up from the basement and planted it in the spot where it had stood for all those years before. Time had turned the bright white background to a soft yellow, but when the headlights of an oncoming car flickered across it the gold lettering still sparkled. Granted, this didn't happen every time. It was as if the sign had a mind of its own and decided who was and who wasn't worthy of discovering the magical house.

Once Drew left others came. The first was Bertram Liebowitz, an elderly gentleman from New York traveling to Georgia to visit his dying sister. With a wiry gray beard and ill-fitting black suit, he was a sorrowful figure indeed. At first glimpse Annie knew his heart was weighted with thoughts of what he was about to lose. He was in need of a sympathetic ear, and she took time to be one.

For two days he sat at the kitchen table drinking cups of dandelion tea and sharing stories of their childhood together. As Ethan and Starr toddled around the room, he mentioned that he and Penelope were also twins.

"No one but another twin can understand the bond that is shared," he said grimly.

Later in the afternoon when Starr climbed onto his lap and tugged at his beard, he found a bit of laughter in his soul and allowed it to break free.

On the third day he left with a bittersweet smile. He'd come with nothing but sorrow in his heart and had somehow found the strength to replace a small part of it with gratitude for the years he and Penelope shared. As he climbed back into his car Annie handed him the snowdrop flower she'd potted for Penelope.

"This plant brings hope and comfort," she said. "The hope is for Penelope and the comfort for you."

He smiled, took the plant from her and placed it on the seat beside him. As he drove off Annie knew that what was destined to be would be, but he would now stand a bit stronger as he passed through the pain of it.

**AFTER BERTRAM THERE WAS A** widow from Kentucky traveling through on a trip to visit her new grandbaby. Bubbling over with enthusiasm, she said this was the first of what she hoped would be many. That woman stayed just one night, and when she left Annie noticed how the potpourri in the center hall had taken on the scent of baby powder.

Two days later a thin girl with bones no bigger than that of a sparrow knocked at the door and asked how much a room for one night would cost.

She had the look of a person who hadn't eaten for days. The skinny jeans she wore hung loose about her thighs. Annie's first impression was that she could be a child who'd run away from home, but it turned out not to be so.

Fearing the girl had little if any money in her pocket Annie replied, "This is a guest house. Travelers are welcome to stay here for free."

The girl stood there with a look of astonishment on her face. "No kidding?"

Annie nodded, invited her in and said she was just in time for supper.

The girl pinched her brows together and asked, "How much for supper?"

"There's no charge," Annie replied. "You're our guest."

When they sat down to supper, Annie noticed how the girl took tiny portions and gobbled them down in no time. Without asking if she wanted seconds, Annie refilled her plate.

"I'm certain your mama wouldn't want you eating like a bird," she said.

"Mama died a year ago," the girl replied. She went on to say that she'd graduated high school and was on her way to Camp Blanding in Florida.

"Me and Tony are getting married," she said with a smile.

Annie sat and listened as the girl told how she and Tony had been sweethearts since the eighth grade.

"We ain't got much money," she said. "But we got each other, and that's a start."

"It certainly is," Annie said, smiling. "A good start."

The clock ticked off an hour and then two. When it struck eight, Annie told the girl she had to get the twins into bed.

"Relax and enjoy your tea," she said. "I'll be right back."

With a squiggling baby tucked under each arm, Annie disappeared up the stairs. Twenty minutes later she returned to find the dishes done and the counter sparkling clean.

"You didn't have to..."

"I know," the girl said. "I wanted to."

They sat together and talked late into the night about the girl's love for Tony and his military aspirations at Camp Blanding. The next day Annie took out the silk dress she'd worn for her own wedding and insisted the girl take it before she left. It was a bit too big and hung loose around the bosom, but the girl looked nonetheless beautiful wearing it.

When Annie stood at the door and waved goodbye, she knew she would forever hold on to the image of the girl's face when she was given the dress. She'd cried and clasped her skinny arms around Annie saying that she would for the rest of her life remember such generosity.

"I am only paying forward what I've found here in this house," Annie replied. "Perhaps one day you too will find a time and place to do so."

"Oh, I will," the girl said. "You can be certain I will."

It was a promise Annie felt sure would be fulfilled.

**THIS WAS HOW IT CAME** to be at Memory House. As the days, weeks and months passed, it evolved into a place where fatigued travelers could come to find a measure of comfort and peace.

Annie often asked her guests how they'd found Memory House. There was no advertising, no commercial listing, just a single sign out by the willow tree. Not one of her guests could answer the question. They'd shrug and say something drew them here, but what it was no one could say.

# Elizabeth's Arrival

Elizabeth Cunningham arrived at Memory House on the first Saturday of December. Early that morning the rain that had threatened for days finally started. It came with a blustery wind and pellets of water that were icy cold and hard as hail. When Annie opened the door and saw Elizabeth standing there with an umbrella turned inside out and water puddling around her shoes, she believed her to be the most forlorn looking woman she'd ever laid eyes on.

Annie gasped. "Good grief!"

She tugged Elizabeth inside the house without stopping to ask what she'd come for. Once she'd caught her breath, Elizabeth said she'd seen the sign and wondered if there was an available room.

The moment she said she'd seen the sign, Annie knew she was a woman in need of help. For some odd reason it seemed vacationers passed by the sign and never noticed it. Only those in need of solace saw the glitter of gold lettering peeking out from beneath the branches of the willow.

As soon as Annie said there was indeed room and they'd be delighted to have her stay, Elizabeth turned back to the door.

"I'll get my suitcase," she said, but Annie wouldn't hear of it. She hurried Elizabeth back to the kitchen, set a pot of dandelion tea to brew and sent Oliver to fetch the suitcase. After a few sips of the tea, Elizabeth kicked off her soggy shoes and started to relax.

"I'm sorry for dripping water all over your carpet," she said.

Annie laughed. "Don't give it another thought, Elizabeth. A bit of water is nothing. The twins carry in clumps of dirt, lizards and frogs all day long."

"Call me Liz," the woman said. "Elizabeth always sounds so formal."

One word led to another, and before long Annie asked what brought Liz to Burnsville. Elizabeth leaned into the conversation and lowered her voice as if she was about to share something very hush-hush.

"Simply put, I got tired of being known as Elliott Winslow's ex-wife. People I hardly knew were looking at me as if I was someone to be pitied. Elliott could have left quietly and moved to another town, but, no, he had to make a spectacle of himself."

"What kind of spectacle?"

"The day after he left me, Fritzi Easton saw him walking through town arm-in-arm with a bodybuilder from the gym. A man, for heaven's sake!"

"Is it possible they were just friends?"

Elizabeth narrowed her eyes and twitched the right side of her mouth.

"Don't I wish!" she huffed. "Nothing is worse than living in a town where everyone knows your husband dumped you to move in with another man!"

A look of concern settled on Annie's face as she listened. Elizabeth caught sight of her expression and gave a weighty sigh.

"See, now, that's exactly what I mean," she said. "Hearing what Elliott's done makes people think I'm to be pitied."

"I'm sorry," Annie said. "I didn't mean to—"

Elizabeth waved the apology off. "No need to be sorry. It's not just you. It was the whole town of West Haven. It happened over a year ago, but with Elliott parading around town with his bodybuilder people can't forget. They mean well and say things like 'You're better off without him,' but that constant look of pity wears a person's nerves to a frazzle."

"Well, rest assured, you'll never see it from me again," Annie said.

"Good," Elizabeth replied then began telling the story of how she'd finally made the decision to move on.

"It happened on a Monday evening after I'd closed the bank, locked up and gone home. I was watching a television show about travel, and, boom, the thought hit me like a stone being dropped on my head."

"Was it the travel part that got to you?"

"Shoot, no. It was the thought of starting over in a whole new life." She gave an impish grin and snapped her fingers. "Just like that I decided to sell the house and look for a new job in a new town."

At first glance Annie had seen Elizabeth as a downtrodden soul, but she had now changed her mind. Liz wasn't downtrodden at all. She was smart, savvy and determined. A person Ophelia would call spunky.

Annie refilled both cups, and they continued talking. By the time the twins woke from their nap, Annie knew that Liz was going to be the branch manager of the Heartland Savings Bank in Dorchester and was looking for a furnished apartment somewhere in the area.

"Something small," Liz said. "An efficiency or at the most a one-bedroom. I don't start my new job until the end of the year, and hopefully I'll be settled in by then."

Listening to the positive way Elizabeth spoke it was easy to believe she had moved beyond the hurt of Elliott's betrayal, but in truth she hadn't. It was like a sinkhole beneath her skin, a thing waiting for the chance to cave in and destroy the new life she was building. When Elliott walked out he took his clothes, his skis, his tennis racquet and her self-esteem. What he left behind was an emptiness that she tried to hide beneath layers of pluck and determination.

**THE RAIN CONTINUED THROUGHOUT THE** evening and into the wee hours of morning. Elizabeth was bone tired when she finally went to bed, but sleep wouldn't come. She snuggled deeper into the comforter and tried to think positive thoughts.

The problem was that the future was still a blank slate. She couldn't imagine the new friends she'd meet, because she'd never met them. She couldn't imagine living in a cozy little apartment, because she'd not yet found it.

*Never mind,* she thought. Anything would be better than living all alone in that big house. At one time "big" meant plenty of room to spread out, to have a sewing room and den, a kitchen with cabinets enough for a gourmet collection of cookware. But after Elliott was gone "big" became a vast emptiness. All those rooms, and she hardly used any of them. Cooking for one was a waste of time, so more often than not she carried home a container of Chinese food or a rotisserie chicken and the Cuisinart cookware remained in the cupboard.

Tears filled Elizabeth's eyes and rolled silently down her cheeks.

*Tomorrow,* she promised herself. *Tomorrow will be better than today.*

# A Running Kinship

Early in the morning, even before the twins started fussing to be lifted out of their cribs, Annie heard the front door squeak open and then close. She slid out of the bed and peeked from the dormer window. The rain had stopped, but she could feel the icy cold air pushing up against the glass. After only a few seconds she spotted Liz jogging down the driveway bundled in layers of clothing with a woolly headband covering her ears. At the end of the long drive she turned right and disappeared around the bend of the road.

Liz jogged to the end of Haber Street then turned onto Lakeside Drive. It was a long road that circled the pond in back of Memory House and came out at the opposite end of Haber. As she ran past the first bend she stopped once and switched the track on her iPod, then continued. Music set the mood, and this morning she had a need for something familiar. It was Jennifer Lopez's album *This Is Me.*

When the first chord sounded she upped her pace. Liz loved running. It was the one time when she thought about nothing but putting one foot in front of the other and feeling the beat of the music pounding in her ears.

Few houses had lights on this early in the morning, and there was not a single car on the road. A newspaper delivery boy pedaled past her and tossed a folded newspaper onto the walkway as he sped by. It was only a few weeks until Christmas, and several houses had decorated trees standing in the window.

*Next year,* she thought. *Next year I'll buy a tiny tree and celebrate Christmas, alone if I have to.*

Elizabeth was hopeful that by then she wouldn't have to celebrate alone. Maybe she would have made a number of new friends, friends she could invite over for a homemade meal. Luckily she'd kept most of the gourmet cookware.

At the end of Lakeside Drive she slowed her pace, and as she swung onto Haber her stride turned to an easy trot. By the time she got back to the house Annie was already in the kitchen, and the twins were in their matching high chairs.

"Did you have a good run?" Annie asked.

"Great!" Elizabeth said through heavy breaths. "I see you've got the little charmers up and rolling."

"They're the ones who get me up." She handed Ethan a clean spoon to replace the one he'd dropped on the floor. "They're usually the first ones awake, but I don't mind because then I know they'll go down for a nice long afternoon nap."

Elizabeth gave a wistful sigh.

"I envy you," she said. "You've got such a lovely family."

"Yes," Annie replied, "I am definitely blessed."

A thousand things crisscrossed Elizabeth's mind at that moment, but she said only that she'd grab a quick shower and join them for breakfast. She hurried to her room, peeled off the layers of clothing, then pulled on a robe and crossed over to the bathroom.

As the cascade of warm water splashed against her shoulders and trickled down her body Elizabeth thought back to the week Elliott left. She'd celebrated her thirtieth birthday a few weeks earlier, and it had been a poignant reminder that her biological clock was ticking at what seemed an accelerated speed. That same afternoon she'd gone out and bought a lacy black nightgown thinking she'd wear it when the time was right. Back then she'd believed the only problem was that after nine years of being together the excitement had gone out of their marriage. How foolish she'd been to think a sexy nightie could relight the fire.

Elizabeth hated these thoughts. No matter how they got started they always circled around to the same question: had Elliott ever loved her?

At first she'd believed he had, but now she honestly couldn't say. Whenever she'd mention it was time to start thinking about a family, he'd dodge the issue. The time was never right. He was pressured at work, or felt they should first get a new car, or questioned whether they could manage on his income alone.

"It's only for a few years," she'd argued. "Once the baby goes to school, I'll go back to work."

That last time he said that he'd think about it and Elizabeth had felt hopeful, but two days later he was gone and it was the end of everything. The end of their marriage and the end of her hoping they'd have a baby.

How unfair it all seemed.

**ELIZABETH STEPPED FROM THE SHOWER,** toweled herself off and returned to the bedroom. Anxious to move on to thinking about something else, she dressed quickly and hurried to the kitchen.

Not long after she and Annie settled at the table with a pot of dandelion tea and a basket of freshly baked scones, Brooke rapped the front door knocker then came in calling for the twins. At the sound of her voice both babies gave a squeal of delight and ran toward the hall.

"Company?" Liz said.

Annie shook her head and hollered for Brooke to come and say hi to Miss Cunningham.

Liz noticed how Annie referred to her as Miss Cunningham. There was the sound of friendship in her voice but no pity, which was a good thing. Perhaps after all was said and done, she'd moved past being the unfortunate woman who'd married Elliott Winslow.

When Brooke came into the room Annie gave a nod toward Liz and said, "I want you to meet Miss Elizabeth Cunningham. She's going to be the new branch manager at Heartland Bank."

Brooke stuck out her hand the same as she'd seen her daddy do.

"Pleased to meet you," she said. "Are you going to live at Memory House?"

"For a little while," Elizabeth said. "Until I can find an apartment."

Brooke gave a knowledgeable nod as if she understood such a problem.

"It's very hard to find the right house. We looked for ages, then found the perfect house right across the pond."

It was all Liz could do not to laugh at Brooke's grown up mannerisms. "Well, that was certainly fortunate, wasn't it?"

"Very," Brooke said. "We're so close I can see Memory House from the balcony in my bedroom." She looked toward the kitchen window and pointed a finger. "See that white house, that's ours."

"My goodness," Liz said, "I think I ran right past your house this morning."

"Why were you running?"

"For exercise. It makes me feel good."

Liz paused. Talking to this little girl was almost like talking to another adult.

"Do you do anything just because it makes you feel good?" she asked.

Brooke hesitated then gave a nod. "Babysitting. I get paid a dollar an hour, but I would do it for free. I like that Starr and Ethan get excited when I come, because it makes me feel special."

Annie turned and joined in the conversation. "You *are* special."

Having waited as long as she could, Starr tugged at the tail end of Brooke's sweatshirt.

"Arbie!" she squealed.

Brooke squatted down. "Not arbie, Barbie. Say buh, buh, buh…"

"Buh, buh, buh," Starr repeated.

"Now say Buh-arbie."

Starr giggled and once again said, "arbie." Everyone laughed.

It was the first time Brooke saw Elizabeth Cunningham, but it would certainly not be the last.

# A Budding Friendship

Throughout the month of December Brooke continued to babysit the twins, and she almost always sought out Elizabeth with some new thought or tidbit of conversation she had to share. Often she arrived before the twins were up from their afternoon nap, and while she waited she and Elizabeth would sit side by side sipping cups of dandelion tea and talking of life.

Brooke told Elizabeth about losing her mama as well as what happened with Eddie Coggan, referring to him only as "the bad man."

"Because of the bad man we moved away, and I had to leave my friend, Ava, and Miss Marta," she said sadly.

Elizabeth gave an understanding nod. "I know exactly how you feel. When I decided to take the job in Dorchester, I had to leave all my friends behind too."

"Isn't it easier when you're a grownup?" Brooke asked.

"Not really," Elizabeth replied. "But maybe it will be once I get settled in my own apartment and start to make new friends. Right now the only people I know are you, Annie, Oliver and the twins."

Brooke grinned at the thought of being on the list of friends.

On an afternoon when the twins napped through until almost four o'clock, Annie brewed a second pot of tea and they all sat and talked. After a little while Ethan started calling to get out of the crib, and Annie went to him. Brooke leaned close to Elizabeth.

"Annie's tea is magical," she whispered. "Did you know that?"

"I was beginning to suspect it," Liz said with a grin.

If anyone asked Elizabeth why she was so drawn to this little girl, she would be hard pressed to answer. At times she thought perhaps they'd met before or crossed paths in some unidentifiable way, because as they sat sharing secrets and cups of tea Elizabeth felt a distinct connection to the child. One night as she lay in bed with her eyes still wide open, a thought came to her. If Elliott had consented to having a family when she first asked, they would have a child just about Brooke's age.

Once that thought settled in her head she could almost imagine a daughter exactly like Brooke, but this child had Elizabeth's dark hair and eyes.

**THE SECOND WEEK OF HER** stay, Elizabeth found an apartment that suited her perfectly. It was a tiny one-bedroom in a red brick building smack in the center of Burnsville, furnished with sleek gray sofas, teal carpeting and abstract prints. Although she preferred the more traditional mahogany styles, the apartment was tastefully decorated. With its double window overlooking a boulevard of coffee shops and boutiques it was actually quite pleasant, the kind of place a person could enjoy coming home to. The only problem was that it would not be available until December twenty-eighth. Given the fact that she was enjoying her stay at Memory House so much, the late availability wasn't much of an issue.

Once she'd paid her deposit on the apartment, Elizabeth had

little to do but relax and enjoy the remaining weeks until she began her new job. Most mornings she rose early and went for a run. Sometimes she ran along Lakeside Drive. Other days she ran along Delaware Street, which took her into the heart of town and past the shops on Washington Street. Always she listened to music on her iPod.

Sometimes it was the sweet sound of Taylor Swift; other days she'd rock out with Lady Gaga. The music made her feel alive. When she ran there was no Elliott, no looking back. There was only the pounding of her feet against the sidewalk and matching her steps to the rhythm of the music.

The days of December fairly flew by, and before Elizabeth knew what happened it was December twenty-second. Brooke would leave the next day for California to spend Christmas with her grandparents.

Elliott had walked out just three weeks before the holiday, so the previous year there was no Christmas. The day came and went without Elizabeth ever getting out of bed. She'd burrowed down beneath her grandmother's quilt and cried from dawn to dark. Never again, she'd sworn. Never again.

Although she barely had one foot settled inside this new life, Elizabeth decided it was time to celebrate. The morning of the twenty-second she left the house early, drove into town and parked in front of the red brick apartment building as if she was already a resident. The weather had turned warm earlier in the week, and the sun on her face felt good. At Starbucks she bought a latte and sat at one of the curbside tables. Pulling her phone from her purse, she went to the Notes app and began making a shopping list.

Annie – Christmas apron & fancy teapot

Oliver – a bottle of cognac for Christmas eggnog

Starr – Barbie doll

Ethan – toy truck

Elizabeth stopped and thought for a moment. She pictured how the boy squealed and toddled off with the Barbie doll when Starr was playing, then deleted "truck" and tapped in a Ken doll for Ethan.

For Brooke...She wanted something special, but what? Elizabeth sipped her latte and tried to remember something Brooke might have mentioned. They'd spoken of so many things, but there was no one item she could pinpoint.

When she'd drained the last of the coffee, Elizabeth left Starbucks and crossed over to the Gift Garden. She'd intended to buy just the apron and teapot, but she came away with a shopping bag filled to the brim. She returned to the car, deposited the bag of gift-wrapped packages in the trunk then continued on down the boulevard. At Vine and Barley, she bought a bottle of Courvoisier Cognac, had it gift wrapped then moved on to Turner's Toys.

The last gift she bought was for Brooke. She'd window-shopped every store in town then walked back to where one thing had caught her eye. She wrote a note on the gift card, slid it inside the box then asked to have it gift-wrapped. When the clerk handed her the tiny box wrapped in silver foil, she tucked it inside her purse.

On the drive home Elizabeth snapped on the radio and sang along with the Christmas carols. For the first time in over a year she felt happy. It was not the same blind happiness she got from running. This was more of a deep down, satisfied-with-who-you-are kind of contentment.

By the time she arrived back at Memory House, Brooke was already there. When the door clicked open, she came racing through the hall and wrapped her arms around Elizabeth.

"I thought I wouldn't get to see you," she said anxiously.

Elizabeth was loaded down with shopping bags, but she bent and kissed the top of Brooke's head.

"Don't be silly," she said. "I wouldn't let that happen."

**THAT AFTERNOON ELIZABETH UNPLUGGED HER** earphones, put the Pandora Christmas music station on her iPod and turned up the volume. She placed it on the kitchen counter, and they all gathered around the table. Annie set out a platter of homemade Christmas cookies and mugs of hot chocolate with honey-sweetened cream floating on the top.

Excited about the upcoming trip, Brooke said, "This is going to be the best Christmas ever."

"It's already the best in a long time for me," Elizabeth said.

That afternoon minutes before Drew pulled into the driveway and beeped his horn, Brooke reached inside her backpack and took out a clumsily wrapped package. She handed the package to Elizabeth.

"I made this for you. It's so you'll remember I'm your friend."

A tear glistened in Elizabeth's eye as she unwrapped the gift. Inside the stuck together paper was a Christmas ball decorated with what looked like red nail polish. On one side it read *Miss Elizabeth* and on the other side *Brooke*. Between the two names was a lopsided heart.

The tear spilled as Elizabeth hugged Brooke to her chest and said, "It's the best present ever."

Then she pulled the small silver box from her purse and handed it to Brooke.

"This is for you. Put it into your suitcase and wait until Christmas Day to open it, okay?"

Brooke hitched her shoulders up in excitement and gave a nod.

"Okay," she said then hurried out the door.

# Elizabeth Cunningham

*It's funny how things you've believed for all the years of your life can sometimes turn out not to be true. I've always thought having a man love me heart and soul would bring me happiness. As a girl I dreamed a Prince Charming would sweep me off my feet and carry me off to a land of happy-ever-after.*

*That's not what happened. Elliott and I had difficulties right from the start. I never recognized the source of our problem and kept thinking that once we crossed this bridge of contention we'd find happiness on the other side. Of course we didn't.*

*Now after all those years of searching for happiness, I find it in a place I stumbled on by accident. I was headed for Dorchester, but that night the rain was almost blinding and I didn't see the exit sign until I passed it. The only thing I could do was to get off at the next exit, which just happened to be Burnsville.*

*Don't ask what led me to Memory House, because I honestly don't know. The only thing I remember is standing on the porch and Annie inviting me in. That very first night I had a strange feeling this was exactly where I was supposed to be. It's got to be fate; there simply is no other explanation.*

*Being here has opened my eyes as to what love is and what it isn't. Brooke is only a child, but I've learned a lot from her. Despite the hardships she's gone through, she still has room in her heart to love her little dog, the twins, Annie and me. I look at her and think if she's brave enough to move forward, surely I can also.*

*Thinking about yourself is what locks a person into feeling miserable. Once you move on to thinking about someone else, you don't have time to concentrate on the thing that's been bothering you. The day I went Christmas shopping, I was so focused on finding gifts to make Brooke and Annie happy that I completely forgot about feeling lonely and forgotten.*

*Next week I move into the apartment, and a few days later I'll start my new job. It's an exciting time, and despite all that's happened I'm happier now than I've been in many years.*

*Before long I'll be leaving Memory House, but I'm not leaving the friendships I've found here. Those I'm going to keep forever.*

# A California Christmas

When Drew called to tell Sylvia and Edgar Green that he and Brooke would be coming to California so she could spend Christmas with her grandparents, there were several moments of silence.

Thinking perhaps he'd lost the connection he said, "Mother Green?"

"I'm here," she replied. "Just checking my calendar. What day did you say you'd be arriving?"

"December twenty-third. It's an early flight, so we'll be landing in Los Angeles at four-fifteen."

Sylvia clucked in disappointment. "The freeway is crazy at that time. Isn't there a flight that's a bit later?"

"The evening flight was totally booked."

"Oh."

He heard another span of silence then a bit of muffled conversation in the background.

"Okay," Sylvia finally said. "I just spoke to Edgar, and we can work it out."

Although Drew felt put out by her lack of enthusiasm, he kept his voice light and casual.

"Great." He rattled off the flight details.

Since this was their first Christmas without Jennifer, Drew was determined not to let it drag Brooke down. Whatever heartache he felt he would keep to himself. Spending the holiday with her grandparents would keep Brooke busy, and hopefully she wouldn't think about the missing piece of their family.

On three different occasions they'd gone Christmas shopping, and by the time they were ready to leave the canvas carry-on was filled with wrapped presents. For Edgar Drew bought a box of the expensive cigars he enjoyed and for Sylvia a bottle of Chanel No. 5, her trademark fragrance.

Brooke did her own shopping, most of it at the Gift Garden. She'd gone back and forth trying to decide on the right gift for Edgar, who was at best difficult to please. In the end she selected a "World's Greatest Grandpa" ashtray even though he never allowed himself to be called anything other than Daddy Green. For Sylvia she bought a lace-trimmed tee shirt with "Grandma" spelled out in rhinestones.

"Grandma is going to love this," she'd said, her eyes aglow.

**WHEN THE PLANE TOUCHED DOWN** in Los Angeles, Drew expected to see Edgar waiting at the luggage carousel. That was the plan. Instead he spotted "Bishop" scrawled on a placard held by a limousine driver.

After he'd claimed their luggage, he walked over and introduced himself.

"I'm Drew Bishop," he said. "Are you here to pick us up?"

The driver nodded, took the suitcase from Drew and then led them back to where the car was parked. Just as Sylvia had predicted the freeway was bumper-to-bumper traffic, and it took almost two hours to reach Glendale.

While the driver was still unloading the luggage, Brooke dashed up the steps and bonged the doorbell. The moment it swung open Daddy Green stepped out. He gave Brooke an affectionate pat on the head and shook hands with Drew.

"Glad you could make it," he said.

By then Sylvia had scooped her granddaughter into her arms and was gushing about how wonderful it was to see her.

"You look just like your mama," she cooed happily.

Brooke grinned. "Daddy says that too."

Sylvia glanced at Drew then, and he saw something in the look. Just a touch of sadness. A moment later she shook herself, and the look was gone.

As Sylvia continued the comparison recalling how Jennifer's eyes had been the exact same blue-green color, Drew carried the suitcases to their rooms. When he returned Daddy Green had a pitcher of margaritas waiting. They gathered at the table on the back patio.

It was a balmy evening, the kind that in Virginia would have heralded the coming of summer. The faint scent of jasmine was in the air, and from time to time a breeze rustled through the branches of the juniper trees in the backyard. After a while darkness settled around them, and the lights flickered on. The fountain came to life and sent an arc of water splashing into the pool. Brooke's eyes glistened at the sight of it. Mesmerized, she watched for a few moments then turned to Sylvia.

"Grandma, this is like a magic house."

Sylvia gave a smile of satisfaction. "Yes, it is. And you could live here if your daddy would allow it."

She expected Brooke to start badgering Drew to do so, but Brooke didn't.

"We have a magical house too," she said. "There's a balcony in my room, and across the pond I can see Miss Annie's house. She has a store and makes *real* magic potions."

Sylvia laughed. "I'm afraid there's no such thing as real magic. It's just an illusion."

Brooke shook her head. "No, it's real magic. Hannah told me so."

Sylvia laughed again then moved on to talking of the huge Christmas tree they were planning to have. Drew shook his head.

"Mother Green, you shouldn't have gone to all that trouble," he said.

"Nonsense! Nothing is too good for my darling little girl," she replied.

The sadness from before came back, but this time Drew saw something else. He saw a longing, and he recognized it. It was the same feeling he had when he missed Jennifer.

Once again the look on his mother-in-law's face disappeared after a few moments, and she turned her attention to the pool. The twinkling of lights, spray of water and changing colors were all preprogrammed into an automated sequence. Despite the hint of melancholy, the evening did have a quality of magic to it. Even Daddy Green, although he was as blustery as always, seemed happy to be with them. He cooked steaks on the outdoor grill, and they ate dinner on the patio.

Drew thought maybe he'd made the right decision after all concerning Christmas.

**THE FOLLOWING MORNING WHEN HE** came downstairs both Sylvia and Edgar were nowhere to be seen, but there was a note on the kitchen counter.

"Sorry to run," Sylvia had written. "A dozen last-minute emergencies at the office plus scads of errands to run. Decorama will be arriving this morning to put up the tree. Have them set it in the center hall. Edgar and I should be home by six or so. Tons of food in the fridge. Help yourself."

Drew plucked a muffin from the basket on the counter then poured himself a cup of coffee. When sleepy-eyed Brooke came down he fixed her a bowl of cereal. Before they'd finished breakfast the doorbell chimed. On the doorstep were two men wearing Decorama tee shirts. One of them was slight of build and only half as tall as the pine tree they were holding.

As if the tee shirts weren't introduction enough the older one said, "Decorama," then asked where the tree was supposed to be set up.

"In the center hall," Drew replied.

He pulled the door back and stepped aside. Huffing and puffing, the two men carried the tree in and then returned to the truck for a dozen boxes of lights and decorations.

Brooke finished her Fruit Loops then came padding through the hall to stand and watch. She was content to stay back as they wrestled the big pine into a stand, but once they began to hang the decorations she grabbed a red glass ball and started for the tree. The older man took it from her hand.

"You're not union," he said. "We ain't insured for non-union."

Drew shot him a look of disbelief. "You're kidding, right?"

The Decorama bully shook his head. "We're a union shop, and that's the rule. Nobody touches anything unless they're union."

The smile faded from Brooke's face, and she again stepped back.

That afternoon the best Drew could do for his daughter was sit beside her as they watched a rerun of *It's a Wonderful Life.* As the final credits scrolled across the screen Brooke looked up at her daddy.

"Is it true?" she asked.

"Is what true?"

"Every time a bell rings another angel gets their wings?"

Drew smiled and gave a barely discernable shrug.

"I don't know," he said. "But I'd like to believe it is."

"Me too," she replied.

**SHORTLY AFTER SIX SYLVIA CAME** hurrying in with a small shopping bag from Glitter, an upscale jewelry store on Rodeo Drive.

"It's a madhouse out there," she said then promised dinner would be on the table in thirty minutes or so.

"Edgar is stopping to pick up shrimp curry." She glanced at Drew. "You do like Indian, don't you?"

"I'm okay with it," Drew replied, "but Brooke's never had it. Jennifer didn't care for curry, so Indian wasn't—"

"That's odd," Sylvia cut in. "I could have sworn she loved it."

**ON CHRISTMAS MORNING EVERYONE GATHERED** in the living room and exchanged presents. Most of the gifts from the Greens were wrapped in the sparkly paper used by Glitter. Drew received a pair of gold cuff links and Brooke a strand of pearls.

"I thought the pearls would go well with this." Sylvia handed Brooke the large box from Neiman Marcus. Inside was a red velvet dress with a layered petticoat beneath the skirt.

"Oh, Grandma, it's beautiful," Brooke murmured. She reached around the box to give Sylvia an appreciative hug. After hugging her back Sylvia shooed her off to change into the dress.

"Having you and your daddy here for Christmas is so special that we've arranged a party to celebrate."

Upstairs, in the privacy of her own room, Brooke opened her last present. It was the small box Elizabeth slid into her hand as she was leaving. She opened the silver paper and lifted the lid.

Inside was a single sheet of notepaper folded over until it was small enough to fit in the box. She lifted the note, and beneath it was an oval-shaped silver locket.

"Dear Brooke," the note from Elizabeth read. "Although we've only known each other for a short while, you've become very special to me so I wanted to give you a Christmas gift that would be special to you. I thought and thought about what would make you happiest, and then I remembered how much you loved your mama. I knew nothing would be as special as always having her close to you, which is why I decided on this locket. Inside there is a place for her picture, and whenever you wear the locket you'll have your mama right there next to your heart. Merry Christmas. With Love, Elizabeth"

**WHEN SHE CAME DOWNSTAIRS BROOKE** was wearing her new red dress with the silver locket hooked around her neck.

"Where are your pearls?" Sylvia asked.

Brooke explained the significance of the locket and said that's why she'd decided to wear it.

"That's such a sweet idea," Sylvia replied. "But the locket doesn't really match. Why don't you tuck it inside and wear the pearls today?"

**BEFORE NOON THE CATERERS ARRIVED** with turkeys, hams and tray after tray of appetizers. By two o'clock the house was filled with people, mostly clients or lawyers from the firm. They came dressed in suits, silk dresses and jewelry enough to weigh a camel down.

With each new arrival Sylvia snagged Brooke's hand and tugged her over for an introduction.

"This is our darling granddaughter," she'd say then start

telling how Brooke looked exactly like her mama when she was that age.

"Having her with us is almost like having our Jennifer back again," Sylvia said over and over again.

Once the full round of introductions was complete, Brooke and Drew became lost in the dialog about rulings, cases and political conundrums. In time they wandered out onto deck and sat in the lounge chairs. A good part of the afternoon was spent calling friends back home. Brooke called Ava, as well as Marta, Annie and Elizabeth. She wished each of them a Merry Christmas and told of what was happening in California.

"The water in the pool changes colors," she told Annie, "and Grandma is having a big party to celebrate 'cause we're here. It's really nice, but I wish I was back home with you and the twins."

Drew was scrolling through the news on his phone, but he heard the wistfulness in her voice. It wasn't a full-out sadness, just a thread of melancholy that wrapped itself around a few words and told a story. Suddenly it seemed the visit to California had not been such a good idea after all.

**FOR THE TWO DAYS FOLLOWING** Christmas Sylvia didn't go into the office but spent a good part of the day on the phone with her associates.

"Check Kilmer versus Horizon," she'd say. "The judgment in that case clearly states..."

According to Sylvia very little went right if she were not available to place a guiding hand on the second-year associate's shoulder.

Drew and Brooke swam in the pool and lounged in the sun. On the afternoon of the third day, he eased his sunglasses down the bridge of his nose and peered across at Brooke.

"I don't know about you," he said, "but I kind of miss being at home."

"Me too," she answered.

Later that afternoon he called the airline and changed their returning flight. They left for home the next day.

**HAD THEY LEFT CALIFORNIA A** day or two earlier Drew would have met Elizabeth when they stopped by Memory House to say hi to Annie. After seeing Brooke's locket and hearing of her fondness for this new friend, he looked forward to such a meeting. Unfortunately by then Liz had moved into her apartment.

# MOVING FORWARD

With the coming of the new year it seemed that everyone's life got busier than before. Elizabeth left the apartment early and pored over the paperwork on her desk for an hour before the bank opened. She developed an instantaneous friendship with the assistant manager, Diane Carver, even though their lives were as different as day from night. Elizabeth was single and lived in a tiny one-bedroom apartment while Diane had a large house, four children and a husband who wanted supper on the table at six-thirty, no earlier and no later.

After Harvey Mossberg, the previous manager, up and left without a word of warning, Diane had taken over handling all of his duties as well as her own. Seeing how efficiently she dealt with the task, the bank offered her the job on a permanent basis. She turned it down.

"It's way too many hours for me," Diane said. "I've got responsibilities at home and a family to think about."

Elizabeth had none of those problems. She came in early and was almost always the last person to leave the bank. In the morning and evening she attended to the paperwork that landed on her desk but during the day she chatted with customers, introducing herself and thanking them for their business. A schedule crammed full of activity was precisely what she needed. As the days and weeks flew by the sorrow in her heart dissipated, and at times she could barely remember what it was that had once saddened her.

The apartment, although furnished nicely, was bare of any personal touches, so Elizabeth began adding knickknacks and throw pillows. On Saturdays she shopped the thrift store and came home carrying books with worn binders or hand-crocheted doilies. On Sundays she cleaned the apartment and rearranged things so they were more to her liking. She moved the comfy lounge chair over by the window so she could sit in the afternoon sun and read, then bought a bookcase to set alongside the chair.

Given the busyness of January, there was only a single Sunday when she had time enough to visit Annie at Memory House. She'd hoped that perchance Brooke would be there, but such was not the case. Like Elizabeth, Brooke had gotten caught up in the hustle bustle of the new year. Missus Kelly, the fourth grade teacher, believed that of all things to be taught nothing would be as helpful as vocabulary skills, so Brooke wasn't babysitting that day. She was at home trying to learn the nuances of synonyms, antonyms, homonyms and idioms.

Although Elizabeth and Brooke didn't see one another for the whole month of January, they continued to talk on the phone. Sometimes it was little more than a quick hello and goodbye. Other times it was long heartfelt conversations that dealt with problems of the day.

Twice Brooke asked her daddy if she might invite Miss Elizabeth to dinner some evening. Both times Drew answered, "Absolutely," but the timing was never right.

The first time she mentioned it, Drew thought back to a time when he also had a Miss Elizabeth in his life. She was his second grade Sunday school teacher, a woman with silver hair a round face and a kindly smile. She handed out gold stars liberally and gave hugs for even the smallest achievement. He imagined Brooke's friend was much the same.

"As soon as I get things up and rolling at the plant, we'll have Miss Elizabeth to dinner," he said. But the days rushed by, and with each one he got more and more caught up in his new life.

He had an excellent eye for color and clarity, and now with him on board Southfield's business had grown by a whopping thirty percent. Customers no longer had to waste a day sitting in the lounge and waiting for the pressmen to come up with an acceptable color proof. They simply turned the task over to Drew, because his exacting standards were far more stringent than their own. Before January came to a close, the plant had added two more pressmen and an evening shift for machine maintenance.

Twice Brian Carson came out to visit the plant, and both times he left feeling justified in his decision to move Drew into this managerial role.

"You're doing a great job," he said, "but be careful you don't get burnt out. Take time for yourself and your daughter. Get to know the community."

The week after Brian's second visit, Drew received an invitation to attend the first Thursday of the month chamber of commerce social mixer. It was touted as a friendly get together where members of the Burnsville, Dorchester and Wayland business communities could exchange business cards and get to know one another. "Green Valley Country Club, 7PM to 9PM" the invitation read.

Drew read the invitation then set it to the side of his desk, uncertain whether he'd be able to go. The question was always what would be on press that day and whether there might be problems requiring him to be available. Plus, there was Brooke to consider. Thursday was a school night, which meant a nine-thirty bedtime.

It was late in the afternoon when Kevin Harding, the plant foreman, brought in a proof of the Garden Depot flyer for Drew's approval. As he dropped the proof in front of Drew he spotted the chamber of commerce invitation.

"You going?" he asked.

Drew had been studying the proof, which to his eye looked a bit heavy on the blue, and glanced up with a quizzical look.

"Going where?" he asked.

"To the mixer on Thursday."

Giving a one-shoulder shrug, Drew answered, "I haven't decided. I'll wait and see what's happening here."

"We get a lot of business from the local community, and getting known around town helps," Kevin replied. "You're the boss, but I think you should go."

Still looking at the Garden Depot flyer, Drew said, "You need to pull back on the cyan. Maybe bring the yellow up plus one."

Kevin nodded and tucked the proof under his arm. Switching back to the subject of the mixer he said, "I'm going. Last month I met Ted Bailey there, and now he's promised us his spring catalog."

"Really?"

Drew thought about it for a few seconds. He was hard pressed to come up with an actual reason for not going. It was a mere two hours; he could certainly get away for that long. Annie would be glad to take Brooke for the night, and if perchance she were unavailable he'd ask Hannah's mom. It was unlikely anything problematic would happen at the plant, and if it did they could reach him on his cell phone. In any event he could swing by on his way home. More than it being good for business, the truth was Drew missed socializing with clients. It was the fun part of being a salesman.

Kevin was halfway to the door when Drew asked, "Mind if I join you?"

"Not at all," Kevin said with a grin. "I've been attending chamber events for years, so I'll introduce you around."

That evening when Drew stopped by Memory House to pick up Brooke he didn't beep the horn. He parked in the driveway, then walked to the front porch and rang the doorbell. Once inside he sat and talked with Annie for almost a half-hour. He told her about the chamber of commerce event and said if she didn't mind having Brooke for the evening, he'd like to go.

"We wouldn't mind at all," Annie replied. "She's a great little helper, and the twins absolutely adore her."

"I assure you she feels the same about them," Drew said. Then he asked if Brooke's new friend Miss Elizabeth might be around the evening of the event.

"She's spoken so fondly of the woman, I'd love to meet her."

"Oh, they've formed quite a bond," Annie replied. "Brooke just naturally gravitated to Elizabeth, which is not at all surprising because she's a lovely person." She went on say that although it was an unusual friendship, it was quite obviously sincere.

Before Drew left, Annie said she would invite Elizabeth over the evening of the mixer.

"I'm certain you'll enjoy meeting her," she said.

**AFTER THE TWINS WERE TUCKED** into bed Annie called Liz and asked if she could come for dinner the following Thursday.

"Brooke will be spending the evening with us, and her dad will be stopping by to drop her off. He'd love to meet you."

"Well, I'd enjoy meeting him too," Liz replied. "Hold on, let me check my calendar."

A few seconds of silence passed as she grabbed the phone and scrolled through her scheduled appointments. Then she huffed with disappointment.

"Oh, darn, I'm busy that evening. A business thing I can't change."

"Maybe next time," Annie said.

"Yes," Elizabeth replied. "Maybe next time."

There was just the tiniest sound of disappointment in her answer.

# Keeper of the Scales

The Keeper of the Scales watched with chagrin. Lifting his gaze to a plain far beyond the landscape of his realm, he looked toward the future. It was still shadowed and gray, which meant nothing was yet ordained.

In the blink of an eye this could change. Once the future was decreed, it would appear in sharp lines and vivid colors. Then there would be no altering the course of events. For now there was a small window of time where he could not change but simply guide the destiny of those he watched over. It could be a few seconds or perhaps a few minutes. It would be less than a day, he was certain.

Although his position of greatness was one that required impartiality, there were certain individuals who touched the heart of the Keeper. Drew Bishop and Elizabeth Cunningham were two such people. Both lives had been weighted with sadness too heavy to be balanced by even the largest stone.

In the mountain of stones bequeathed him, the Keeper willed his hand to find the one he was searching for. The stone was a rarity, seldom seen and almost never used in a plan such as he had in mind.

He stretched his long fingers forth and plucked out a stone the color of a ruby. This stone was darker in color and with a density greater than any other. He lifted it into his hand and felt the weight. It was good. This stone could do what no other could.

He narrowed his eyes, and with all of his power concentrated into a single thought he called forth a bolt of lightning that struck the stone.

For a moment it burned hotter than the sun. The edges crumbled to dust as the stone began to take shape. Then with a thundering crack it split into two pieces. Each piece was shaped like one half of a heart.

It was as he'd willed it.

He placed one half of the heart on Drew Bishop's scale and its matching counterpart on the scale that belonged to Elizabeth Cunningham. He could do nothing more. If the ruby stone failed to work, their destiny would be left to fate.

# THURSDAY

Most days Drew wore a zippered leather jacket and an open collar shirt to the plant, but on the Thursday of the chamber of commerce meeting he left the house wearing his camelhair blazer and a burgundy print tie. For the first time in almost a year he'd pulled the jacket from the closet, and it felt good to be wearing it again.

Once he was in the plant he removed the jacket and hung it on the back of his chair, but the feeling of being dressed for an occasion remained with him. It was like the old feeling of walking into a customer's office and knowing he was going to make a sale. It was a feeling of confidence. A feeling that something good was just over the horizon.

The day passed rather uneventfully, and at six-thirty he left with Kevin Harding. Confident that there would be no crisis during the next two hours, Drew rode with Kevin who would drop him off back at the plant at the end of the evening. Brooke was spending the night with Annie, so he'd have time to duck back into the plant and check that everything was indeed running smoothly.

When they arrived at the Green Valley Country Club the reception room was already filled to overflowing. They eased past a waiter carrying a tray of hors d'oeuvres and joined a group of men standing near the entrance. Kevin slapped a friendly hand on the back of a man in the group then did a round of introductions.

"Drew is our new plant manager," he said.

Jack Schroeder stuck out a hand. "Northern Virginia Electric. Glad to have you joining our group."

There was some conversation about a tri-city summer festival the chamber was planning. Then they moved on to another group and another round of introductions. Chamber membership chairman Peter McMillan could talk a man into deafness, and once he discovered Drew was the plant manager at Southfield he started badgering him to print the Saint Andrew's Sunday bulletin for free.

"Southfield doesn't really do that kind of printing," Drew said. "We're mostly color work and longer runs."

Of course nothing he said dissuaded McMillan, and in the course of the conversation Kevin spotted a friend and wandered off. For several minutes Drew stood there half listening and half scanning the room in search of Kevin.

That's when he saw her.

She was standing on the far side of the room with her face turned toward him. He smiled, and he could swear she returned the smile. He pulled out the last business card in his pocket and handed it to McMillan.

"I've got to go," he said. "Call me next week, and we'll talk about it."

While McMillan stood there stuffing the business card into an already overcrowded wallet, Drew disappeared into the crowd. He eased his way past clusters of people and ignored the din of conversations. Halfway across the room he lost sight of her but continued in that direction. Moments later she reappeared.

Now she was turned sideways and he was looking at her profile. She laughed at something someone in the group said then wrinkled her nose and turned away. Then he saw only the back of her head with hair the color of autumn, a mix of browns and golds and coppers. A waiter with one last sea scallop on a tray offered it to him as he squeezed by but Drew shook his head and kept moving, seeing her, losing sight of her, then finding her again.

Then suddenly and yet not suddenly at all, he was standing there with his face turned to hers. He looked into her eyes, eyes that were the rich brown of melted chocolate, and was at a loss for words.

"You look so familiar," he stammered. "Have we met somewhere before?"

Elizabeth gave a soft chuckle.

"I think if we had met before we would both remember it," she said. She fixed her eyes on his, smiled and stuck out her hand. "Liz Cunningham, Heartland Bank."

When Drew took her hand in his he felt a tremor in his heart. It was the kind of rumble felt moments before an earthquake.

"Tonight's basket of cheer was donated by Joseph Rodolfo of Rodolfo's Restaurant!" the emcee said over the loudspeaker just as Drew said his name. "So when you're looking for good Italian food, remember Rodolfo's."

Elizabeth leaned in. "Sorry, was that Hugh Jessup?"

Drew laughed and shook his head.

"Drew Bishop," he said, but the loudspeaker was crackling again.

"Drew?" Elizabeth repeated.

He nodded.

For several minutes they tried to chat between announcements of the next chamber meeting and charitable endeavors that needed assistance, but it ended up being only a few words here and there. It was enough.

"Well, since we've supposedly never met before and aren't in the same business, would you mind if I called you for something other than business?" Drew asked.

Again she smiled at him, and again he felt the thundering of his heart.

"I'd like that," Elizabeth said. Then she reached into her purse, pulled out a business card and handed it to him. "Liz Cunningham, Branch Manager" it read.

At the start of the evening Drew had a pocket full of business cards, but one by one he'd handed them all out. Now he was left with only an empty pocket. He gave an apologetic smile and stammered something about giving his last card to the fellow from Saint Andrew's.

By the time the loudspeaker died down, a number of the guests were already out the door. Elizabeth made no attempt to leave; neither did Drew. But as they stood there talking, Kevin tapped Drew on the shoulder.

"Let's get going," he said. "My car is blocking Henry Larimore's."

Again Drew apologized. "I'll call you."

"I'll look forward to it," she said, but there skepticism in her eyes.

As he and Kevin were on their way out the door Drew looked back, but by then Liz was gone.

# Elizabeth

*There are times when you meet someone you think is truly special, and you can almost swear the earth has moved beneath your feet. I had that kind of feeling when Drew smiled at me from across the room. Then when he came over, I thought for sure this was something meant to be. When he asked if we'd ever met before, I almost told him I had the exact same feeling. Because I did. I felt like we had a connection, the kind that links one person to another. It wasn't just that he smiled or came over; it was like his hand reached out and touched my heart.*

*Obviously I was wrong.*

*The bit about not having a business card is as old as the hills. When Muriel Willis went to the Housewares Trade Show, she fell for the same line and ended up with a guy who had a wife and seven kids. They went together for three years before she found out the truth, and when she finally did it almost broke her heart.*

*And the friend telling him it's time to leave, that was another thing. It's like the pre-planned emergency call for when a date is turning sour.*

*No, thanks. After what I went through with Elliott, I am not about to get mixed up in another fiasco. I've finally gotten my life together, and I'm feeling good about who I am. Being single and living alone is better than having your heart torn out by a man with swept-under-the rug intentions.*

*If this Hugh or Drew or whatever-his-name-is does actually call, I'll just say I'm too busy to play games. Chances are he won't even call, so I probably don't have to worry about what I will or won't say.*

# THE BIG SURPRISE

When Kevin dropped him off at the plant, Drew headed for his office rather than starting for home. It wasn't necessary and he knew it, but it was something to do. Something, perhaps, to take his mind off the woman he'd met.

He chatted with Pete, the evening foreman, for a few minutes, took a second look at the Kline's catalog they were running, then settled at his desk and scanned through several e-mails. He looked at each one then clicked "Mark unread" and moved on to the next one. All were things that could be done the next day, and tonight he simply had other things on his mind.

It was ten-thirty when Drew arrived home. He came through the garage and snapped on the kitchen light. Without Brooke around, the house seemed eerily silent. Even though she was usually in bed and fast asleep by this time, tonight it was different. Tonight the silence picked at Drew's thoughts.

Try as he might, he could not get Liz out of his mind. He lowered his face into his hands and closed his eyes. The image of her was still there. He pictured the velvety brown of her eyes, the crooked little smile that hiked the right side of her mouth higher than the left and the touch of her hand in his. He felt something he didn't want to feel. Something he wasn't ready for.

The following week would be the one-year anniversary of Jennifer's death. It was too soon. He had Brooke to think about. First and foremost, he had to be a father, a man dedicated to his child, not a man giving himself to passion. But still…

Drew pulled Liz's business card from his pocket, laid it on the table and sat there studying it. He'd said he would call; shouldn't he at least do that? But then what?

Realizing sleep would be impossible to come by, Drew went to the cupboard and took out the tin of dandelion tea Annie had given him. He thought back on the weeks they'd spent at Memory House and how she'd served him a cup of the tea every evening. She'd said it was a brew good for relaxing the mind, and he had in fact slept like a baby. He dropped the silken tea pouch into a mug then poured boiling water over it and waited. As he stood there watching the water go from clear to the blushed yellow of a tea rose, he thought of both Jennifer and Liz.

They were different in so many ways. He pictured Liz with her dark eyes and a cluster of autumn colored curls framing her face; then he thought of Jennifer, so like Brooke, with the summer sky reflected in her eyes and hair golden as the sun. Yes, they were different and yet in an odd way alike.

Once the tea was ready, he stood alongside the counter and sipped it slowly. On any other evening he would have sat at the table but tonight he was too edgy, too full of thoughts and feelings he couldn't understand. At long last when weariness overtook him, he trudged upstairs and climbed into bed.

**HE HEARD THE VOICE AND** recognized it as Jennifer's.

"You're making this far more difficult than it should be," she said.

"You're wrong," he argued. "How can there be an easy answer when I have you and Brooke to think about?"

"You don't—"

"Don't what?" he asked.

"You don't have me. I'm just a memory." She turned to him, her eyes soft with a look of serenity. "I said this day would come; now it's here."

"I don't understand," Drew said. "What's here?"

"The happier life I promised."

"I'm not looking for a happier life," he replied. He reached out to pull her into his arms, but there was nothing to hold on to. She was there but not there.

She smiled a bittersweet smile. "It's time to move on. You've found someone who will love you and Brooke as I did. Let go of the past and look to the future."

Although nothing moved but the soft breeze that ruffled her hair, he felt her hand touch his heart and then pull away.

"Stay with me!" he cried.

"I'll always be with you," she whispered. "As a memory."

He felt her lips brush against the side of his cheek as she had done a thousand times before; then she moved away from him.

"Wait," he called. "I need to know what you want me to do!"

When there was little more than a shadow of where she'd stood, he heard her final words.

"To find happiness, look through our child's eyes," she said.

After that there was only a blinding whiteness.

**PULLING HIMSELF FROM THE DREAM,** Drew rubbed the sleep from his eyes and sat up.

It was already seven o'clock. He hurried downstairs, set the coffee pot to brew then came back up for a shower and shave.

Afterward as he sat at the kitchen table his eye caught sight of Liz Cunningham's business card. He picked it up and slid it into his blazer pocket. For a reason that he couldn't readily identify, he'd decided to wear the camelhair blazer for a second day. On the drive to work he thought about the dream and about the feeling that stirred his heart when he held Liz Cunningham's hand in his.

By the time he pulled into his assigned parking spot he'd decided.

Not wanting to seem overanxious, he waited until almost ten then dialed the number on the card she'd given him. The phone rang twice. A youthful voice answered.

"Heartland Bank," she said. "How may I help you?"

He asked to speak to Liz Cunningham.

"May I ask who's calling?"

"Drew Bishop." He hesitated then, trying to make it sound like a legitimate business call, added, "Southfield Printing."

"Please hold, I'll see if she's available."

The woman pushed mute then buzzed Liz's office. "Drew Bishop of Southfield Printing is on line one; are you available?"

Liz hadn't expected him to call, so she wasn't prepared. She didn't say anything for a moment, and the girl asked if she should get one of the customer service reps to handle the call.

"No," Liz answered. "Put him through."

His voice sounded nicer than she remembered.

"I'm sorry for running off last night," he said. "My assistant manager's car was blocking someone else so—"

Liz was still undecided as to how she felt about Mister Drew Bishop, so her voice was a bit on the cool side.

"Yes," she said. "I heard him tell you that."

Drew caught the hint of an attitude in her answer and wondered if maybe he'd made a mistake.

"That was my first time at a chamber event," he explained. "Kevin had offered to introduce me around, and since I'm rather new in town—"

Liz laughed without meaning to. "I'm new in town too. I've only been at the bank for about two months."

"Five months for me," Drew admitted.

From that point on the conversation became lighter and cordial. They talked for almost ten minutes; then he asked if she could get away for lunch. Although she'd brought a sandwich from home figuring she'd eat at her desk, Liz said she had no plans.

**THEY MET AT RODOLFO'S AND** sat across from one another in a brown leather booth. As they settled in Drew asked if she'd like a glass of wine.

She gave a mischievous grin and said, "Okay, but just one. I have to go back to work this afternoon."

He laughed. "So do I." He motioned for the waitress then turned back to Liz. "You like red, right?"

"How did you know?"

"I didn't, but since that's what you were drinking last night..."

"Good guess," she said, smiling again, this time at the fact that he remembered.

For a short while their conversation centered on the town, the business community and the spring festival the chamber of commerce was planning. When the first glass of wine was finished, they ordered a second and a pizza to share. Without ever realizing it was happening, Liz let down her guard. And when Drew told of how he'd seen her from across the room and given away his last business card to break free of Peter McMillan, she giggled like a schoolgirl.

Smiling at the sound of her laughter, Drew leaned in and said, "Luckily I made it over there before you got away."

"I wasn't trying to get away," Liz replied.

Drew was handsomer than she remembered, and without the loudspeaker crackling in her ear the conversation took on a soft and easy flow. It was able to move from one subject to another without any bumps or blank spots. When he asked what brought her to town, she said the job at the bank and left out any mention of Elliott or the scandal he'd caused.

"I've been in banking for my whole career," she told him. "I started out as a teller with Connecticut Trust and worked my way up. When this job came along I felt it was a great opportunity."

With his eyes fixed on her face he asked if she was happy living in the area.

That was the thing she liked. The way he looked at her. It was a look that said more than words ever could.

"Very much," she replied. "I found a wonderful little apartment, and I'm starting to make friends."

"This is an easy place to make friends," Drew said. "I've spent most of my career as a lone wolf salesman, and I didn't realize how different it is being part of a team. It's a big change, and I must say I'm enjoying it."

He added that the job allowed him to spend more time with his family.

Liz's spine stiffened. "Family?"

"I have a daughter." Drew reached into his back pocket and pulled out his wallet. He flipped it open to the photograph of Brooke and handed it to Liz. "This is—"

"Brooke," Liz said, finishing his sentence.

Drew's eyes grew big as he sat there looking thunderstruck. "How did you—"

Liz's mouth curled into a lopsided grin. "I'm Miss Elizabeth. But Brooke is the only one who calls me that."

"You're kidding!"

"No, I'm not. I met Brooke when I stayed at Memory House."

"Wow." He shook his head in amazement. "This is almost unbelievable. You're nothing like I imagined Miss Elizabeth to be."

Uncertain of what he meant, Liz said, "I hope you're not too disappointed."

Drew gave a deep-throated laugh. "I'm not at all disappointed, I'm delighted." He chuckled and shook his head again. "Miss Elizabeth. Imagine that."

When the shock of it began to wear off he asked, "But how did you—"

"When Brooke came to babysit the twins, she and I used to talk…" Liz hesitated then let her thoughts come to the surface. "I never had any children, and Brooke is an easy child to love."

Drew nodded. "Yes, she is."

A look of caring remembrance settled on Liz's face. "Brooke and I both had an empty spot in our hearts, and I suppose our relationship filled that spot for both of us. I've become very fond of her."

She allowed her eyes to linger on his face and in a soft voice added, "I hope that's okay."

"Okay?" Drew laughed. "It's flat out wonderful!"

Liz exhaled a deep sigh of relief.

Although it would be months before he would tell Liz of the dream he'd had, Drew knew this was what Jennifer meant when she said "to find happiness look through our child's eyes."

**DREW DIDN'T GET BACK TO** the plant until after three that afternoon, and when he finally did get there he went in whistling. By then he and Liz had decided not to tell Brooke that they'd met but to wait and let her do the introduction.

# Dinner Guest

That same evening Drew asked Brooke if she was still interested in having Miss Elizabeth over for dinner. She gave an enthusiastic nod and asked when.

"Well, the plant is a bit slow right now," Drew said, "so I was thinking maybe this weekend. How about Sunday?"

"Yes, yes, yes!" Brooke squealed. "We could make a fancy dinner with cake and ice cream..." Her eyes sparkled as she ran through a dozen different thoughts of what they could serve.

"Before we start planning a big fancy dinner, don't you think you should call Miss Elizabeth and ask if she can come?"

"She'll come," Brooke replied confidently. "I'm sure she'll come." Taking her cell phone from her pocket, she pulled up the Contacts menu and tapped Elizabeth's name. "You'll hear how excited she's going to be," she said and hit the Speaker icon.

Liz answered on the first ring. "Hi, Brooke."

Not slowing down for any formalities Brooke asked, "Can you come to dinner on Sunday?"

Liz chuckled. "Does your daddy know that you're asking me to dinner?"

"He knows. He's the one who said to do it."

"Well, then, I think it's a fine idea, and I would love to come."

Brooke turned to Drew, "See, Daddy, I told you she would say yes." The ideas for all the possible things they might make for dinner began spilling out of her.

"My goodness," Liz said, laughing, "that sounds more like a banquet than just an ordinary Sunday dinner."

Drew stood and listened as the conversation went back and forth with talk of biscuits, chicken, cake and ice cream. There was something about the way Liz spoke that reminded him of Jennifer. She didn't cajole or talk down to Brooke; she treated her as an equal, someone with thoughts and ideas worth listening to. It was easy to see why Brooke had developed such an affection for her.

**ON SATURDAY MORNING BROOKE WOKE** bursting with ideas for what she now called the dinner party. When she sat at the breakfast table she had a notepad beside her plate.

"I'm going to make a menu, like in restaurants," she announced. "And we can use the fancy dishes."

That afternoon she and Drew went grocery shopping together, and it was all he could do not to laugh at the seriousness with which she addressed the task. As they went from the butcher counter to the bakery corner, she told every clerk about the dinner party.

"We need a nice plump chicken," she told the butcher, and Drew knew this was something she'd heard her mama say.

The remainder of the afternoon was spent making preparations. While Drew cleaned and straightened the house, Brooke set the table, rearranging things over and over again.

**ON SUNDAY AFTERNOON WHEN THE** doorbell bonged at precisely three o'clock, Brooke shouted, "I'll get it!" and ran.

Drew followed along but stayed behind as she pulled back the door. Liz was standing on the porch with a cake carrier in one hand and a potted plant in the other.

"A little something for your house," she said and handed the plant to Brooke.

As Drew watched he felt his heart quicken. Wearing an ivory colored jacket with a lacy scarf tucked around her neck, Liz looked more beautiful than he remembered.

She caught sight of him standing in the background but kept her focus on Brooke's face when she said, "Thank you for inviting me."

Brooke tugged her inside then turned to Drew.

"Daddy, this is Miss Elizabeth," she said proudly.

He held back the grin he felt inside and kept a straight face as he stepped forward.

"Drew Bishop," he said and stuck out his hand.

Liz slid her hand into his, and he held on to it longer than was customary.

"Brooke has spoken of you often," he said. "It's a pleasure to finally meet you."

"Tell Miss Elizabeth what we're having for dinner, Daddy."

Drew laughed. "I'm afraid it's a long way from gourmet, but we're dealing with single-dad cooking here."

Brooke hiked her shoulders up and gave a squeal of excitement. "It's roasted chicken with stuffing inside! I helped make the stuffing!"

Liz's eyes crinkled in the corners as she smiled. "Did you know roasted chicken is my favorite?"

Brooke nodded. "I remember you told me that."

**THE DAY WAS BALMY FOR** February, more like what to expect in early April. With the sun warm against their shoulders, they sat on the back deck. Drew poured two glasses of cabernet and filled a third with ginger ale, and Brooke carried out the two small trays of hors d'oeuvres they prepared and explained that one was a recipe they'd found in her mama's cookbook.

"It's called sausage puffs."

That afternoon Drew and Liz both held back and let Brooke draw them into the various topics of conversation. They spoke of school, jobs and the recreational things they liked to do. They talked of places they lived and traveled to, and Drew told of how he used to be on the road from Monday through Friday.

"I'm glad to be settled in a job where there's none of that now," he said.

"I'm glad too," Brooke echoed.

Before the evening was over Liz spoke of the spring festival the chamber of commerce was planning.

Drew gave her a sly wink and said, "Oh, are you a member of the chamber?"

He said he'd recently joined and looked forward to the possibility of seeing her at the next meeting. As he spoke he caught the look on Brooke's face. She was beaming.

After dinner the three of them cleared the table together. Since they'd used the good china with a silver rim, the dishes didn't go in the dishwasher. Drew washed them by hand, Liz dried them and Brooke carried them to the cupboard.

It was almost nine when the evening finally ended. Liz bent and kissed Brooke then gave Drew a casual hug.

"I've had a wonderful time," she said.

"We did too," Brooke replied happily. "Can you come again next week?"

Liz laughed. "I think that's something you'd better ask your daddy."

Drew reached out and took her hand in his; it was something he'd wanted to do all evening.

"Daddy would like to have you come again next week also," he said.

"Then it's a date," Liz replied. "Only this time, no fussing over such a fancy meal. I'll bring a casserole, and you can put together a salad."

**A SHORT WHILE LATER BROOKE** went off to bed, and when Drew came to kiss her goodnight she asked, "Daddy, did you like Miss Elizabeth?"

"Yes," he answered. "Very much."

"Good," she said with a smug smile.

# Season of Love

In the weeks that followed Drew saw Liz often, sometimes for lunch and sometimes for a drink after work. On several occasions Brooke spent Saturday night with Annie and the twins, and on those evenings the couple went dancing or to a show.

Every Sunday there was a family dinner at 1220 Lakeside Drive. Over time this became a casual thing where they spent the afternoon cooking then settled at the wooden table in the kitchen. Brooke pulled recipes from her mama's cookbook and claimed this or that was her favorite dish; then they'd try to duplicate the taste as she remembered it.

When Brooke said corn pudding was her absolute favorite, Liz came with a box of muffin mix and a ready-bake recipe. Liz insisted she was not a great cook, yet she taught Brooke how to make fluffy biscuits that Drew swore were light enough to float off the plate. Once the dishes were cleared and the pots washed, they'd generally pull out a game board and play Monopoly, Scrabble, Clue or Sorry.

**By the time March turned** into April and buds of green began to sprout on tree limbs and garden beds, the three of them were having dinner together almost every evening. Some nights it was only a pizza, but it was a shared pizza, which made all the difference in the world.

Often as Drew sat at the table with Brooke finishing up her homework and Liz checking her e-mails, he thought back to a year earlier and remembered the anger that had bristled off of Brooke, perhaps off of both of them. They were alone together, each with heartaches too heavy to bear alone and too private to share with one another. They were a family but not a family.

How different it was now. There were times when Drew wished the moment or the evening could last forever, that they could go on this way day after day with nothing ever changing. But theirs was a delicate balance, and any one change could throw everything off.

It was too soon, he told himself. Brooke loved Liz now, but was it because she saw Miss Elizabeth as her friend? What if something changed? What if Liz stepped in to take Jennifer's place? That thought rumbled through Drew's mind time and time again. On evenings when he stood at the window and watched Liz back out of the driveway and disappear into the darkness, he inevitably wondered, *Is it really too soon?*

Part of him wanted things to forever remain the same, but the greater part of him wanted more. He wanted to sense the weight of her lying beside him in the bed, to feel the warmth of her skin against his. He wanted to know that in the morning he'd open his eyes and find her there. He wanted to look to the future and know they would grow old together, sitting beside one another with a thread of contentment tying them together. But more than he wanted anything for himself, he wanted happiness for Brooke.

And so it remained as it was. Friendships continued to be friendships, and passion was held at arm's length. Sometimes on a school night when Brooke went to bed at nine-thirty, Liz stayed for a while longer. When the house was silent and steeped in shadows, she and Drew sat on the sofa snuggled together like two lovesick teenagers. When he held her in his arms and covered her mouth with his, Drew felt the thundering of his heart and each time he wondered again, *Is it really too soon?*

**WHEN SPRING TURNED INTO SUMMER** they began to have picnics on the back lawn, and on the first Sunday of August they invited Annie's family to join them.

The day dawned with an abundance of sunshine and enough of a breeze to make it comfortable. Liz arrived early that morning carrying a basket filled with homemade salads, muffins and cookies. When she came through the door Drew took the basket and leaned down to kiss her cheek as he often did, but she turned and his mouth came down on hers. It lingered there and became more passionate than he'd intended.

It had been too long. With summer came later bedtimes and less private time. He felt a yearning that was impossible to suppress.

"Tonight," he whispered in her ear.

She smiled, gave an almost imperceptible nod then turned to look for Brooke. She found her in the yard and gave Brooke a hug.

"So are you ready for today?" she asked.

"Yes," Brooke answered. "Daddy bought a croquet set, and I'm going to teach the twins how to play."

By the time Annie, Oliver and the twins arrived, the redwood table was heavy with dishes of food, the chairs were set out and the croquet wickets were hammered into the ground.

After lunch the grownups leaned back in the Adirondack chairs with their chilled glasses of dandelion tea and watched as

Brooke chased the twins back and forth across the yard. When Starr finally hit a ball through the wicket, the cheers could be heard across the pond.

"Brooke is like a little mother," Annie said as she laughed. "It's a shame she doesn't have a younger sibling."

The words were hardly out of her mouth before she regretted saying them. She saw how Drew averted his eyes from everyone, and Liz's cheeks turned the color of sunburn. With another lighthearted laugh she turned the thought off, saying with two rambunctious toddlers she should be careful what she wished for.

The conversation moved on, but the thought was out there.

It's funny how something you believe no one else knows, something that's been kept private in your heart, can all of a sudden make you feel as if you are standing naked in the midst of a group. That's how Liz felt at that moment. She wondered if her maternal desire to be more than a friend of the family was written on her face. At the same time Drew also was wondering if his desire had been that blatantly obvious.

That evening Liz stayed later than usual. It was ten-thirty before the excitement of the day wore off and Brooke fell asleep on the sofa. Drew lifted her into his arms and carried her to bed. He covered her with a blanket and turned on the nightlight then closed the bedroom door as he left. Sitting next to Liz, he snapped off the television and took her in his arms.

"I'm sorry about today," he said. "I hope you know I feel just as you do, but with Brooke—"

She pressed her finger to his mouth. Not waiting for the explanation that was to come, she gave him a shallow smile then said, "I love Brooke too. I would never ask you to do anything that might bring her sadness."

Drew kissed her full on the mouth and felt the pounding of his heart.

"I love you, Liz," he whispered. "You know I do."

With his hand pressed to her back, he felt the sigh of anguish that rattled up from her chest.

"I know," she said softly. "That's what makes this so difficult."

**IN THE EARLY FALL LIZ** asked Drew and Brooke to come to dinner at her apartment.

"I'd like to have the fun of making dinner for you this time," she said.

That week she bought a folding card table, pushed the club chair into a corner, moved the coffee table to the bedroom and set the table in the center of the living room.

When they arrived the table was draped in a fine linen cloth and set with crystal glasses, china plates and silverware. In the center of the table was a squat vase with a tiny bouquet of pink carnations. Drew had been there on earlier occasions, but this was the first time Brooke had been to the apartment.

"How come you don't live in a house?" she asked.

Not wanting to address the issue of a big house being the type of place where a person can get lost in their own thoughts, Liz laughed and said this size apartment was perfect for her.

"You know a place is right when everything you own has just the right spot to sit in."

"But it can happen different too," Brooke replied. "When we found our house it had all the furniture already in it, so there wasn't any place for our other furniture to sit."

"Well, I guess that was a problem, wasn't it?" Liz replied.

Brooke thought for a moment then shook her head. "No, it wasn't a problem. We decided the new furniture fit us better anyway, so Daddy told the moving man to leave the old furniture in the old house."

Liz laughed. "That was a very good solution. You're quite the problem solver, aren't you?"

"When I have to be," Brooke said as she climbed into her seat at the table.

With the chairs pushed up under the table it had seemed as though there would be plenty of room, but once Drew pulled out the chair and tried to sit it was a tight squeeze.

"No problem." He turned the chair sideways and sat with his long legs stretched out to the far end of the sofa. "You know, Liz, this apartment is as charming as you are, but it's the size of a dollhouse."

"Daddy's right," Brooke said. "We have a big house with lots of room. Why don't you come live with us?"

Liz bolted up from the table claiming she thought the soufflé was burning. Before Liz returned, Drew explained that such a thing would not be proper unless a man and woman were married.

That's when Brooke came up with her great idea.

# The Love Potion

Two days later when Brooke jumped off the school bus in front of Memory House, she had twelve whole dollars she'd saved in her pocket. When she bolted through the door she spied Annie working in the apothecary. Instead of hurrying back to see if the twins were up from their nap, she turned and went into the shop.

In a near breathless gasp she said, "Hannah told me you make magic love potions. I want to buy a bottle."

With a look of astonishment stretched across her face Annie replied, "Aren't you rather young to be needing a love potion?"

She started to explain at this age it might feel like love but it was simply a crush, and she'd have a dozen or more such occurrences before true love came along. Brooke cut in before she had a chance to finish.

"It's not for me," she said. "It's for Daddy."

Such a thought made Annie suspicious. Drew was not the type to believe in love potions or magic spells. He was by nature a practical man. He was one of the few who could walk by the potpourri in the hallway and smell only the flowers in it.

"Did your daddy tell you to buy him a love potion?" she asked.

Brooke gave a quick shake of her head. "No, he doesn't know, so you've got to keep it a secret."

Annie came from behind the counter and squatted down to talk to Brooke. Suppressing the chuckle she felt inside, she kept her expression dead serious.

"In a case such as this," she said, "it's important that I know all the facts so I can make sure to give you the right love potion."

"There's more than one?"

"Indeed there is. There's the potion of forgiveness, the one for first love..."

As she spoke, Brooke studied Annie's face for any trace of trickery and seeing none, she explained.

"Miss Elizabeth has to live in a very small apartment because she's not married to Daddy. If I could make her and Daddy fall in love they'd get married. Then she could come and live at our house."

Holding to an expression of seriousness, Annie said, "I can see you've thought this through. But are you sure you want Miss Elizabeth to live at your house?"

"I'm sure!" Brooke said. "She's my friend."

"If Liz and your daddy get married, then she'll be more than a friend. She'll be kind of like your mom. You think you'd be okay with that?"

Images of Jennifer flickered through Brooke's mind. She remembered how they would shop together, read stories and bake cupcakes that made the whole house smell good. But most of all she remembered the way her mama tucked her into bed each night with a kiss and a wish for sweet dreams. She remembered the way her mama would hold her tight and make her feel like nothing could ever go wrong. These thoughts curled her mouth into a crooked little smile that was oddly reminiscent of Liz's.

She nodded emphatically. "Uh-huh, I'd be okay with that."

"Well, if you're absolutely sure..."

Brooke broke into a wide grin. "Then I can buy a bottle of love potion?"

"Yes," Annie replied. "But you'll need the Happiness Forever potion that's strong enough to make a man propose. That takes time to prepare."

"I can wait."

"Instead of just standing here waiting, why don't you play with the twins and keep them busy for a while so I have time to make it?"

"Okay," Brooke said and hurried off.

Perhaps Annie would not have made such a rash promise were it not for the fact that she'd seen the way Drew and Liz looked at one another, the way he reached across and touched her hand or her arm every chance he got, and the passion that passed through layers of clothing when he sat next to her and pressed his thigh against hers. She had seen it and knew they were in love with one another. It was so obvious even a blind man could have seen it.

Something prevented them from getting married, and Annie thought she now knew what that something was.

As soon as she heard the laughter of Brooke playing with the twins, Annie pulled her cell phone from her pocket and called Drew at the office. It wasn't unusual for Annie to call, but this was the first time she'd phoned him at work. At the sound of her voice Drew became alarmed.

"Is something wrong?" he asked.

"No," she said, "but I do have a situation you should know about."

She warned him that Brooke would be coming home with a bottle of love potion that evening.

"It's just honey, orange blossom and hibiscus, but she believes it's a love potion. Brooke plans to slip it into your tea this evening so you and Liz will fall in love and get married."

"You're kidding."

Annie chuckled. "No, I'm not." She explained the conversation she'd had with Brooke.

"Apparently Hannah told her I could make magic love potions, and she's convinced that's what it will take for you and Liz to get married."

"Wow," Drew said. "I can't believe it!"

Although she could already sense the happiness in his voice, Annie said, "I hope this is good news."

"It's great news. I would have asked Liz to marry me months ago, but I was concerned about Brooke accepting it."

"I can assure you that's not a problem. I asked Brooke if having Liz as her mother would be okay, and she said yes. Actually she seemed pretty happy with the thought."

"Thank you," Drew said reverently. "It seems like a small thing to say when you've given me a gift that will change our lives, but—"

"Actually, this isn't a gift from me, it's from Brooke. And if I might add a word of advice, let her go on believing in the love potion. It never hurts to have a bit of magic in your life."

**That evening after the dishes** were cleared from the table, Brooke volunteered to make a pot of tea.

"It's a special tea Miss Annie gave me," she said and disappeared into the kitchen. She returned carrying a tray with two of the Lenox china cups filled to the brim and a small plate of cookies.

"The good china?" Drew feigned a look of astonishment. He looked at Liz and then back at Brooke. "Is this a special occasion?"

Brooke gave a smug grin. "Maybe."

"Do you want to tell us about it?"

She shook her head. "Not yet."

Although it was barely eight o'clock eight Brooke said she was really, really tired and trudged off to bed. Halfway up the staircase she peeked down to see if the love potion was working. Drew caught sight of her from the corner of his eye, so he leaned over and kissed Liz full on her mouth.

**LATER THAT EVENING HE EXPLAINED** all that had happened. When he finished telling of Annie's call, he sighed and said, "They claim that out of the mouths of babes..."

He let that thought hang there for a moment then added, "I guess Brooke saw something we were too blind to see."

Without saying anything more he went down on his knee and took her hand in his.

"I love you, Liz," he said. "I loved you the moment I first saw you. I can't explain how it happened or why, but that evening when we shook hands I knew we'd be spending the rest of our lives together."

Her eyes filled with tears. "I had the same feeling." She lifted his hand to her mouth and planted a kiss in the center of his palm.

Drew felt the thundering of his heart for he knew the answer even as he asked the question.

"Will you marry me? Say yes, and I'll spend the rest of my life trying to make you happy."

"You won't have to try very hard, because just having you love me is what makes me happy."

"Is that a yes?"

"Of course it's a yes!"

He kissed her mouth then held her so close he could feel her heartbeat matching time to his own.

Liz stayed until almost three o'clock in the morning, and as they sat on the sofa talking of the future she came up with a plan. Keeping her voice low in the event Brooke slipped back to listen, she whispered her thoughts. Drew chuckled and said such a plan was ingenious.

# A Second Proposal

The next morning Brooke woke earlier than usual and was bursting to know what happened. Still in her pajamas she hurried downstairs and found Drew just setting the coffee on to brew.

"Good morning, Daddy," she said cheerfully.

"Morning." He stifled a yawn and pulled a mug from the cupboard. "You're up kind of early, aren't you?"

"Kind of." She sat there eyeing him as if she expected to see some physical change. When none became apparent she asked, "Did you and Miss Elizabeth do anything special last night?"

Drew straightened the curl pulling at the corner of his mouth and turned to her with a poker-faced expression.

"It's funny you should ask," he said. "Just after you went to bed, Liz and I were sitting on the sofa drinking the tea you made, which by the way was delicious—"

"Thank you. Then what happened?"

"I got this really good feeling in my heart, and when I looked at Liz I knew I was falling in love with her."

Brooke's eyes grew big and round. "Really?"

He nodded. "Yes, really. Don't you think it's strange that after all these months I just up and fall in love with her like that?"

Wearing a grin that stretched from ear to ear, Brooke said, "It's a little bit strange but very nice."

"Nice, yes, but now what?"

"Why don't you ask her to marry you? Then she could live here instead of that tiny little apartment."

Drew fingered his chin thoughtfully. "I'm not so sure she'd say yes to just me. After all she started out as your friend."

"She drank the tea, didn't she?"

"Yes, but what does that have to do with—"

"She'll say yes," Brooke said confidently. "I'm positive she will!"

Drew feigned a look of concern and shook his head as if he was doubtful of such a thing.

"Maybe if we asked her together. You know, so she'll realize that we both want her. I bet then she'd say yes."

"But she can't marry me."

"Well, not legally marry you, but by marrying me she'd get you in the bargain. I think that's something she'd appreciate."

Just as Drew expected her smile grew wide, and she exclaimed that it was indeed a very good idea.

**THAT EVENING DREW PROPOSED TO** Liz again. This time it was slightly different. He spoke of how they would be a family, and Brooke was standing beside him when he went down on his knee. When Liz said yes, he pulled a diamond solitaire from his pocket and slid it on her finger.

Afterward they celebrated with a glass of champagne. Even Brooke had a taste of the bubbly and she got to stay up until ten, even though it was a school night.

**THE FIRST WEEK OF NOVEMBER** they were married in the Good Shepherd Church. A week earlier the leaves on the trees turned shades of gold, red and brown, and with the stiff breeze of the previous day many had fallen to the ground. The crunch of dry leaves could be heard underfoot as attendees arrived at the church. Being they were newcomers in town Liz and Drew thought it would be a modest gathering, which is not what happened.

Annie and Oliver came and sat in the very first pew. Ophelia, who loved a wedding, also came, along with several of the friends Liz met during her stay at Memory House. Every employee of Southfield Printing was there along with the tellers from Heartland Bank. Nine of the neighboring families on Lakeside Drive came as did Alice Swift, the widow with a tiny apartment across the hall from Liz.

When the organist stomped down on the first chord of the wedding march, there was not an empty seat to be had.

**FIRST DOWN THE AISLE WAS** Brooke. She carried a nosegay of pink roses and wore a dress of ivory silk, the color and fabric identical to Elizabeth's. She walked with the measured steps they had practiced, and when she reached the end of the aisle she glanced back to see Elizabeth and Drew following arm in arm.

Since this was the second marriage for both, Elizabeth decided not to wear a traditional veil. Her dress was a soft swirl of ivory silk, and her hair was pushed back with a band of seed pearls. She carried a small bouquet of white roses. When they reached the altar Liz handed her bouquet to Brooke.

Pastor Willoughby was the first to speak.

"We are gathered together to join Elizabeth Cunningham and Drew Bishop in holy matrimony," he said. Then he bowed his head and recited a prayer asking that the lives before him be blessed with goodness. After the prayer he said the vows taken that day were not simply those of a man and woman; they were the foundation of a new family.

Brooke, like Liz and her daddy, had written her own vow. When Pastor Willoughby invited her to speak, she turned to Liz and in a clear childlike voice said, "Miss Elizabeth, thank you for marrying Daddy and being my mom. I promise I will love you and be your true friend."

A hushed sigh came from the congregation as Drew stooped and hooked a heart-shaped locket around her neck.

Elizabeth and Drew then turned to face one another and spoke words they had written.

"I give you my promise to love you forevermore," Liz said. "I will love you, honor you, share your dreams, make your family mine and, God willing, walk beside you until the end of my days."

Drew in turn promised to love, honor and cherish Elizabeth until the end of time.

"I marry you with my eyes wide open," he said. "You have helped me let go of the past and embrace the future. Thank you for making me laugh again. Whether it be good or bad that comes our way, you will forever be my partner in life."

They exchanged rings, and as they shared a kiss the organ came to life and the church bells began to chime.

**IT WAS A SHORT HONEYMOON,** just three days in New York City. They saw a play, had dinner at the Rainbow Room and spent an afternoon browsing through the quaint shops in the East Village. Kevin Harding was more than qualified to watch over the Southfield Plant in Drew's absence and Diane was capable of managing the bank, but the truth was Drew and Liz were both anxious to get home and begin their life as a family.

On the drive back to Virginia they decided to make their first Thanksgiving together a memorable one, and as it turned out it definitely was. In all they had 30 people at the table, which wasn't a single table but all three of the redwood lawn tables squeezed together. It stretched from the far wall of the dining room through an archway and well into the living room.

That afternoon the sounds of happiness coming from the Bishop house could be heard at the far end of the pond. When the guests left they all agreed that never before had there been a grander Thanksgiving. After the dishes were cleared and everything put away, the Bishop family dropped wearily on the sofa and reminisced about the day.

"Best Thanksgiving ever," Liz said.

Drew smiled. "We have a lot to be thankful for."

Brooke stretched her arms over her head and yawned. "I'm sleepy. I'm going to bed." She stood and started toward the stairs.

"Put your jammies on," Liz called. "I'll be in to say goodnight."

Brooke looked back and smiled.

"Thanks, Mom," she said.

The last time Brooke had called Liz Miss Elizabeth was the day of the wedding. Before the three of them started back down the aisle, Brooke had already decided that Miss Elizabeth was now Mom.

And so it was.

# In a Place Far Away

The Keeper of the Scales watched as Elizabeth kissed Brooke good night, and a pleasant feeling of warmth settled in his heart. With a single stone he had taken the fragments of disaster and from them created a family. It was good.

He lifted his eyes and scanned the celestial landscape. Silver threads, more numerous than the stars, stretched across the sky. They were invisible to the human eye, but still they connected one person to another—a neighbor, a friend, a stranger from a faraway land.

There was no foreseeing what would travel through each of those threads. Joy? Perhaps. Tragedy? Possibly. It was something not even his great eye could see. He could only keep watch and ply his stones when a scale became too heavily weighted on one side or another.

He reached his fingers into the wide sash of his robe and pulled out a small aquamarine stone that sparkled with the brilliance of a diamond. This was the stone he'd selected for Elizabeth a decade earlier. At that time the balance of her scale wavered from moment to moment. He'd seen her tears and felt her sorrow but knew the time was not right. Given the wisdom of centuries, he knew before he placed this precious stone on her scale he had to first find balance for her. At the time, with a thunderous sigh, he'd tucked the stone into the folds of his sash and waited.

The Keeper saw Elizabeth settle next to Drew on the sofa. Then he took the stone in his hand and gently placed it on the happiness side of her scale. The scale tipped in that direction.

Before another year passed by Elizabeth would have the baby she'd always wished for.

*If you enjoyed reading this book, please post a review at your favorite on-line retailer and share your thoughts with other readers.*

*I'd love to hear from you. If you visit my website and sign up to receive my monthly newsletter, as a special thank you, you'll receive a copy of*
A HOME IN HOPEFUL

http://betteleecrosby.com

*Silver Threads is Book 5 in the Memory House Series.*
*Other books in this series include:*

MEMORY HOUSE
Book One in the Memory House Series

THE LOFT
Book Two in the Memory House Series

WHAT THE HEART REMEMBERS
Book Three in the Memory House Series

BABY GIRL
Book Four in the Memory House Series

# Also by the Author

*The Wyattsville Series*

SPARE CHANGE
Book One

JUBILEE'S JOURNEY
Book Two

PASSING THROUGH PERFECT
Book Three

THE REGRETS OF CYRUS DODD
Book Four

*The Serendipity Series*

THE TWELFTH CHILD
Book One

PREVIOUSLY LOVED TREASURES
Book Two

WISHING FOR WONDERFUL
Book Three

*Stand Alone Stories*

CRACKS IN THE SIDEWALK

WHAT MATTERS MOST

BLUEBERRY HILL

# Acknowledgments

*But now abideth faith, hope, love, these three;*
*and the greatest of these is love.*
*1 Corinthians 13:13*

When I first started in this business, I thought I would sit down, write a book, publish it and wait for the rave reviews to come rolling in. Needless to say, that is not how it works. The truth is that even the most skilled novelist is only as good as the people who support her. I am fortunate in working with a team that I consider the best in the business. Not a single day goes by when I don't thank God for providing me with a pathway that has brought these people into my life.

This is especially true of Coral Russell, the Bent Pine Publicity Director. She is a friend, a partner, a publicist extraordinaire, a finder of new technology and perhaps most importantly a believer in all I do. To say thank you is woefully inadequate, for she is quite often the wind that carries my words to readers, friends and fans across the globe. From the bottom of my heart, I will forever be thankful for having met Coral.

I am equally blessed in knowing Ekta Garg, a super-talented editor who somehow manages to catch my mistakes without ever losing sight of my voice. Ekta's attention to detail constantly pushes me to go deeper into the story and I believe I am better because of this challenge.

Thank you also to Amy Atwell and the team at Author E.M.S. They are like the proverbial Fire Department, always there to help put out the fires. Thank you Amy for turning my manuscripts into beautifully formatted pages and for being so wonderfully organized and dependable.

I also owe a debt of gratitude to the loyal fans, friends and followers who buy my books, share them with friends and take time to write reviews. Without such fans my stories would grow dusty on the shelf.

Lastly, I am thankful beyond words for my husband Dick, who puts up with my crazy hours, irrational thinking, and late or non-existent dinners. I could not be who I am without him for he is and will always be my sweetheart and greatest blessing.

# ABOUT THE AUTHOR

**AWARD-WINNING NOVELIST BETTE LEE CROSBY** brings the wit and wisdom of her Southern Mama to works of fiction—the result is a delightful blend of humor, mystery and romance.

"Storytelling is in my blood," Crosby laughingly admits, "My mom was not a writer, but she was a captivating storyteller, so I find myself using bits and pieces of her voice in most everything I write."

Crosby's work was first recognized in 2006 when she received The National League of American Pen Women Award for a then unpublished manuscript. Since then, she has gone on to win numerous other awards, including The Reviewer's Choice Award, The Reader's Favorite Gold Medal, FPA President's Book Award Gold Medal and The Royal Palm Literary Award.

To learn more about Bette Lee Crosby, explore her other work, or read a sample from any of her books, visit her blog at:

http://betteleecrosby.com

Made in the USA
San Bernardino, CA
14 June 2018